ALICE THE DAGGER
THE WONDERLAND COURT SERIES

ASHLEY MCLEO

To all the broken women and girls who became and will become warriors.

CONTENTS

CHAPTER I

A curse on my hips!

I shifted to the right, hoping the dagger on my left hip would slide over the window frame and allow me to shimmy inside with greater ease. I probably should have taken the blasted thing off before trying to shove myself through a tiny window, but you know . . . hindsight and all.

Why does this have to be the only way into this stupid home?

The mark, a shifter mafia leader, must have thought no one would come after him while he was on the toilet. And honestly, it was a good assumption.

How many people could scale four stories, and squeeze themselves through a window barely bigger than a chihuahua-sized doggie door?

I was among the few, and I'd only chosen this route because Xavier wanted this job done fast. What that dang vampire wanted, he usually got.

My fingers gripped the windowpane, and I pushed. Inch by inch I wiggled my way forward, until the next thing I knew, I was flying over the toilet and headed straight for the floor. Thankfully, my hands had remained in front of me. Air flew from them, cushioning my fall so I didn't break my face.

Still, I hadn't acted quickly enough to eliminate *all* the evidence of breaking and entering. The sound of my landing rang through the bathroom, loud and telling.

I leapt up and froze, waiting to see if anyone in the mansion had heard. Shifter ears were particularly sensitive. When no footsteps or voices came closer, I breathed a sigh of relief. I'd gotten lucky.

Taking a moment to readjust my dagger, I caught my reflection in the mirror. My long, white-blonde braid had gone *seriously* astray in my struggle with the window.

I huffed out a breath and deftly fixed it. Even the most despicable marks—and they were all pretty nasty individuals—deserved more respect than being done in by someone who looked like hell.

Once I was presentable, I moved to the door and twisted the knob slowly. Entering the hallway, I scanned left and then right before turning in the direction of the master suite. Quick glances inside every room I passed confirmed that they were empty of people. Actually, they weren't just empty. Most reminded me of staged rooms in a furniture store, cold and un-lived in.

I'd taken a right turn when confirmation that I was

closing in on the mark hit my ear. Music, identifiable as a song from the first *Godfather* movie, trilled through the hallway, punctuated by bursts of male laughter.

The Godfather, how typical. He's probably taking pointers.

I rolled my eyes and pulled my dagger from its scabbard, careful to keep the tip away from my skin.

Shifters were formidable foes, their senses unparalleled. They were also strong and could outlast most of their opponents. Especially when the shifter was a 250-pound alpha wolf, and his opponent was a 140-pound demi-fae.

But not even shifters could survive the batrachotoxin my employer purchased from South America for jobs like this one. Still, even with the aid of poison, I had to be silent as the night to succeed.

I called air again, and bid it to create a buffer along my skin, holding in my scent. Only when I was sure that defense was secure did I begin walking, dagger poised in my striking hand.

Once I reached the door to the theater room, I peeked inside.

An exhale left me. The alpha wolf was alone. This job would be much less messy than I'd expected.

I pressed the air buffer as far out as possible, bidding it to muffle my sound as well as my scent. Then, with bated breath, I tiptoed toward the brown leather sectional.

I had the good luck of arriving right in the middle of a scene riddled with gunfire. The sound system was on point, loud and crisp and perfect for covering my tracks. And, unsurprisingly, the alpha wolf was cheering and howling with laughter at every grizzly death.

Geez, this guy's a disgusting asshole.

As I got closer, the scent of popcorn, buttery and delicious, filled my nostrils. I approached the couch and was close enough to distinguish the alpha's gray hairs from the brown when the wolf-shifter turned slowly and stared me dead in the eyes.

"You're a little young, aren't you?" He spoke without a trace of fear in his well-lined face.

"I've been around the block a time or two," I replied coolly.

A corner of his lips lifted. "We'll see about that. Get her, boys."

My stomach dropped as the air shimmered with magic and suddenly, two figures appeared at the edges of the couch. Hulking wolf-shifters with pistols aimed straight at me.

I flew into motion, rebounding off the couch and into a roundhouse kick that clocked the closest wolf straight in the temple. As he fell, I swiped him with the dagger before twisting and hurling it at the other attacker. The blade landed on target—between his eyes—and he fell too. I yanked the dagger out of his skull, and was about to burst out of my crouch when the *click* of a gun cocking stopped me.

"Who sent you?" the alpha demanded.

I turned my neck ever so slightly to look at him, and he growled.

"Don't move an inch, faerie. Now, answer me. Who sent you?"

"My boss. I don't know who wants you killed, but they hired us for the job."

I gave him a longer explanation than was necessary. It bought me time to figure out what to do. At this range, he wouldn't miss me if he pulled the trigger.

"You aren't around when he takes the jobs?" the alpha pressed. His need to learn who'd betrayed him was written all over his face.

"No. My boss called me today." I tilted my head to the side as if I was thinking something over, hoping to deflect from my slight repositioning my dagger. "Maybe around five. So whoever wants you dead must have come in before that. It's usually someone close to the mark. Who wasn't around you today?"

His brows furrowed, unable to resist the urge to recall his day.

Knowing that I wouldn't get another chance, I pushed a gust of air at him—straight in his eyes.

The gun went off, but I was already out of the line of fire, ducking and then hurtling over the couch. The alpha opened his eyes milliseconds before my blade sank into the side of his neck.

Blood spurted everywhere, splattering the rich brown leather of the couch, and my clothes. I pressed my lips together. I hated the thought of someone's blood on my clothes.

A heartbeat later, the alpha fell. When he stopped breathing, my shoulders relaxed.

One more bad guy down.

Knowing that the alpha was no longer roaming the streets of L.A., doing shady criminal stuff to innocents, made what I had to do a *little* easier.

At least, that's what I told myself so I could look in the mirror.

* * *

The door to my apartment whined open.

"I'm home!" I sang out, aware that no one would be there to welcome me. It was just a habit from the days when there had been someone here, someone to love and call mine. And though those days were gone, for some sick reason or another, I still felt comfort in the ritual.

Moving into the kitchen, I laid my scabbard on the counter, pulled a jug of OJ out of the fridge, and drank straight from the carton. After a brief examination of my meager rations, I settled on making mac and cheese with frozen peas tossed in for nutritional value.

Once the water was on the stovetop, I went to change. As soon as I stepped foot into my bedroom, my shoulders lowered and my heart rate slowed.

Despite Xavier's warnings, I liked to keep a window

cracked open to feel the fresh air on my face and watch the way my veil-like white curtains fluttered in a breeze. My bed was a massive canopy, also surrounded by gauzy linen. Sheepskin rugs littered the floor, and a teal pod chair, perfect for reading in, sat in the corner.

Unlike the shell I presented to the outer world, which included an all-black attire and hard attitude, this place was all softness and light and air. I loved it and hoped that when my contract with Xavier was complete, I could bring a bit of this feeling out into the world with me.

I stripped, releasing my wings from the bindings that allowed me to pass as human. I hated wearing the straps, but visiting an aether-blessed fae, the only type of fae with the ability to construct glamours to conceal such features, cost time and *a lot* of money. So much money that organizations like the government and fae academies often had an aether-blessed fae on retainer—but not Xavier Doru. When the vampire did hire one, he thought the money the fae demanded was better spent hiding my pointy ears.

His reasoning was sound. If my wings were rendered invisible, and therefore freed from their bindings, I'd still have to be careful that they didn't hit anyone in crowds. The bindings were more practical than a glamour, even if they were annoying and stifling.

Immediately, my clothes got tossed into the trash. I couldn't wear them again without thinking of the shifters I'd killed.

After a hot shower to rinse the blood off my body, I

wrapped myself in a loose, soft robe that gave my diaphanous gold-veined wings a little room to breathe, and padded barefoot to the kitchen.

The water was boiling, so I poured in the noodles. I'd just finished stirring them when a knock came at the door.

My spine straightened, and I dashed to the counter where I'd set down my dagger.

As soon as I unsheathed the cold metal, a chuckle came from the other side of the door. "It's me."

I exhaled in annoyance. Xavier.

I flung the door open to find the ice-blond vampire leaning against the entryway, looking as cool as a cucumber.

"How did you know I was home already?" I asked, unable to shake the idea that despite all our talks of trust, he'd bugged my place. After all, there was precedent.

Jax, my ex-boyfriend, knew that Xavier had been spying on him, but he'd never done anything about it. Well, nothing except live at my apartment until the day his contract was up, and then skip town without so much as a goodbye.

Asshole.

My heart clenched. It still hurt to think about Jax, the one person I'd thought I could trust. He'd been the first guy I'd given myself to and thought I loved. My best friend . . .

But I should have known better. No one wanted this

life. Everyone who aged out of their contracts left as soon as they could. Why would Jax be any different?

I should have guarded my heart. Over the years, I'd learned many times that the ones closest to us had the power to hurt us most. And yet, in the face of my first love, I'd forgotten. Like a prize idiot.

"Our client called," Xavier said, ripping me from my own misery. "They wanted to thank you for a job well done. I did the math. Your place isn't far so I figured you'd already be home."

I blinked. That was fast. Too fast.

"They already know he's dead? But it's only been—" I glanced at the clock above the stove. "Forty-five minutes since I left."

"The mate was in the next room." Xavier's lips curled up as shock flitted across my face. "I see you didn't realize she was present. You're losing your touch, Queenly."

I rolled my eyes and stirred the noodles again. "Please. I'm the best assassin you have. Just because I didn't check all ten-thousand square feet of that monstrosity doesn't mean I'm losing anything. It means that I was more direct—more lethal—than usual."

Xavier chuckled. "I've always appreciated your inclination to get down to business."

"In that case, why are you here?"

The vampire flopped onto my hard gray couch and planted his feet on the coffee table adorned with various sci-fi romance novels that I was halfway through. "What?

We've known each other for so long! We can't be pals? Paint each other's nails?"

Pals? That was a laugh, coming from a vampire who I'd once called Father, only to receive a long lecture about how Xavier was better than both of my parents because he would never leave me—as long as I stayed in line.

Not long after that, the lonely child I'd been had signed away her freedom. My desperation had cost me greatly, and I'd been paying the price ever since.

"I don't do pals, Xavier. You know that."

"I've been meaning to bring that up. It's something you should consider. In the real world, people appreciate being smiled at now and then." He shook his head. "Maybe I should have let you get that cat. It might have softened you up a bit."

My teeth ground together. His refusal to let me buy a kitten was a major sore spot. "This may not be made of silver but I'm sure I can do some damage with it." I picked up my dagger and waved it at him. "Tell me what you want or get out. I've had a long day."

He leaned forward and placed his elbows on his knees. "New job came in, and you've been requested. No details yet, but they'll come in soon enough. Swing by my apartment at eight in the morning. I'll have travel arrangements sorted out by then."

I arched an eyebrow. "But I just finished a job."

Xavier shrugged. "Money is money. Surely you understand?" He gestured to the empty room as if he was trying to make a point that he didn't need to make.

I wasn't yet a legal adult, so I lived in an apartment Xavier rented for me. Each month, I paid him rent. After that sum was gone, I survived on the difference between the money my jobs brought in and what it took to pay back my other debts to the vampire. Debts I had to repay or risk being hunted down by a team of fellow assassins or a vampire clan. I'd seen both groups hired for those who broke their contracts, and they always found their mark. As a result, I understood the value of money well. It bought freedom.

I also understood that Xavier was a cheapskate, and I couldn't wait to age out of my contract. When that day came, and I could legally get an apartment on my own, I'd pay off the last of whatever I owed Doru and walk away. And I'd *never* look back.

I exhaled a long breath. "Why didn't you text me?" The noodles were almost done, and I moved on autopilot, adding the frozen peas for thirty seconds before transferring the mix to a colander then back into the pan. I added an obscene amount of butter, followed by the nuclear orange cheese powder, and stirred.

"I need you at my place early, and you would sleep through a bomb, Queenly. I couldn't risk you missing the text."

Touché.

"Fine. I'll be by tomorrow. Now, if you'll excuse me." I began pulverizing the cheese clumps. "I'd like some personal time."

Xavier stood, a shit-eating grin on his face. "Until tomorrow, blondie."

I scowled at the hated nickname, and was about to retort something cutting when the sound of the front door shutting hit my ear.

Looking up from the pan of mac and cheese, I found myself alone yet again.

CHAPTER 2

I parked my car a few blocks from Xavier's beachfront apartment in Santa Monica. As I got out to hoof it the rest of the way, I huffed, wishing the vampire didn't love being in the thick of things. It would make my life so much easier if he lived in the 'burbs and had a damn driveway.

Or even better, if Xavier would just tell me my next mission over the phone.

At least it was early, so there were fewer cars and people around than there would be around midday, when people tended to flock to the beach. I wouldn't have to worry about the nightmare crowds, because by then, I'd be long gone.

Stalking my next mark.

I inhaled deeply, trying to dispel my annoyance at having to take another job so quickly. We were usually given at least three days to recuperate, and I'd wanted to use them all. But apparently, Xavier knew I'd bounce as soon as possible, and he wanted to utilize my skills while he still could.

Eight days . . .

My shoulders loosened as the idea of freedom bolstered me, and the fresh ocean scent filled my nostrils, calming me. Since I was young, I'd loved the ocean. I felt a kinship with it, like I'd grown up with that big blue expanse watching over me, which was odd because until recently, I hadn't lived anywhere near the beach. I breathed in again and a shiver of pleasure dashed through me. As I was a few minutes early, I considered dipping my toes in the sand so I could pretend I was on vacation.

My lips curled up slightly. *Wouldn't that be something? A real vaca—what the actual hell?!*

I blinked as a white rabbit dressed in a cobalt-colored waistcoat, with a pocket watch hanging from the jacket, hopped out from behind a bush.

"Nooooo, I'm too young to go crazy."

I rubbed my eyes. When I pulled my hands away, the rabbit was still there. Actually, he'd come closer, and was now standing four paces from me.

I reached for the dagger I usually carried on jobs, only to remember that I was in public and it wasn't there.

What I'd planned on doing with it was anyone's guess. It wasn't like the rabbit was bothering me. Making me question my sanity, sure, but even then—I was just hallucinating a rabbit.

Or maybe he was a pet? My lips twitched. That had to be it. This was L.A., and people with stupid amounts of money dressed up their pets all the time.

"Did you lose your owner, buddy?"

"*Owner?*" The rabbit stood on his hindquarters and grabbed the pocket watch.

"Holy shit," I breathed. Had the rabbit *spoken?*

"What's this nonsense about owners? Oh, nevermind! If we don't hurry, we'll be late!"

Unable to believe what I'd heard, I looked around.

No one was nearby to verify if I was, in fact, losing my marbles.

"Did you hear me, Alice?" The rabbit thumped his foot and shook the watch. "We will be late!"

I cleared my throat. "Excuse me, but did you say my name?" I glanced from side to side again. "What are you, a rabbit-shifter, or something?"

I'd met a lot of shifters. They were usually larger, more ferocious animals, especially the seedier kind. I'd also encountered a few bird-shifters, but never a rabbit. Although that didn't mean they didn't exist.

It was the only explanation for the creature in front of me.

"I'm not some common shifter! I am a *pooka*!" The rabbit glowered up at me with luminous golden eyes. "And you're late! We must get moving!"

A pooka . . . my shoulders relaxed slightly. That was some sort of fae race. One that was less common than the better known elves, faeries, or pixies.

The rabbit hopped closer, and pulled at the hem of my jeans. "Come now! We must leave. You're la—"

"Late. Yeah, you said that," I cut him off. "But to what? And actually, can we take this conversation into the park? I'd rather not let any humans see me talking to a rabbit. Xavier would have to hire a mind witch to erase their memories. He hates working with witches." I gestured to the left, feeling much too out in the open to be talking to a rabbit—or pooka, whatever—in broad daylight.

Without waiting for the rabbit to respond, I walked around the shrubbery and into the park.

He followed a moment later, hopping down the path I'd chosen with a huffy look on his face. "*This* is not the right way. We should go the opposite direction!"

"Why? And to where?"

"To the Wonderland Court!"

I stopped dead in my tracks and barked out a laugh. "The Wonderland Court? But why?"

"You are Alice Queenly, a fae brought up under the supervision of Xavier Doru, vampire lord, are you not?"

Xavier, vampire lord? I'd never heard Xavier described like that—at least not from others. *I* often thought of him as my overlord but there was no way I'd admit that out loud.

"Sure, that's right," I said slowly.

"Then you are *precisely* who I seek." The rabbit put his little paw on his hip. "Word has it that the queen has sent mercenaries to find you. For your safety, we must leave now! We're already late!" He held up his watch and shook it in my face.

My confusion cleared.

I didn't know much about Faerie, the otherworldly realm named after the first fae race who had settled there. And I definitely didn't know a thing about pookas, but I had plenty of experience with hired men.

I'd pissed someone off—a queen.

I was about to tell the rabbit that if some queen sent men to deal with me, then good luck to them. I'd kick their asses. But I swallowed my cocky proclamation when, after a particularly vigorous shake of his watch, I focused on the clock face.

It was eight o'clock.

"Xavier will be furious!" I whirled around and broke into a sprint.

"Alice! Come back!"

I twisted but didn't stop. "Thanks for the heads-up, but don't worry about me. I can take care of myself!"

He said something else, but I was already too far away to hear, and wasn't about to turn around for clarification.

Xavier *hated* waiting, and I didn't want to piss him off. An angry vampire was the worst.

I was out of breath when I reached Xavier's building and pressed the call button for his apartment.

He picked up, but said nothing.

"Sorry, I got held up," I said, knowing it was better to admit the wrong right away.

The buzzer sounded, and I pushed the door open.

Throwing a wave at the armed security guard on duty, I dashed past the front desk, and into the elevator. I pressed the button for Xavier's floor, leaving my finger on the pad so it could scan my print. One soft beep confirmed my access, and the elevator shot up fifteen floors.

I arrived at the door to the vampire's penthouse as he opened it. His jaw, normally stone-like, was set even harder than usual, and his eyes narrowed.

"I'm five minutes late and that includes my apology," I said, trying to sound as if I wasn't worried how he'd respond. "Deal with it."

"You're lucky I need you today, Alice, because I don't just *deal*."

I gulped.

No, Xavier didn't deal with unexpected matters well at all. He was a control freak, and someone always paid the price for things that inconvenienced him, no matter how big or small. While he'd never laid a finger on me, I'd witnessed his cruelty among my peers—the other orphans he'd raised into killing machines.

I was glad the younger children in his care were far away, studying and practicing tricks of the trade in the country mansion Xavier owned. Had they been nearby, I would worry about them.

"So, what's the job?"

Xavier gestured to his raised drafting table that overlooked the Pacific Ocean.

Two guns glared up at me amidst a bunch of disorganized papers fluttering in the breeze from the open window. Once again, the scent of salt filled my nostrils.

My chest loosened a bit. I might not have gotten to chill at the beach this morning as planned, but at least I could enjoy this spectacular view for a few minutes.

Xavier lifted a plain manila envelope just as a bee slipped in through an open window and buzzed around his face. He swatted at it before turning his attention toward me.

"Your new mark is more dangerous than most. This contains everything you'll need to know to bring him down. You'll have to travel to Beijing, and our client wants it done by the end of the weekend. Your flight leaves in two hours."

"*Two* hours?" My voice rose an octave. Getting to and through LAX was difficult enough, but I wasn't at all prepared to leave. "Are you cra—holy crap!"

Xavier's vampire reflexes kicked in as he grabbed a gun. Only a millisecond later, I moved for the other, as a flash of white appeared in the air next to us and fell to the floor.

"How many times do I have to tell you we're late?" The white rabbit landed cleanly on the ground, and hopped right in front of me, not at all deterred by the guns pointed at him.

I lowered my weapon. "How did you even get in here?"

"I told you, I'm a pooka! I flew in." The white rabbit gestured to the window, cracked open only two inches.

My eyebrows pulled together. "Okay, I'm going to need some clarification on that."

He snapped his "fingers," and suddenly, he was no longer fluffy or white or in the cobalt waistcoat, but a black horse with a blue blanket on his back. One stomp of his hoof, and the figure changed again, this time into a gray Persian cat with a blue collar.

The cat remained there only for a second before it was replaced by a bee buzzing around my head and screaming, "You're late!" in a tinny voice.

Well, that explained how he'd gotten in the window.

"So, you're a shape-shifting fae who can take multiple forms?" I clarified.

"Yes," the pooka said and returned once again to his rabbit form. "Most of us can change into many creatures —at least a dozen. Each individual pooka has their preferences and limits, but we're much more adaptable than your common shifter."

"Okay, I get it now. Although I am still not sure why you're here."

"That you don't understand anything is obvious." The rabbit's golden eyes shifted to Xavier. "Would you like to clear up a few things Mr. Doru?"

I was about to retort that me not knowing *anything* was

rude and just ridiculous, when Xavier gulped. His face was much whiter than normal, which made my eyes pop open.

I didn't think I'd ever seen Xavier intimidated by anyone in my life. And now a *rabbit* was making him anxious?

Xavier stepped forward. "She still has eight days with me."

The rabbit gave a single hop, and his balled-up fist shook at the vamp. "*Eight days*! Is that all you've got to say for yourself? She's been in your care for thirteen years, and clearly knows nothing about her heritage or the rebellion, and you want to quibble about *eight days*?!"

The rabbit pulled out a fluff of white hair. "This is blasphemy! And what's worse, it's putting me even further behind!" He extracted the golden pocket watch from his waistcoat again, glanced at it, and let out a scream. "Oh gods! She'll have my head!"

My eyebrows furrowed, not sure what to make of that last statement, but needing answers. Sane ones.

"Xavier, when he says heritage, what's he talking about?"

"He's—" Xavier's mouth snapped shut as the rabbit hopped onto the drafting table.

"The vampire hasn't told you for thirteen years, and he clearly doesn't want to tell you now." The rabbit glared at Xavier. "Despite the dangers, a few fae have journeyed from Wonderland to this realm and back again. Over the years, sightings came from these travelers. Rumors flitted through the rebel ranks that he's been using you in ways that we would not approve of."

His rabbit eyes remained pinned on the vampire in a way that far larger creatures wouldn't dare. "Until now, I didn't believe them. *Obviously,* I was wrong. This sort of treatment nullifies the contract."

"What do you know of the contract I signed?" I asked, gaining the rabbit's shocked attention for a second.

"The contract that *you* signed? I know nothing of the sort." The rabbit scowled at Xavier before his eyes snapped back to me.

"However, I am knowledgeable about the contract your parents signed." My spine straightened at the mention of my parents, but the rabbit didn't notice and continued on. "The one that stated the vampire was supposed to raise you in hiding. *Safely* in hiding. You were to be taught how to defend yourself by one of the best fighters in this land. Your warden took things a few steps further than intended."

"She learned to fight and defend herself with the best," Xavier butted in. "In fact, she—"

"Shut up, Xavier," I said. For once in my life, he actually listened, which only made my spidey senses tingle harder. I turned my attention to the pooka, determined to get to the bottom of this. "If you're so concerned about me, why have I never seen you before. Or heard from my family? Why did it take you thirteen years to check on me?"

"Yeah, Rabbit." Xavier crossed his arms over his chest. "What took you so long?"

The rabbit scoffed. "The channels from Wonderland into this world are controlled by the Red Queen. It took slipping past the kraken and sneaking into another court to open a portal to enter this world! I've since convinced a witch of your world to reopen one of the old portals to Wonderland, but only for a brief time."

The rabbit glanced at me. "That being said, if you wish to reunite with those who care for you, your true family, we must go *now*."

My true family? My heart lodged into my throat.

I'd long given up discovering my family, or where I'd come from, but occasionally I dreamt about it—kinda. My dreams came in flashes, most of which were long gone when I woke. But the sound of my mother's voice, and a visage of a woman with long, white-blonde hair like mine, always remained when morning came.

"Do you want to meet your loved ones, Alice? The rebels who have been fighting to make the world you were born into a better place?"

"Rebels?" I said the word as if I'd never heard it before. "My family members are rebels?"

"Yes. Rebel leaders. They're always in danger. Hence why they brought you here, to protect you—or at least *try* to protect you—from violence." The rabbit was studying my face carefully, trying to find tells in the cool facade Xavier had trained into me.

Who was this rabbit kidding? Every orphan wished to

find their family. Now that I had a partial answer as to why they'd left me, and it was a good one, that desire was already growing more intense.

I had a million questions they needed to answer. More than anything, I wanted to see them again, to have a *chance* to remember a bit of my past.

"I have her until her eighteenth birthday." The gun twitched in the vampire's hand. "And I have an important job planned."

I looked at him incredulously. "I'm sorry?! You've been using me for nefarious purposes when you weren't supposed to, and now you're going to try to keep me here?"

Xavier's eyes narrowed. "I may have stretched the truth, but you're the one who signed to work for me. *You* made that choice."

Damned vampire. My fist clenched.

I'd been a child barely able to sign my name when he'd started training me. I'd seen how Xavier seemed to love the other assassins. How he treated them with respect. I'd wanted that too—wanted to belong.

But I wasn't a child anymore, and I was done with this vampire.

I tossed my gun on the table, and placed a hand on my hip—sure that if he retaliated, I'd be able to hold my own. "And right now I'm making the choice to break my contract. I'm out, Xavier."

"That gives me the right to hunt you," the vampire growled, more pissed than I'd ever seen him.

"If you want to try to stop me, just remember this," I arched an eyebrow. "You taught me well, made our boundaries clear. We're not *family*, this is business." The vampire's eyes widened as I threw his words back in his face. "If you come after me, I won't hold back."

"Hold back?! You owe me, Queenly. I fed you, housed you, and clothed you!"

My lips pressed together. At that moment, I wanted nothing more than to stick a stake in Xavier, but of course, he didn't keep stakes in his apartment. Or silver, or anything else that was deadly to him. And I didn't have my dagger, so decapitation was out.

He isn't worth it, anyway.

"And I *killed* for you. Actually, consider me not killing *you* the rest of my repayment." I turned to walk toward the door.

"How dare—"

I whipped back around to face the man who raised me. "No! How dare you lie to me about my parents and tell me I should be grateful!' I thrust a finger at him. "You'd better watch yourself from now on. When I get back, we're going to have words."

The vampire stared into my eyes for a few long, dangerous, seconds before replying.

"Fine. You're released from your contract. But you should know, Alice, I raised you the best way I knew how." Xavier glanced at the pooka, his lips pursed in frustration at having lost his best assassin and cash cow. "No doubt where you're going, your training will come in handy."

"Whatever. Do me a favor, and stay out of my life." I strode toward the door. "Come on, pooka. Show me the way to Wonderland."

CHAPTER 3

The pooka transformed into a mini-poodle wearing a blue sweater. I cradled him in my arms as we strolled past the security guard, and into the wilds of L.A.

More people crowded the sidewalks now. Two speed walking grannies dressed in sweats straight out of the eighties and carrying one-pound weights stopped us before we got very far. They wanted to pet the poodle, and I couldn't say no, so I was forced to make small talk until the old biddies moved on.

Finally, we reached the park I'd pulled the rabbit into earlier. I set him down and began wiping off a few strands of white fur that clung to my black shirt and leggings.

"That was so embarrassing. Don't think I'm ever doing that again," I said, looking at the poodle's ridiculous poofs. "I'm much more of a cat person. They're less needy. A pittie would work too. Fewer people approach you when you're with one of them."

The poodle transformed back into a rabbit, and rolled his eyes, which cut through my annoyance and made me giggle.

Who thought they'd ever see a rabbit roll its eyes at them?

"Follow me, Miss Queenly."

Rabbit began hopping down a path. After a few minutes, the stretch of grass gave way, and we were in a manicured garden dotted with cedars.

"Are we looking for a door, or what?" I asked.

Unless they were demi-fae, like me, most people in our realm weren't allowed to enter Faerie. And even if you were demi-fae, you had to have an excellent reason to enter the other realm. Familial obligations counted, but I could have never claimed that before. One of the other valid reasons was a job that sent you from one world to the other.

"Of a sort." Rabbit shook his head. "Xavier truly failed us. How is it you know so little about Faerie?"

Beats me. I didn't even know that I was born there.

Oh my God!

"Rabbit?"

The pooka twisted. "My name is Herald."

"So sorry I didn't intuit that."

Rabbit—Herald—scowled. "You had a question?"

"If I was born in Faerie, that means I'm full-fae, right? Not demi-fae?"

"Of course. To be exact, you're a pure blood faerie, the fae race our realm is named after."

I stopped in my tracks.

Herald said it like it was nothing. But to me, it was massive. All my life, I'd believed I was a mixed race demi-fae without a family. When really, I was the daughter of full-blooded rebel faeries.

WTF . . . mind blown.

The rabbit didn't seem to notice my revelation, and kept hopping down the path until he stopped in front of a tree with a wide trunk.

Herald smiled. "Ah! The witch stayed true to her word."

"We're here?" I glanced about but didn't see a single thing that looked like a door or a portal.

"Right here!"

Herald ignored the sign instructing people to stay out of the garden surrounding the tree, and hopped over the flowers and toward the trunk. He placed his paw on a woody knot, and a hole slightly smaller than a manhole cover popped open.

I blinked as a bright light flooded out of the tree.

My mouth fell open. "A witch did that?"

"With a fae. Portal magic is complex, and the best way we've found to keep them open is to have two magicals work their powers on opposing sides and blend them. Of course, permanent Faerie holes look nothing like this, but we're working under the radar."

"Will this disappear later?"

"Absolutely. Once we pass through, I'll instruct the fae whose magic kept it open to end the enchantment. If we keep it open, one of the queen's men might find it."

Something dinged in his pocket, and an alarmed expression came over his face. "Oberon's ears! Heads will roll! Come, Alice!"

With that, Herald leapt into the hole and disappeared from sight.

I peered down after him. Only darkness stared back, making me gulp. It wasn't the endless blackness that scared me. No—I'd learned to use that to my advantage, to be one with it. Sometimes it even felt like an old friend.

But the unknown? That scared the hell out of me.

It would be easier to stay here, go on another job, maybe two if the vamp insisted, and soon enough be free of Xavier. Free to do whatever *I* wanted, with no obligations to anyone or anything. That way, no one could ever hurt me again.

But another opposing dream stared me in the face. My family. Fae who only put me in Xavier's hands to protect me.

I had to meet them. So, before I could change my mind, I shoved myself through the hole.

Blackness swirled around me as I plunged. Air whipped through my white-blonde hair, and goosebumps charged over my skin. My hands flailed out, trying to grab onto something, a rock to slow the momentum, a root, *anything*.

Nothing popped up.

That is, until my right shoulder slammed into something hard, and the sound of an instrument—a piano?—hit my ears.

I released a gasp, and at that very instant, light beamed through the darkness as if someone had turned on a light switch.

A trumpet flew past me, followed by a teapot leaving a trail of teacups swirling through the air in a circular motion. Flags, balloons, and playing cards adorned the walls of the tunnel like photos.

I shook my head as another barrage of objects soared past, this time a hookah with a stuffed dog attached, apparently smoking.

Whoever created this portal must have been on drugs. Or maybe —oh shit!

The floor came in sight, and I realized I was going way too fast if I wanted to land and live. I didn't see any Herald-splatter below, but that didn't give me hope. The pooka could've easily changed from a rabbit to a bug or something with wings. But I didn't have that option. As always, my wings were strapped to my back.

I reached for my powers of air and brought a gale of wind up under me, fighting against gravity. It wouldn't be enough to save me from hitting the ground, but it slowed my fall a little.

As the floor came at me, I braced for impact, closing my eyes and hoping that I'd escape broken bones.

I landed with an *oomph*, and bounced up and back

down softly. My eyes snapped open, and I looked down to see what I'd landed on.

"What the hell?"

A massive crimson cushion that hadn't been there a moment ago sat beneath me. Next to it was a small table—another object I hadn't spotted—and on top of the table were two items. One was a wee bottle of purple beverage. The other, a single-bite teacake.

Well, that's weird.

I glanced around, taking in the room. It was twenty feet in diameter, and circular. Ten feet above my head, small windows peppered the wall to allow in light and fresh air. A single door stood facing me, no larger than a mouse hole.

Herald was nowhere to be seen. He must have transformed and exited through the door, forgetting in his time-obsessed haste that I had no damned idea where I was going.

"Wonderful." I shoved myself up off the cushion.

I circled the room, keeping an eye out for an alternate exit. On my third sweep, I had to admit that things looked bad. As far as I could tell, there was only one way out, and there was no way in hell I was squeezing my curvy hips through it.

I knelt on the ground and tried to twist the tiny knob. And wouldn't you know it, that sucker wasn't only too small to fit through, it was locked.

"How does he expect me to get out of here?"

I scanned the room again, and when my eyes landed on the table, I jerked back.

Something had changed.

Now, a small, gold key gleamed up at me from between the tiny bottle and teacake.

"Curious." I tilted my head and made my way to the table.

The key wasn't the only thing that had changed. The bottle now bore a label I was positive hadn't been there before, and words had appeared on the top of the teacake.

I picked up the bite-sized dessert and read it. "Eat me?"

My attention went to the bottle's label. "Drink me?"

I uncorked the bottle and sniffed. It didn't smell of any poison I knew of, but that probably didn't mean much. I was in Faerie, poisons could be totally different here.

I moved on to the key. It wasn't labeled, because duh, it was a key, but this time, I noted its positioning, right between the cake and the bottle. How they got there, I had no idea. Still, there had to be a reason for their existence. Seeing as I was in Faerie, a place that unlike the human world was open with magic, I figured the cake and the drink were probably tools to help get me out of the room.

"Should I try one first? Or both at once?"

The liquid in the bottle suddenly glowed.

I picked it up. "I can take a hint. Bottoms up."

I tilted the bottle back and took a sip. Right away, my insides contorted, and a sense of being wrapped in saran wrap came over me. It was uncomfortable, the most constricting sensation I'd ever experienced.

And then, suddenly, I began to shrink.

"Holy shit!" I screamed.

I blinked and lost three inches, and it was only a breath later that five feet seemed like a dream. After thirty seconds, I was no taller than the table, and by the end of a full minute, I was toddler sized.

My heart rate thundered as everything in the room got progressively larger. I did not like this. Not one bit. My teeth ground together as I reached about a foot in height. *When is this ever going to end?*

Finally, I stopped shrinking when I was about four inches high. The bottle I held was as tall as me, and the weight of it nearly knocked me over.

I scrambled to right it, spilling a little in the process. Once I found my feet, I blinked, taking in my new world.

I nearly winked out of existence!

Shaking off my nerves, I strode over to the door, and turned the knob to exit the room.

The handle clicked to a stop, and my stomach sank as my stupidity set in.

I'd left the key on the table. The table which, at my diminutive size, now resembled a mountain.

"This is delightful," I grumbled, stomping back to the table and examining the legs.

After a brief study, I concluded that I could probably

climb them. The issue would be getting atop the surface of the table. I scratched my head, unsure the maneuver would even be possible.

"Knew they should've sent me," a high-pitched and prideful voice shot through me.

I whirled around, but found no one.

"Or both of us," a second voice, slightly more high-pitched than the first, said. "I'd have *loved* to help."

"Oh, please, Dum! You know I would have been perfect for the job. I'm much more of a go-getter than you or that stupid pooka. He transformed into a fly and forgot her here! Probably worried about being on time again, the fool."

"And you seem set on confusing the heck out of the poor thing," Dum retorted. "Alice! Look up!"

My eyes drifted upward, which was a great deal farther than it had been minutes ago, and widened when I found two pixies sitting on a windowsill.

"Oh, hi." I blinked up at them.

"Hello. I'm Tweedle Dee, that's two words, if you please!" The pixie with short, red hair and a matching dress stood and curtsied as she introduced herself.

"And I'm her twin sister, Dumtalora." The pixie with blue hair down to her tiny butt, and a dress to match, threw me a wave.

"Hi, Tweedle Dee and Dumtalora." I said the names slowly, hoping they were some kind of joke.

"Oh, you can call us Dee and Dum," Dumtalora said

quickly. "Obviously, our names are a bit of a mouthful for you."

Now someone named Dum thinks I'm slow? Oh, the irony.

"You two wouldn't be able to help me out here, would you?"

The pixies slipped off the window ledge. Their retracted wings popped out, and they fluttered in midair.

"We can help you get the key," Dum said.

Embarrassment crashed over me. Why hadn't I just unstrapped my wings?

Some faerie I am . . .

"Yeah, that would be great."

They beamed at me before landing next to the key. After a scuffle over who would hold it, they discovered that it was too heavy for one pixie anyhow, and shared the burden.

A minute later, they landed in front of me and dropped the key.

"Oh my! We need to exercise more!" Dum clutched her side and bent over as if she'd run a marathon.

"For once, I totally agree." Dee fanned the back of her neck with her red mane.

"Thanks." I lifted the key effortlessly, which told me that despite our sizes being equal, the pixies were kinda weak. "Now, time to get outta here!"

I slung the key over my shoulder and spun toward the door.

"Hold on!" A shriek came from behind me, stopping my heart before I'd even taken two steps.

"What?!" I twisted around, thinking maybe one of them had had a heart attack from exertion. "What happened?"

Dee shoved Dum. "Nothing. She's just being dramatic." The red-haired pixie rolled her eyes and lifted off the floor.

I watched as she soared up to the tabletop, grabbed the teacake, and floated to me. She handed me the cake, and suddenly my hands were very, very full.

"She didn't want you to forget this."

"What does it do?"

"Returns you to your normal height," Dee explained. "Obviously, you can live a fine life at our size. Heck, I have a date with an elf later this week. He doesn't mind at all that I'm small. Especially when I—"

"Thanks!" I shouted over her. "I appreciate the help, but I should be going."

I strode over to the door, intent on getting out of there, nibbling on the cake, and finding Herald again so he could take me where I needed to go.

I had to set the cake down to maneuver the key in the lock, but eventually I got it, and the lock clicked open. I dropped the key, picked up the cake, and marched through the door.

As soon as I stepped foot on the other side of the portal, I gasped.

This place burst with color and life and scents and sounds unlike *anything* I'd ever seen.

"Not many people enter Wonderland Court anymore."

I twisted to see Dee soar through the small door, and blinked.

In my world, I'd entered a tree, but in Faerie, I'd exited out of a tower at least ten stories tall. The contradiction confused me, but considering all the crazy stuff I'd passed on my way down the rabbit hole, I decided I needed to roll with it.

"But when they do, they always have that reaction," Dee finished, landing beside me.

A second later, Dum followed.

"I bet. In my world, trees are generally only green, or orange and red in autumn. But they're definitely never pink or blue or purple," I told them, taking in the assortment of vegetation in front of me. "And those sounds . . . what am I hearing?"

It sounded like a cross between a cat's yowl and a dog's bark. Totally alien to my ear.

"That's a bandersnatch," Dum said. "There are only a few left in the wild. You're lucky to hear one. They rarely make noises because they don't want to be captured."

Who does?

"Well, I guess I'd better grow." I was ready to be back to my normal size and leave the pixies behind.

Keeping in mind how little of the liquid I'd drank, and how small it had made me, I took only a tiny nibble of the teacake.

The reaction was instantaneous. My bones extended and thickened by the millisecond as I shot up.

When I stopped growing, I looked around. Everything seemed normal, like it had been before I drank the purple liquid.

Actually, I might've gained an inch or two. Go me. I grinned.

Now back to normal height, I noticed a path leading into the woods away from the tower, and made my way over to it. I'd just entered the woods when I felt the slightest weight land on each of my shoulders.

Oh no, this is not happening.

"What are you doing?" I asked Dee and Dum, both of whom were positioning themselves so they could ride with their legs comfortably dangling down the sides of my arms.

"Coming with you," Dee replied.

"Yeah, except I work alone so . . ."

I didn't finish before she started laughing. "Oh, right. There was talk that you'd probably insist on that, considering what you've become."

"And what's that?" My stomach tightened defensively.

I didn't want people to gossip about my occupation. Or tell my family before I met them.

"A warrior. One not scared to take back what we need." Dee crossed her arms over her chest and gave me an impressed look.

All of a sudden, I felt more friendly toward her. Being called a warrior was better, more socially acceptable, than being called an assassin. Still, I didn't want them tagging along.

"Okay, well, the rumor mill was right. This warrior works alone. So, hop off, pixies."

"If we do, how are you going to find those you seek?" Dum chimed in.

"I—"

A group of gryphons charged through the forest in front of us. My mouth fell open as I watched the beasts, part eagle and part lion, run gracefully through the forest. Their scent, earthy, a bit like petrichor, as if they'd just been flying through a storm, and also something unnamable—at least to me—filled my nostrils.

The pixies were right. I was out of my depth.

The phone in my pocket wouldn't work, or help me navigate. I knew I was in Wonderland Court, but not where that court was in Faerie. I didn't even know if the stars were the same here. Or the cardinal directions.

And come to think of it, now that I was in Faerie, shouldn't I be getting sick? Most people who visited Faerie from my world became ill on their first trip to the fae world.

"Why don't I feel funny? I'm from the human realm. Shouldn't I be feeling Faerie drunk?"

Dum gave me an understanding smile. "You were born here, Alice. Even if you haven't been back in a while, Faerie is in your blood."

"Theoretically, anyhow," Dee said sassily.

I glared at her, but couldn't retort, because the little

shit was right. I didn't feel at home here. "Fine. You can come with me. But only until I find Herald, and he introduces me to my family."

The pixies exchanged a glance before Dee held out her tiny hand.

I lifted my big one to hers, and she grabbed the tip of my finger to shake.

"We're in this together!" she beamed. "And now that you've agreed, I should tell you that you're going the wrong way."

CHAPTER 4

We'd been trudging through the woods for hours by the time we exited the forest path onto a larger road. My eyes trailed down the lane.

If we went right, there was nothing but a stretch of dirt road, but on the left, a building—a house, by the looks of it—rose in the distance.

"Go that way," Dee commanded and pointed in the direction of the house. She was definitely the bossier of the two pixies and had been directing me for almost the whole journey.

"Who lives there?"

"No one anymore. The last occupants left years ago," Dum said, her mouth downturned and a tear beginning to sparkle in her eye. "That's a sort of memorial. A very, very sad one."

"Okay," I said, not wanting to dig deeper.

Xavier didn't put much stock in fragile things like feelings, and he had raised me with a grit-it-out mentality. I never had quite met his expectations, my own emotions were often too strong to deny. But I was quite good at brushing aside others' emotions and, as a result, when I was inclined to care, other people's emotions made me uncomfortable. I never knew how to best support them.

Probably because I wanted to avoid talking about why the house made Dum sad, we reached the building in no time at all. Up close, its derelict state grew more obvious. The roof had caved in, and many bird nests lined the openings of each window. A stench that reminded me faintly of compost and rotted wood teased my nostrils.

But the strangest thing was the long table spread out over an expansive lawn. It could have easily seated twenty people, and by the looks of it, at one time, it had. Teacups, cake platters, and plates rimmed with gold ran the length of the wooden surface, all of them covered in dirt, and most chipped or broken.

I took in the table, ignoring the pangs of hunger that the idea of food elicited, and shifting my attention to the front door, still cracked open on its hinges. "It looks like people got up mid-party and never cleaned up . . ."

Dum burst into tears, making me cringe, so I turned to the other pixie.

Dee shot her sister a disapproving look and shook her head. "They didn't come back because the Red Queen either killed them . . . or worse."

Herald had mentioned the Red Queen. Was she the

same woman who'd sent people after me? I'd been so caught up in dreams about my family that I'd never asked for clarification. Now seemed like a good time to change that.

"Why? And is the Red Queen the same one who is after me?"

"I'm afraid so." Dee pressed her lips together. "The people who gathered here were the first rebels to oppose the Red Queen. Their bravery cost them their heads."

"I see." My throat tightened as sadness rippled through me. I felt as if I should say more, but what? If the people who perished here had been rebels, they probably knew my parents, but I didn't know them. What could I say that would really matter?

"Don't worry," Dee remarked. "It'll be eerie inside, but not gruesome."

Brushing off that she'd misread my emotions for fear or hesitation, I twisted to face her. "Excuse me? Why do we need to go inside? I thought you said this was a memorial."

On the other side of me, Dum picked up a lock of my hair and tugged lightly. "Before you enter more populated areas, we need to cover your hair. It's too much like your mother's. People will be on the lookout for it."

I cocked my head. I supposed that made a little sense. I rarely saw others with hair as white as mine, and if my mother was a rebel leader . . .

"It doesn't take dye well," I warned them, recalling the time I'd tried to dye it purple to piss Xavier off and get out of a mission. The color had barely lasted a day before fading to nothing. "Never has."

"We're not looking for dye," Dee said, and pointed to the front door.

I sighed and followed their directions. The door creaked when I pressed it open wide, and I shuddered as we stepped into a dank smelling entryway. Old homes weren't my thing. Even less so if they had history like this one did. Ghosts definitely lived here, and while there wasn't much that scared me, ghosts gave me the creeps.

If they decided to get hostile, neither daggers nor my magic could harm them.

"It's just like I remember," Dum sighed.

"Let's hope Ernie's creations have not been looted," Dee said cryptically. "Go up the stairs, Alice."

I climbed the bowed steps, keeping a sharp eye out for rotting floorboards. Shockingly, everything held up, and when I reached the top, Dee directed me to the second room on the right.

"What is this place?" I asked as I opened the door and came face to face with hundreds of hats in every style imaginable.

"A workshop." Dum leapt off my shoulder and began flitting around the room. Dust flew from some of the hats in her wake, filling the air.

"So this is how we'll cover up my hair?" I wrinkled my nose to keep from sneezing.

A lot of the hats were crazy flamboyant and not my

style, but I guessed I'd wear them—if it was the only way to get close to my family.

"What about this one?" Dee held up a bright green top hat adorned with flowers.

"Too flashy." I gestured to my all-black ensemble. "I prefer black."

"*Boring!*" Dee said, but placed the top hat back on its hook.

I nixed a few more options, all too colorful or large for my taste, before I found the perfect one.

It was a black boater cap with a simple gold ribbon wrapped around it. There was enough room in the top of the hat for me to tuck my blonde braid out of sight. Only the wisps near my ears would be visible, and there was nothing I could do about them except pull the hat down low.

"I didn't think it would work, but it kind of does." Dum tilted her head to take in my new accessory.

"I don't know." Dee shot a longing glance at the green top hat embellished with purple and orange butterflies on the rim. "Seems a shame, considering Ernie was known for his color and flair, but I guess it is best to be unassuming during our travels."

"Yes, and on that note, we should go," Dum said.

Finally, I thought, and followed the pixies from the room.

Once we hit the road again, we walked for miles and miles, until after cresting a hill, a town appeared.

I woke up the pixies, who'd been napping on my shoulders. These two were pint-sized freeloaders.

"Where—oh! We're almost to Heartstown!" A bright smile lit up Dum's face.

"Is that here?"

"No, this is just a village before we cut through another bit of forest." Dum waved at the trees behind the quaint settlement. "Heartstown is another hour through the woods."

An hour?

When I'd left my apartment that morning, I'd assumed I'd grab something to eat on the go. Now that I'd been walking all morning and afternoon, my belly was tight with hunger. I wouldn't be able to deny the pangs for much longer. Heck, at this point I'd even take a greasy spoon diner, the type of place I usually disliked. I found their lack of healthy options frustrating, but I was so starving that I'd deal.

"Can we stop here for food?"

"Ohh, Oberon's ears, this place has the most delicious food!" Dum squealed as she placed her hands on my chin to stabilize herself, and swung forward to look at Dee. "We have to take her to the Oyster House!"

"It's the best tavern around," the other pixie agreed, "but we must be careful. The Oyster House is rough and tumble, and we don't know where Carpenter's allegiances lie."

"Allegiance? Do you mean you think he could work for the queen?"

"Unfortunately, yes." Dum's face twisted into an expression of indecision. "Alice, we'd love to take you to the Oyster House, but if we do . . ."

"You can't call yourself Alice," Dee cut in.

"But . . . why? No one knows me here."

"Most know your family, though," Dum said. "If Carpenter is in league with the Red Queen, he'll tell her you're here. That could mean trouble."

Clearly, these pixies didn't know me very well. Trouble was my middle name. But I didn't want to put them in danger and pretending to be someone else was easy enough.

"I've got this, girls. Back home, I playact on jobs all the time." I grinned reassuringly. "Just call me Camilla."

The pixies shared a glance that told me they were not convinced, but I was their ride, and my stomach ached with hunger. I wasn't taking no for an answer.

Tilting my chin up and rolling my shoulders back, I strode up to the Oyster House and walked in like I owned the place.

And then I stopped dead in my tracks.

"Oberon's ears, we should have warned her!" Dum moaned. "Now she definitely looks like an outsider."

"About the *enormous* stuffed walrus in the middle of the pub?" I whisper-hissed, taking in the figure in front of me. "Yeah, a heads-up would have been nice."

It would have been one thing if the walrus was simply stuffed and lounging on a fake iceberg. But this walrus was easily three times the size of a normal walrus. It sat there, its mouth gaping open wide, with dozens of empty oyster shells filling it. Someone had even applied some shells to its skin, indicating a grotesque degree of overindulgence. Worst of all, the beast's eyes had been gouged out, and hung a sign around its neck proclaiming the animal to be a "glutton".

"Sorry, Al—Camilla," Dee said. "It's a long story. We'll tell you later. For now, grab a table. And don't stare at anyone."

"Anything to get away from that," I mumbled and stalked over to a table in the far corner.

Although I did my best to avoid eye contact with the dozen other patrons in the tavern, it was impossible not to notice the ugly trio of fae in the opposite corner. Their faces were young and smooth like children's, but they were hunched over like old men, making a gross and confusing juxtaposition.

When I sat down, I sighed. The tavern stank like beer, and the chair wasn't the comfiest, but after miles of walking, I'd take it. I leaned back, prepared to relax, when I noticed that the ugly fae weren't the only ones staring anymore.

Everyone was.

I groaned. "I hope we don't find trouble here, but if shit hits the fan, you two should stay out of the way."

"You haven't seen our teeth, have you?" Dum leapt off my shoulder, onto the table.

"Excuse me?"

Dee jumped down to join her sister, landed lightly,

and spun to face me so that the skirt of her red dress flung up a touch. A tiny growl left her throat, and I watched as her canines dropped much like a vampire's would.

"Excellent," I said. "But that's like a pinprick on someone my size."

"Not if our venom seeps into their bloodstream," Dum declared proudly. For the first time, she sounded a lot like her sister.

"I didn't realize," I said, impressed.

"Pixies always get the rap for being cutesy," Dee remarked with a sassy snap, I guessed to emphasize how badass pixies were. "We're not as scary as someone like you, but get a swarm of us on the attack, or even a handful, and you'd be dead in a minute."

The hubris in her voice made me shudder. "I'm glad I have you on my team, then."

"You'd better be," Dum said. "Because here comes a spriggan." Her eyes darted up to meet mine. "Remember, you're not you-know-who. Play it cool like you're a traveler."

"Afternoon." One of the three ugly creatures I'd seen before pulled up a chair before I could agree to Dum's plan.

I leaned back, slightly repulsed. Not only was the guy hard to look at, but his sour smell, strong enough to cut through the scents of fish and beer, made me want to puke.

"You must be new around here," the spriggan said.

"What makes you think that?"

He gestured down to my feet.

I glanced down at my Converse sneakers. *Well, damn.*

It wasn't like I'd planned to tumble into Faerie when I got dressed that morning.

"Just coming back after a long stint of visiting family in the human world."

"Your demi-fae family doesn't come here?" His voice was tight, like he couldn't believe such an insult. Probably a fae elitist then.

"Nope. This place makes them sick. Plus, the closed portals make it too difficult."

The spriggan leaned back and tented his fingers on the table.

It was a power move I'd seen Xavier use many times. The spriggan was trying to figure me out, while giving the impression that he had everything under control.

I mirrored his actions, which prompted him to arch a bushy blond eyebrow.

"That's interesting. Most demi-fae jump at the chance to visit the world of their ancestors. They'd do anything to get here." He twisted toward his friends and waved them over.

My stomach sank as they rose from their seats. The spriggan wasn't buying my story, and wanted to investigate further.

Time to go on the offense.

"I'm sorry, but my friends and I are trying to get a

bite to eat." I gave him a don't-screw-with-me smile. "And if you don't mind, we'd like privacy."

The spriggan leveled me with his gaze as his youthful lips curled up. "Them's regal words for a girl from the human world."

The pixies gasped at his use of the word "regal".

Regal? I knitted my eyebrows. How could anything I'd said be construed as such?

"In fact," the spriggan continued as his friends joined him, "almost seems to me like you're someone our master would want to meet."

There was no way in hell I'd go anywhere with this creep.

I reached for my dagger before I remembered I hadn't worn it this morning when I drove to Xavier's place.

I refrained from sighing. That was unfortunate, although in no way a deal-breaker. My dagger made things easier, but truth be told, all I needed was my hands and my magic to kill a man.

Although the advantage of surprise never hurt, either —particularly when I was outnumbered.

A little test . . .

I leaned closer to the spriggan, thankful that I'd worn a low-cut shirt and a good bra that day. "It seems like you're threatening me."

As I'd hoped, the spriggan's eyes flitted to my chest for a second. There was interest in his gaze, and considering that his face looked so young, it was pretty disgusting. But

I couldn't let this fae's appearance hinder me. He might have the face of a child, but in body, he was grown.

The next time the same opportunity arose, I'd be ready to capitalize on it.

"Not if you come willingly." The fae behind the leader patted the circles of rope that hung off their hips.

The leader grinned. "You have two options. Agree to use the rope, or I can bind you with magic. Can't promise I won't slip up on the magic from time to time, though." His voice dipped suggestively, and I readied myself.

When his gaze predictably traveled to my cleavage again, I sprang into action.

I flipped the table in the leader's face and leapt high into the air. Two powerful roundhouse kicks took out the spriggans behind him.

The moment I landed, the leader had recovered, tossing the table to the side, and was preparing to attack. But he hadn't been counting on my pixie friends.

Dee and Dum were already on him, attacking his baby-smooth face with their tiny fangs.

The spriggan screamed bloody murder, and all around us, the tavern erupted into chaos. Fae, all of them male, ran at us. Punches were thrown, magic released, and curses spat, but my girls and I showed them what was up. In just over a minute, every single patron in the bar was lying on the ground, either passed out or moaning.

"That didn't go as we'd hoped," Dum said, biting her bottom lip as she cast a glance around the room.

"Not at all," Dee remarked, kicking a man in the

eyeball when he tried to rise. "We should get out of here. I doubt anyone will be eager to take us on again, but it's still best if we put some distance between us."

I agreed, but I also refused to leave without sustenance.

Taking charge, I marched down a long hallway into the kitchen.

There was only one guy there, singing to a tune coming from a strange bird who seemed to be able to play songs. He was a massive man, his back turned to me as he stirred a pot of mussels. A platter of sliced bread and at least three dozen shucked oysters sat next to the stove, ready to be taken out to customers.

"Hey!" I shouted over the bird. "We need some food to go."

The man turned.

He looked nothing at all like I expected. Then again, who would expect *anyone* to have a tattoo of a hammer on their cheek?

"You'll get served when I'm ready," the cook said.

My arms crossed over my chest, and I leveled him with my gaze. "Go take a peek at your dining room—my handiwork. Then you can reassess what you just said to me."

The cook arched a brow, but I didn't budge. I was young, but I'd learned from the best, and knew exactly how intimidating I could look. Few people took me on, and the ones who did were idiots like the spriggan.

As expected, after only a few seconds of standing my

ground, he dropped his spoon into the pot and lumbered over to the door. One peek later, and the cook, who belatedly introduced himself—'Eddie Carpenter at your service'—provided us with a sack of sandwiches and, at my request, a few golden fae apples to go.

"Thanks, Eddie," I said, leaving the kitchen. "See you around."

"Hopefully not," he remarked.

"You have good instincts, my friend." I toasted him with the bag, and left the Oyster House.

CHAPTER 5

"You two didn't mention that those teeth shred the heck out of food." I watched, captivated, as Dum devoured her fourth hunk of meat with all the grace of a ravenous wolf. The girl might be tiny, but dang. I'd hit my limit a half hour ago. The pixies, on the other hand, were still going strong.

"We don't like to advertise that our table manners could use work." She flicked away a tiny shred of meat from where it had landed on her breast.

I laughed. I hadn't wanted the two around at first, but I'd changed my mind—a little. If I had to have guides, at least they were badasses and provided good comedy.

We fell into silence as I huffed up a mile-long steep hill. Although I was fit, the hours of travel had started to take their toll. By the time I got to the top, I had to stop and place my hands on my knees to catch my breath.

At least there's a view.

A short distance away, the dense vegetation of the forest broke, and a city rose behind it.

"Please tell me that's where we're going?" I panted.

"It sure is," Dee said through a mouthful of bread. "That's the beautiful capital of Wonderland Island, and seat of the Red Queen's court, Heartstown."

The origin of the city's name was obvious. Many of the buildings had windows in the shape of hearts. Occasionally, multicolored trees popped up between the structures, also pruned to resemble hearts. And then there was the show-stopper—the castle.

The red and white motif was unmistakable in the sea of browns, tans, and creams. Its turrets and spires soared toward the sky, all topped with gold hearts. Large gardens surrounded one side of the castle, while on the other side of the palace, an ocean spread before us, glimmering a strange green-blue.

"Someone has a thing for hearts."

"The queen," Dum said. "The rebels call her the Red Queen because she's made so many heads roll, but she prefers to be called the Queen of Hearts. The castle is Heart Castle."

I snorted. "Sounds delusional to me."

"You have no idea," Dee replied.

I descended the long hill. Gradually, the trees began to thin, and a sign proclaiming that we'd reached the boundaries of Heartstown appeared where the path split at the bottom, although it didn't indicate which way would take us to the city gate.

Actually, would we use a main city gate? I was searching for rebels. Surely discretion would be valued. I furrowed my eyebrows. "Which way?"

Dum pointed me in the right direction. "We'll stop by rebel headquarters first. Most who believe in our cause congregate there—not all together, of course." Dum added the last bit after I arched my eyebrows at her. "We'll introduce you."

"Will my family be there?"

"Almost everyone will be. They've been waiting for you." Dee glanced away quickly, as if she'd heard something in the woods. I checked my other shoulder. Dum seemed to have heard it too.

I listened, but didn't hear a peep and figured the pixies had keener hearing than me. I brushed off the awkward pause and kept on moving.

As we approached the wall of Heartstown, the pixies directed me around the side, away from the main gate. From there, they led me to a hole in the wall not much larger than the window I'd squeezed through to break into the alpha's home the day before.

I sighed. "There's not a less guarded gate we can go through? I'll knock out the soldiers. Or maybe I can climb a tree and hop over?"

Dum's gaze flicked up to me, and she gestured to my shoes. "Bad idea. We don't want anyone manning the gates, even the least important of them, seeing you yet. Someone might recognize you, and call for help."

"Yeah, now hurry up before someone spots us," Dee commanded.

I have to stop climbing through teensy places, I thought as I shoved myself through the hole, pinching my hips and covering my clothes with stone dust in the process.

Once I was on the other side, I tried to wipe my clothes off so as to be presentable when I met my parents. As I did, I scanned my surroundings.

It was clear to me that we'd entered on the sketchy side of town. Buildings looked like they were about to fall over, and rats stared at us like they owned the place. Which they probably thought they did, considering the piles of trash lining the street.

"Won't be long now!" Dee sang as she soared through the hole. "We're almost there."

And she was right. Rebel headquarters, apparently also known as the home of someone named Henri Hatter, turned out to be a derelict, sprawling, two-story house only a few streets away from the city wall.

"So, this is it?" I asked as we stood outside the rusted gates.

"Isn't it the perfect disguise!" Dum exclaimed. "Henri's father bought it so his son could be close when Hatter was at court. Now, leaders of the resistance live here."

Dee leapt off one shoulder to join her sister on the other. "You know, Alice hasn't actually expressed interest in being a rebel. Perhaps you shouldn't go around spreading insider knowledge?"

I blinked. Of course, she was justified. I *didn't* want to

join their resistance. I only wanted to meet my family and get some answers. But the idea that the pixies might not trust me stung.

"Oh! Stop it, Dee!" Dum scowled at her sister. "She won't say anything. Will you, Alice?" The softer of the pair blinked up at me innocently, waiting for my assurance.

"No," I decided on the spot. "I won't."

"See! Now let's go inside. Henri is waiting for us." Dum's cheeks pinked. "We're later than expected because of Herald leaving you, but you're here all the same!"

When we got closer to the building, its run-down nature was even more obvious. Curls of paint threatened to fall off the walls, and I swore I could hear the squeaking of mice.

"Are you two sure that this is the place? Sounds gross inside."

"That's just Dormouse and Tim," Dum replied.

"Uh, okay. Why do they sound like chipmunks?"

"They're mice! Not chipmunks!" Dum said with a laugh. "They just have naturally high-pitched voices like me and Dee!"

Mice . . . Like real mice? I swallowed, a little grossed out.

"They're on our side," Dee said, looking as unbothered by the rodent party going on inside as her sister. "Go on."

Still skeptical, I knocked lightly so as not to break down the door. Another chorus of squeaks came from within, and a few seconds later, the door squealed open.

A rabbit stood there, but not the one I'd followed into Wonderland. This one had brown fur, a distinct lack of a waistcoat or pocket watch, and a scowl on his face.

"What happened to Herald?" the brown rabbit said, his gaze oscillating between Dee and Dum.

"I told you that you should have sent me! The idiot left Alice at the tower!" Dee exclaimed. "I had to save her!"

"*We*," Dum corrected. "We had to save her."

"I would like to put it out there that I didn't actually need saving. I would have figured out the cake/bottle thing."

It was probably a lie, but I wasn't about to meet my parents for the first time in ages, and let them think I was a damsel in distress.

"I'm March Hare," the brown rabbit replied, taking no notice of what I'd said. "Come inside before someone sees you." He turned and made his way down a long, dark hallway.

March Hare's gait was somewhere between a hop and how normal people walked—one foot gliding smoothly in front of the other. It was so strange and mesmerizing that I didn't even hear the voices we were approaching until the hare led us into a large room filled with paintings in various stages of doneness.

Three new people stood before us, in the middle of what appeared to be a heated discussion. Well, '*people*' was a loose term. While they talked like people, dressed like people, and even walked like people, two of the three beings weren't people.

Two mice stood on the table, both dressed in long shirts—one red, one yellow—as they munched on crumbs and chatted up at a man with a sheet of long, black hair that covered his face.

"No!" the black mouse wearing yellow squealed. "We should—"

March Hare cleared his throat.

The mice turned, and the man's head snapped up. Striking green eyes locked with mine, making my breath hitch in my throat.

Is he for real?

The guy, with his razor-sharp jawline, a muscular build, and long, black hair that flowed just past his shoulders, was almost too much to take in. Add in the translucent wings veined with emerald and gold that juxtaposed delicacy with brawn, and he was officially the most handsome man I'd ever seen.

Not a human man. A faerie, like me.

"Good afternoon," the man's deep baritone rumbled, making my heart rate kick up as he walked over. His eyes continued to bore through me in an odd way.

It's like he's looking at a ghost . . .

"I'm Henri Hatter. This is my home. The black mouse is Dormouse, and the one wearing red is Tim."

"Alice. But I think you might already know that."

Henri's lips twitched up at the corners. "Welcome to Heartstown, Alice. Would you mind chatting with me?"

He gestured to a pair of tatty chairs that sat before a hearth filled with fire.

"Sure . . ." I said, "although I came here for a specific reason." I cast a glance around but didn't see anyone else in the room. Nor did I hear others moving about elsewhere. "My family . . . are they here?"

"Of course," Henri replied. "You always preferred to get down to business."

I cocked my head. "Excuse me?"

"We've met before, Alice. Long, long ago." Henri smiled, and my heart skipped a beat when two deep dimples appeared in his cheeks. "Come, let's talk." He turned, and for the first time, I was presented with Henri's backside.

And boy oh boy, what a glorious backside it was. Two tight balls of muscle flexed one after the other as he walked toward the hearth.

Realizing I was staring like a hard-core creeper, I blinked and shook my head. *Get ahold of yourself, girl!*

I squared my shoulders, and followed Henri to the threadbare armchairs. He offered me the one that looked more cushiony, and I accepted, sliding into it gracefully.

"How are you finding Wonderland Island so far?"

My eyes widened a touch. Small talk? Was this really happening? I'd waited years to talk to my family. I didn't have time for this crap.

"Well, to be honest—"

"Don't tell him about the Oyster House!" Dee whisper-screamed in my ear. "Please! They'll never trust me with a job like this again."

I wanted to retort that they hadn't trusted her with this job to begin with, but seeing as I might need the pixies' expertise to get out of Faerie, I didn't want to burn that bridge.

"It's interesting," I said, "but to be honest, I'd like to get on with this and meet my family."

Henri's face tightened. "Humor me. Did you run into anyone on your journey?"

My lips pressed together, annoyed at his insistence that we delay my reunion.

"I arrived in a strange tower and took a walk through the woods. On the way, I came across a beat-up old house with an abandoned tea party. That—"

Dum groaned, and I paused, noticing that she wasn't the only one who had reacted to my mention of the tea party. Hatter's face fell, and he lifted a hand to his heart, as if I'd wounded him.

"But other than that," I continued, not sure what to do about his display of emotion. "It was uneventful."

The man nodded and shook himself, as if having to pull himself from a pit of some deep emotion. Had he been at that tea party?

"Perfect," Hatter said before I could work up the courage to ask. "We hoped for an easy journey. I apologize that Herald was not as good of a guide as we would have liked. He can become frantic at times . . . Particularly if he's short on it."

"Where was he going in such a hurry, anyway?" I asked, unable to help myself.

Henri chuckled. "Herald is part of the rebellion, but he works inside the castle, too. He's the Red Queen's crier. Seeing as she's having a croquet match today, he needed to be present."

"So why send him to get me?"

"I thought it was smart because he's the most versatile of us, since he's able to shift into anything. But now I see how wrong I was. Dee and Dum, you two did great." Henri gave them a brilliant smile.

Dee and Dum let out matching high-pitched, flirty laughs. "Oh, it was nothing, Hatter!" Dee said, and I swore that her voice was deeper, more sultry, than before. "Happy to help." Her wings fluttered a little in my ears.

Henri beamed brighter, oblivious to the effect he was having on their tiny pixie hearts. "Thank you. Now, Alice, let's get down to the reason we invited you here."

Hatter twisted toward a side table and picked up a small book. He flipped through a few pages before stopping and turning the book to face me.

What was this, story time? No freaking way. My patience, which admittedly wasn't the strongest to begin with, had worn thin. I was done with the niceties and chit-chat.

"Where are my parents?"

Hatter's green gaze locked with mine, nearly mesmerizing me as he shifted in his seat.

"Well?" I asked, not about to be thrown off track by a

hot guy. "If they sent for me, why aren't they here? They're rebels, right?"

Henri cleared his throat. "I didn't want to have to tell you this without a backstory, but I can see you don't wish to hear that."

He closed the book and leaned forward so that his elbows rested on his knees and his tented hands pressed to his lips.

The room fell totally silent, and a distinct sense of unease trickled through it, making me clench my jaw.

"The truth is, your parents died years ago." He spoke the words quickly, like he was ripping off a bandage.

I blinked, stunned, before shooting to my feet. "You lied. Why?"

"We need your help." Hatter stood. "You see, Alice, your parents were the king and queen before the Red Queen unseated and killed them. You're the true heir to the crown. You still have—"

Barely registering his words, I grasped for my dagger, my protection, the one thing I could count on. But it wasn't at my hip, so instead, I thrust a finger at him. "You brought me here under false pretenses."

"We brought you here to meet your parents' supporters, and return you to the throne."

"Well, maybe you should have asked about what I wanted," I snapped. The others reared back at my tone. "Because I never asked for a crown, asshole."

I spun and fled the room.

CHAPTER 6

After years of training under a vampire, I was very fast, and confident that I could lose Hatter in the crowds of Heartstown. My breathing remained even as my feet pounded uneven cobblestones. Without caring much where I went, as long as I put distance between me and Henri, I ran through the run-down neighborhood, weaving between buildings, and hopping dilapidated fences.

Fae of all races, sizes, and shapes watched me flee. The thought that perhaps one could help me leave this place entered my mind, but I dismissed it.

Why would I want help from any of them? So far, every fae I'd spoken to had deceived me.

They're all liars. They—

I stopped dead in my tracks.

No. They couldn't have, because the fae were unable to lie.

I spun around and spotted a creature who I thought was a brownie, judging by his nut-brown skin, masses of hair, and perfectly round belly.

"You!" I rushed up to him. "Who was the queen of Wonderland before the Red Queen?"

The brownie looked around from side to side and gulped.

"Tell me!"

"T—th—the Red Queen has always ruled Wonderland." The brownie stuttered.

I blinked. Impossible. The fae were long-lived, but not immortal. Only vampires and the old gods were immortal.

But *if* it was true, then Hatter had lied. How?

"Are you sure?" Because that doesn't seem very—"

"She's enchanted them."

I looked up to find Henri standing in front of me, and immediately raised my fist, ready to pummel the shit out of him.

When I punched, he caught my hand. Our arms shook as we fought each other, eyes locked together for long seconds that made me uncomfortable. Finally, I broke the connection, ripping my fist from his grasp.

"How did you keep up?" I glared at him.

Henri fluttered his wings. "Flying is faster than running, especially above crowds."

Ugh, wings! I really must unbind mine.

"Whatever. What do you mean she's enchanted them?"

"You won't run if I tell you?"

I glanced at the brownie, who had taken a few steps back. His body trembled, and sweat dripped down his face.

Was he reacting to me? I knew that I could be intimidating, but still, this was drastic.

"It's the spell. He told a lie, which our kind can't do unless we're under a spell or some other magical influence." Hatter gestured to me. "Which you probably have experience with, given your profession?"

He was right. Even though I'd thought I was demifae, once every moon cycle Xavier had made me drink a potion that allowed me to lie. In fact, I'd done so just days ago. Xavier always said it was because he couldn't take the slightest chance that my fae blood would make my missions more difficult. Now that I knew I was a pureborn fae, I recognized that I wouldn't have been able to lie at *all* without the potion.

This guy, Hatter, was clever—and apparently not a liar.

But if my parents are dead, who am I supposed to be meeting?

"Fine. I won't run, but why did you lie to me? In fact, why even bring me here? I could have gone on, oblivious to all this."

Thanks to the potion in my system, that last part was a total lie. I'd wanted to meet my parents for years, and probably would have sought them out eventually.

But Hatter might think it was the truth.

"Let's go this way," he gestured toward a park with

hedges sculpted in the shape of hearts, and masses of rose bushes with bright red blooms. "No talking until others can't hear. And put this on." He shoved a black cloak at me.

"What? Why?"

"Your hair. You lost your hat while you ran, and the color is too much like your mother's. It's drawing attention. Now that you know who she was, surely you understand?"

A female fae walked by, her eyes trailing down my braid with interest. I frowned and slung the cloak over my head.

We were deep into the park when Hatter spoke again. "Your parents were the previous rulers of the Wonderland Court, although you'll be hard-pressed to find a layperson who believes it."

"But how could she spell them like that? Fae are elemental—even if they're aether-blessed, that's so many people. The Red Queen would need—"

"A witch," Henri finished. "She has two powerful witches on her counsel. Along with a few other sorts of creatures who don't normally live in Faerie. When the Red Queen began her reign, they released a mist. Everyone who didn't flee and came in contact with the mist forgot all about your parents. In that way, the Red Queen wiped out your parents' legacy almost entirely in one fell swoop."

My teeth ground together. "I'll kill her."

Hatter's eyebrows arched. "That's sort of what we

were hoping, actually. That you'd join the rebellion and be able to take her down. Then you could claim your birthright."

I had no intention of joining any rebellion or becoming queen. I'd been honest when I said I didn't want a crown. All I'd wanted was to meet my parents, hopefully like them, and learn about my life before Xavier. I certainly didn't want to lead a kingdom.

However, now that I'd learned about my parents' murder, I couldn't deny that I felt another desire coming on.

The need for vengeance ran hot and thick through me, and I would damn well get it. But to take down a queen, I required information. For the time being, I decided it was better to let Hatter believe that I might become a rebel and queen.

"How many remember the truth?"

"The rebellion members, of course," Hatter said, visibly relieved by my response. "There are others, too, but not many. I would say that out of the thousands who live here, little more than two hundred on Wonderland Island remember. Many fled Heartstown and live in the wilds."

"But what about the other courts? There are dozens, right?"

"The Red Queen has surrounded our island with monsters that she controls. Few fae can get on or off," Henri replied, his tone dipping into sorrow. "Other courts remember your family, but none have stood up to help us.

One, the Dark Court, has actually allied with the Red Queen."

The Dark Court. In my world, there had even been talk of it. It was said they worked with demons to help take over the human realm in the recent war. Their attempts had failed, but it had been close—dangerously close.

"Okay, fine. So people don't remember my family. That still doesn't explain why you lied to me. Or how."

Hatter's gaze flicked to mine, and he inched closer. I tried to ignore the scents of leather and spice clinging to him. "No one lied."

I was about to pull away, when his hand landed on my wrist, stopping me.

"No one said that you would meet your parents, only your family. And rumor has it that your sister lives. The Red Queen is hiding her."

I blinked as I took in the words. "I don't have a sister."

"You do. Her name is Elise. She's two years your junior and almost your mirror image, save for the hair. Hers was always darker."

I tilted my head. "How is it you expect me to believe that? Why would you be able to recall my sister when I can't?" My fists clenched as frustration arose at the black expanse of my pitiful memory.

"The enchanted mist never stripped me of my memories, because my father, Ernie Hatter, worked at the palace before the Red Queen took over. He ordered me to be taken far from home, like you. Many of our parents did that. Unfortunately, like your family, my father died at the Red Queen's hand." Hatter peered out over the garden.

"That abandoned tea party you saw on the road, that was my father's childhood home. After he hid me, he fled there, hoping that the Red Queen wouldn't follow." He shook his head. "A fool's hope. But then again, my father was a hatter by profession as well as by name. As such, he truly was a little mad.

"The Red Queen came for him while he, March Hare, and Dormouse dined with friends. Only March Hare and Dormouse walked away that day—though they were not unscathed either."

A lump rose in my throat, but I swallowed it back down, determined not to show my sympathy to the person who'd tricked me.

"If your father worked at the palace, then he must have known my parents."

"He was your mother's personal hatter." Henri sniffed, and once again his emerald eyes found mine. "We both spent a lot of time at the castle. I remember you and your sister vividly. And even if I didn't, I would know that you existed, because I have this."

From his pocket, he pulled out a locket. He opened it, and two photos stared up at me. One was of a man wearing a flamboyant hat, and the second was of three young children.

The kids, a black-haired boy with burning green eyes, and two girls, one with white-blonde hair, the other with light brown, were all crammed on a throne, smiling mischievously, as if they knew they weren't supposed to be there. The moment I laid eyes on the smallest child, something broke inside me. And a single precious memory floated into my mind.

Elise ran through ornate corridors—the palace halls probably—as I chased her. Flowers adorned our hair, and we were both laughing. Shadowy onlookers smiled indulgently.

"Elise—" I gulped. "She's real."

How could I forget such a thing? Such an important person? It didn't seem right, or possible.

"Yes, she's real," Henri echoed. "Although no one has seen her for thirteen years. Word has it that the Red Queen keeps her imprisoned in the Dark Court."

I could think of only one reason the Red Queen, a woman who had gone to such extremes to convince others she was the natural ruler, would keep my sister alive.

"The queen wants leverage over me, because she knows I'm not dead."

Hatter nodded. "I think so too. What's more, she probably believes that when you return, having your sister will be the bargaining chip she needs to spare her own life.

"Hmm." My lips pressed together as anger at the queen who'd stolen my life and future began coursing through me. "Too bad for the queen, I've never been much of a bargainer."

CHAPTER 7

"We're so sorry for not telling you everything, Alice!" Dee's high-pitched voice rang out as Hatter led me back into his great room. "But no one trusted us with the job as it was! We had to follow command."

"Yes! So, so, so sorry!" Dum added, her blue eyes filled with tears.

I grunted, not quite ready to forgive the pixies I'd almost considered friends.

"Oh, Hatter," Dee turned to Henri. "I'm so relieved that you caught her before something *terrible* happened."

"Of course he did," Dum fluttered her lashes at Henri, and smoothed her dress.

Apparently, both pixies were done begging forgiveness. It was back to their regularly scheduled programming of flirting with Hatter, their sexy rebel leader.

"Even if Alice can run as fast as a bandersnatch, Hatter is an *athlete*," Dum cooed. "Our wings couldn't keep up, but I had faith that you'd catch her, Henri."

Hatter chuckled. "I don't know if I'd call myself an athlete. I only exercise so I can paint for hours without tiring." He crossed the room to pick up and right an easel I'd knocked over when I raced out of the house.

My eyes trailed over all the paintings. There had to be at least twenty. Had he made all of them?

"So modest, too," Dee purred as she landed on my shoulder.

I rolled my eyes.

"Don't be jealous, Alice. He's known me longer and has always had a bit of a thing for me," Dee hissed in my ear.

I scoffed, my tone little more than a whisper. "Right. And when you get married, how is that going to work? You're not exactly height-compatible."

"Pfft. I've been on dates with tall guys before. I'd even grow a little. For Henri, I'd do almost anything."

"Anything, huh? How about—"

"What are you two gossiping about?" Henri asked.

My mouth snapped shut, and heat dashed across my cheeks.

"Yes, Alice. What *were* you saying?" Dee said, her voice sickly sweet.

"I was wondering . . ." I paused because Hatter was watching me with those intense green eyes that made me shiver. "When will we get started with this whole killing the queen thing?"

"Oh, you told her?" Dum looked relieved. "Good. I hated keeping secrets from my new best friend!"

Although my heart had frozen over upon learning that everyone had manipulated me, those words melted it a little.

Damn pixies and their cuteness would ruin my rep.

"Alice, I'd like to show you something."

As soon as Hatter turned his back, Dee leaned in close.

"Should I tell him what you were really about to say —hey!"

I shoved her off my shoulder and she plummeted with a squeal until her wings caught her.

"That was—"

"Warranted," I hissed, and then batted her away before joining Hatter, who was pulling a cloth cover off one easel.

"What's this?" I asked, taking in the painting.

"A map of Wonderland Island. Or as close to a reliable map as I can create."

With all the vibrant colors and strange shapes, it didn't look like any map I'd ever seen. But then again, today I'd seen forests with trees of every shade. Obviously, things in Wonderland were unique.

"What are all the animal-looking things?" I pointed to a pack of what seemed to be cat-dog hybrids.

"Those are bandersnatch."

So that's what we heard on the way there. Weird looking things . . .

"And those?" My finger moved to the ocean where tentacles emerged from the deep blue.

"Kraken." Hatter gestured to the sea creature "Both are types of creatures under the queen's influence."

"What does she use them for?"

"The Red Queen rarely leaves her castle. Instead, she relies on soldiers—some official, some not—and enchanted animals to keep the peace. Her appearances have grown even more sparse in the last year. We think perhaps that's because of the threat you pose."

My lips curled up. Too right. "We'll have to get me a weapon before I sneak into the castle and take her on. A dagger, preferably. I left mine back at home."

Henri put up a hand. "Hold up. One thing at a time. A dagger?"

"It's my weapon. Back home they call me Alice the Dagger. It's all I need to defeat the Red Queen."

"But why would you need that when you're aether-blessed?"

I arched my eyebrows. "I can't control aether."

He twisted to face me, his expression incredulous as he held up a finger. "One. A dagger will *not* be enough against the Red Queen." Another slender digit popped up, joining the first. "And two—you might have forgotten . . . which I don't quite understand . . . but you most definitely can use aether."

I scoffed, annoyed at his presumption that he knew my magic better than I did. "I'm sorry, but I've broken up vicious underground shifter rings. I've taken on vampire clan leaders—*ancients*. Most recently, I survived a damned *demon war*. All that without the use of aether, which absolutely would have been useful. That said, I'm pretty sure I can handle a fae queen with a dagger."

Hatter was studying me, listening to my every word, but his face revealed none of his thoughts. Was he impressed? Scared?

After a quiet few seconds, he sighed. "Why they chose Doru to watch over you, I'll never understand. You're too young to have experienced all that."

My lips parted in shock. "You can't be much older than me."

"Three years older. I used to throw it in your face all the time when you tried to boss me around." Hatter smiled faintly. "And don't take this the wrong way, I'm sure your experience will come in handy, but I'm also positive that it won't be enough."

I crossed my arms over my chest. "Why not? If the Red Queen stole the throne, then she probably can't use aether either. Isn't it usually a trait of the hereditary royal line?"

"Yes. Royals, but occasionally, an extremely powerful fae just pops up."

"And is she one of those anomalies?"

Hatter pressed his lips together and turned back to

the painting of Wonderland Island. "No, but she is your aunt."

My hand flew to my stomach. It felt like someone had sucker-punched me in the gut. My aunt?! This person, this queen who overthrew my parents—*killed* them—was related to me?

"I see you don't remember that either," Hatter murmured. "I'm sorry to be the bearer of all the bad news."

"Why is that? Why don't I remember anything?"

"I suspect that when they hid you in the human world, they had a mind witch block your memories. It would be too dangerous to have a small girl talking about her family when the Red Queen was on the hunt."

That sounded reasonable. Before Xavier ground it out of me, I used to be more talkative—chatty, even. No doubt I would have spilled about my parents if I remembered them.

Henri sighed. "Well, I have to say, learning that you don't remember how to use aether changes things."

"Uhhh, it's not that I can't recall it," I corrected him. "It's that I never could."

"It's not that at all."

I placed my hands on my hips. "Oh? And how would you know?"

"Because as a child, you used it all the time."

Yup. Definitely annoying that he remembered things about my past that I had no recollection of.

Seeing that I wasn't going to respond, Hatter continued. "In light of this new information, I think we'll have to go with plan B."

"And what, may I ask, is plan B?"

Henri's eyes shifted to the painting, and his long, slender fingers traveled to the pack of bandersnatch he'd pointed out earlier. "We go after the queen's precious babies and draw her out of her fortress." He gestured to the chair in front of the fire. "You'd better take a seat. This might take a while."

A while? Try *hours*.

The sun was setting and Hatter was still telling me what he knew about the creatures the queen controlled. Although the information was my key to avenging my family and finding my sister, after three hours, I couldn't wait for him to finish.

Thirty minutes later, he was still going strong, so I took things into my own hands.

Drawing on all my acting skills, I stretched my arms wide and released a fake yawn.

Just as I'd hoped he would, Hatter stopped the Wonderland lecture and asked Dum to take me to my room.

My room—in *his* house.

As someone who didn't like leaning on others, I wasn't sure how I felt about that. Plus, there was just Hatter being Hatter, that set me on edge.

The guy was gorgeous and kind, but also unnerving. He knew me too well, and I didn't like that either. But seeing that the Red Queen wanted me dead, I couldn't deny that rebel headquarters was the safest place to gather my thoughts.

And make a plan.

"Once you have a nice rest, you'll be good as new," Dum said cheerily, her tiny feet lightly kicking my upper arm as she perched on me.

During Hatter's lecture, the pixies hadn't left me alone. They sat on my shoulder and braided my hair, or brought me snacks. Clearly, they were trying to repent.

I hadn't forgiven them, but seeing as I understood their point about being underestimated—as a female assassin, that was always the case—I softened sooner than usual.

"I hope so," I said, playing along as I glanced at a row of painted portraits we passed. Each one depicted fae of various races, some I couldn't even identify, looking dignified and serious.

I shook my head. *This morning, I was heading to Beijing. Now I'm in Faerie.*

"It's okay if you need to sleep in tomorrow. We're not on a strict timeline. Although I have to say, you're doing much better than most people who visit Faerie. Which I suppose makes sense. You're not visiting. You're coming home!"

Even though Dum was trying to lift my spirits, her words frustrated me.

The world I'd been born into felt so alien. Intellectually, I understood why a mind witch would want to erase a child's memory to protect them. But did they need to take *everything*?

Dum tapped my shoulder. "Alice? Can you hear me? Take a right here."

The cloak I wore, which initially hid my hair, but later became a blanket during Henri's lecture, tripped me up as I turned on a dime. Dum jostled on my shoulder.

"Sorry," I mumbled as she caught herself.

"No worries. You have a lot on your mind." She smiled at me before pointing to the next door. "And here we are! This one's yours."

Only two rooms remained until we reached the end of the hall.

"Who stays in those?" I pointed to the room next to mine, and the one across from it.

"Henri is next to you, and the other one is . . . empty." Her voice dipped, indicating a sad tale I didn't inquire about.

I had too much on my mind as it was, and being next door to Henri . . . my stomach twisted.

Dum's wings fluttered as she lifted off my shoulder. "Do you want company? Or are you going to rest?"

"I'd like some alone time."

Her shoulders fell a little. "Okay. There's a bell inside you can ring if you want food or water or anything. Someone will be happy to get it for you."

"Thank you."

She threw a wave, and left me alone.

My door creaked as I pushed it open, and upon first glance of my room, my eyebrows flew up. The space before me was very similar to my room back home.

The canopy bed was veiled in the same gauzy material, furred rugs lined the floor, and fresh air floated in from a window, just like I liked it.

Of course, there were differences too, but even the differences resonated inside me as familiar and right.

A fireplace sat in the far-right corner with two gold-colored chairs in front of it, and a stack of books on the table in between. My gaze traveled left, scanning the rest. On one side of the bed, a mirror hung above a small vanity—an overly girlish piece of furniture, in my opinion. There was another door, either leading to a closet or bathroom.

The wall opposite the bed wasn't a serene cream like the rest, but covered in wallpaper that drew my eye. I moved toward it to get a better look. A pattern of white roses set in dark teal stared back at me.

My hand floated to my lips. *White roses. Why does that feel so familiar?*

I jumped as boots thunked on the floor down the hallway, breaking my spell. I dashed back to the door, closing it softly.

The footsteps continued to come ever closer, passing by to stop at the end of the hall. The door to Hatter's room opened and shut.

I let out a breath I hadn't realized I'd been holding. I

didn't want anyone to see me like this, out of sorts and unsure, least of all Henri.

No. I needed to pull myself together, to get under control.

And decide my next course of action.

CHAPTER 8

It took longer than usual for me to decide what to do. But in the end, I decided to go as I usually did. Alone.

I'd never fought an aether-blessed fae before. Most lived in Faerie, where they could claim royal lineage and the benefits it gave. The ones in the human realm were few. They were also, generally, privileged and lived private lives because others coveted their powers over the aether.

And for good reason.

While almost all races of fae, and most demi-fae, could manipulate at least one of the other four elements to some degree, aether was a whole different animal. The fifth element was the most deadly. It was pure energy and creation, said to come from the life force and will of the old gods themselves. If one mastered it, they could potentially do whatever they wanted.

Even suck your soul right out of you.

I shuddered as I perched on the edge of my windowsill. I could use four elements, two of them formidably. And yet, I knew that if this queen was a strong aether-blessed fae, I was screwed. However, if she was only moderately talented at manipulating aether, I stood a chance.

Maybe.

I leapt out of the window. Using air magic to soften my landing on the cobblestone, I rose and huddled against the building. After a quick glance up at Hatter's window to ensure I hadn't been spotted, I tiptoed toward the main street.

It didn't take long to determine which direction I needed to take. In the distance, the castle glowed a brilliant white as it towered over the shorter buildings in Henri's neighborhood. Torches illuminated every tower and turret so that the painted hearts were as clear at night as they were in the day.

My fists clenched, taking in the place where my parents would have raised me.

Soon they'll be wiping the hearts off of those towers. There will be no trace of the queen left.

I pulled the cloak Hatter had given me over my head, and took to the main street.

Despite the late hour, the city was bustling. Vendors hawked street food, and fae milled around outside establishments, talking and listening to the music coming from inside.

A few males cat-called at me as I passed. I wanted to

shoot them the bird, but the gesture would probably mark me as an outsider, and I needed to fit in. So instead, I settled for my most intimidating glare and continued in the direction of the castle.

It was in a moment of giving a man my 'piss off' death glower that I ran smack dab into a fae with outrageously long ears, a towering physique weighed down by a doughy middle, and no wings. An elf.

"Oh!" I cried out, taken aback as the elf grabbed my arms and righted me.

"Best watch where you're going." His eyes locked on my face, clearly liking what he was seeing. Behind him, a few friends smirked. "The streets can be a dangerous place for a pretty thing like you."

"Thanks for the unsolicited advice." I jerked back, out of his grip.

"Apologies, I—" He threw up his hands in what was sure to be a half-hearted apology, and in doing so, knocked off my hood. The elf stopped speaking and his friends—all seemingly elves too—began muttering amongst themselves behind him.

My heart rate quickened. That reaction couldn't be good. Lightning fast, I pulled the hood up, and took a dozen steps back.

"Where were you going in such a hurry?" the lead elf asked, his eyes narrowed. "Let's talk."

"I don't want to," I replied, distancing myself further.

The leader smirked. "Why don't you save yourself the trouble of bruising your perfect skin, darling, and come with us? We only want to ask you a few questions about your snowy top. Maybe show you a good time."

Snowy top. Damn my luck.

These assholes were the queen's men, and clearly they weren't going to let me go. I needed to handle them, and fast.

I swung into action, charging straight for the largest man in the front, and hurling myself into the air. In a practiced move, I flung my legs out feet-first and slammed into his chest. He fell back into the fae behind him with an *oomph,* but not before I pulled the sword from his belt and darted a few feet away.

Because the leader was so large, he toppled three of his men as he crashed down. However, two had remained on their feet, and kept their wits about them, pulling swords from behind their backs, and pointing them at me. Fire erupted in their opposite hands.

My heart leapt into my throat. I didn't know these opponents. They could be strong with every element as well as steel. It would be six against one, and not knowing their strengths and weaknesses meant I held *no* advantage.

I spun on my heel and ran.

"Get her!" the leader shouted.

I sprinted through the streets, not bothering to remain on trajectory for the castle. Their footsteps pounded against the cobblestone behind me as they lay chase.

I divided my focus, half on the sounds of the fae following me, and half on my surroundings. I needed to find something that would give me a leg up against my opponents. Or a way to hide or lose them. It was dark and difficult to tell exactly what was around me, but up ahead, there appeared to be a well-lit intersection with bags of flour or rice lining the sides.

I could work with that.

My feet slapped against the cobblestone as I pushed my speed to breaking point, desperate for any extra inch I could put between me and the gang. The moment I crossed into the intersection, I sliced open a bag, and called on the wind.

A puff of white filled the air, and I thanked my lucky stars.

Not rise. Flour. Even better.

I emptied the bags of white stuff and sent it soaring in a tornado through the intersection as the men reached it. One yelled, and the blade I wielded found his throat. As the others coughed and sputtered, I silenced them too. I did this six times total, until only the sound of my beating heart and the rushing wind filled my ears.

I called off the tornado to check that the men on the ground were dead. One look told me that they were, and a soft pang of emotion flitted through me. They'd have given me up in a second, but I did not relish killing. Never had.

Still, I did what I had to do to survive, and that wasn't going to stop. Not wanting to be around when other fae entered this area, I sprinted away. I'd put an easy ten blocks between me and the crime scene before I ducked into an alley and crouched behind a barrel smelling of fruity wine.

My breath was heavy and my heartbeat erratic as I wiped a stream of sweat off my forehead.

"That was unexpected," I muttered as I ripped open the cloak for some air.

"Not to me," a masculine voice rang out.

I shot up out of my crouch and spun to take in the alley. No one was there. Or at least, no one that I could see. I squinted at the ground, but through the darkness couldn't spot a pixie or any other tiny fae race either.

"Up here," the voice said again, and my gaze lifted.

I scowled.

Henri was sitting atop the building opposite me, his gossamer wings spread and shimmering in the moonlight.

"You eliminated one issue, but what are you going to do now?" Hatter asked. "Try to take on the Red Queen all by yourself?"

My scowl deepened, and I threw a dismissive wave. "You have no idea what I'm capable of."

"Well, I know that you snuck out of my house with skill. If I hadn't put a ward on the window to protect you, I'd never have realized that you were gone. And I did just watch you massacre six elves, so it seems that I know a little," Hatter replied as he shoved off of the building and fluttered to the ground. "You know, Alice, we have the same goal."

I looked at the ground.

"Our methods might be different," he continued, "but

we both want vengeance on the Red Queen. Why are you so intent on working alone?"

"It's how I was raised to do things. It's easier that way."

"You mean, alone you're not at risk of getting hurt?"

I cringed, because Hatter had hit the nail on the head.

Henri sighed. "We can go to the castle. I'll show you why I think it's better that we work to draw the Queen out, but if you think I'm wrong, we'll attack tonight."

I arched an eyebrow.

"Fine, *you* can attack tonight. You can do it your way, and I won't interfere." He held out his hand. "You're going to have to hold on tight."

"Wait, you expect me to fly with you? In your arms?"

Although part of me hated the idea, I couldn't deny that another part, the feminine part that I often squashed to protect my heart, shuddered in delight.

"You can't take off that cloak to use your wings."

"What if someone sees us? Wouldn't it be better to walk?"

He shook his head. "The street gang that chased you is one of many on the lookout for known rebels . . . Or people who have distinguishing characteristics like yours. And once others find the bodies, they'll search the streets for the killer."

"We can use the rooftops."

Hatter extended his hand again. "I promise this is better. Faster. Put your back to me so you have a full view, and you'll soon understand why."

My eyes narrowed, but he was probably right that soon the alarm would sound. The quicker I worked, the better.

"Fine." I moved closer to press my back to him.

Hatter wrapped one arm around my waist. Instinctively, my body wanted to shiver, but I repressed the response.

He took one of my hands. I almost pulled it away, but he stopped me. "Don't let go, whatever you do. If they spot us, they might try to shoot us down. If I have to fight back," he wiggled the arm around my waist and something squirmed in my stomach. "I'll make do battling with this hand. But if you hold on to my other one, you won't fall."

"Do you think I have a death wish?"

His wings fanned out, and we lifted into the sky. Wisely, Hatter flew straight up into the low cloud cover of the night, and then toward the castle. It was such an expansive building that the lights burned brightly even through the clouds.

When we were directly above it, Hatter spoke. "I'm going to drop now. We might not get to linger, it depends."

"On . . . ?"

"You'll see. Just be prepared. I might shoot back up very abruptly."

I nodded. "I'm ready."

He descended like an anchor in the ocean. The sensation was thrilling, and I had to admit, a bit scary.

Hatter's hand was my only safety net, and I didn't know him. Testing our trust hundreds of feet in the air seemed particularly risky.

The clouds thinned, and the castle came into full view. It took only a couple seconds longer before figures became apparent.

My breath hitched.

I'd expected the castle to be guarded, but not like *this*.

Soldiers lined the gates, not to mention every entryway, every window and tower. There had to be at least five hundred standing there, looking out into Heartstown.

"There are wards up too," Hatter said, his voice soft. "Knowing that, do you still wish to infiltrate tonight?"

"No." I knew when I'd been beat. "I have more planning to do."

Hatter didn't respond, only lifted us back into the clouds, and we soared away from the castle.

CHAPTER 9

The next day, I woke in a tangle of sweaty sheets, my breathing tight, only to find myself alone in my bedroom at Hatter's place.

"A dream," I murmured, the nightmare I'd just had fresh in my mind. The girlish screams still ringing in my ears.

Elise, my sister, was being carried away on the back of a dragon. The Red Queen was with her, cackling like a crazy woman. Repeatedly, I'd tried to fly after my sister, but never managed to leave the ground because soldiers, their chests emblazoned with hearts, stopped me every step of the way.

"Didn't happen," I assured myself, though of course, a similar scenario might well have happened years ago. "She's safe . . . Somewhere safe . . . We'll find her."

I stayed in bed a few minutes more before slipping out

of the sheets and dressing. My heart rate was still faster than normal, and no matter what I did, I couldn't seem to bring it back to normal, to control myself. I hated that idea. Though, in the past, I'd performed unspeakable acts, I was usually able to keep my emotions in check. Not last night.

And not now either. Not only did I feel dread for my sister's fate, but as what I'd done last night settled in, I also felt increasingly foolish about trying to take on a well-guarded castle all by my little lonesome.

I'd let my emotions get the better of me. I'd never acted that irrationally when Xavier assigned me a job. Theoretically, I should have treated this the same.

It was a damn rookie mistake.

So I decided to put on my big girl panties, find Henri, and convince him that recon needed to begin today.

When I reached the bottom of the stairs, notes from a twittering flute and stringed instrument floated at me from behind the green door leading into the great room. I was about to push open the door when someone's voice rose up alongside the instrumentals.

My lips parted, and I tilted my head. Hatter sang a tune. One that, judging by its mention of courts and trolls and rolling hills, originated in Faerie. His voice was full and rich and deep—so mesmerizing it raised goosebumps along my arms.

The guy was handsome, strong, smart, and had golden pipes? Yet another indicator that life wasn't fair.

I heaved a sigh and pushed the door open only to stop dead in my tracks.

Hatter wasn't just singing along to a record, but painting at the same time—because of course he was. Even from where I stood, the painting looked like a masterpiece, a landscape filled with otherworldly colors portraying Faerie.

"Do you ever sleep?" I asked, my jealousy growing. The only skills I had of any note were related to killing.

"That I do," Hatter sang, keeping in tune with the music before setting the brush down and grinning like sunshine at me. "But I was restless last night. I woke up hours ago needing to get some energy out."

I crossed the room. "Restless? Does that mean we're finally going to take action today? Find the Red Queen and off her?"

Hatter's smile fell, which was no surprise. My wording was harsh, crude even. That's what came from being raised by a vampire who not only had a predilection for blood, but got paid for spilling it. I was sometimes too hard for polite company. For rebels too, it seemed.

"Sorry, that came out wrong."

"No, it's fine." Hatter went to pull a needle of a record, silencing the music. "We want the same thing. You're just a bit more blunt about it. But no, there will be no killing today."

Feeling out of place and wanting a distraction, I gestured to the easel. "Where is that?"

"Wonderland Island, the southern tip. I haven't been there for years, haven't been much anywhere outside of Heartstown. But the southern part of the isle is so beautiful that I could never forget it."

"Why haven't you been there?"

"Travel is restricted and often monitored." Hatter glanced up at me before placing his paint pallet on the small side table. "Rebels sometimes go on missions, but we have to be careful and send people selectively. Getting people off of the island, to a portal in another kingdom, is extremely dangerous. Coming back is easier because magicals from the human world can help. But unless there's something very important to warrant the journey, it's best to simply go about our lives."

I understood what he meant, though from a different perspective. I was usually hired to off a mark by people that they loved, because the mark was acting abnormally. Spurned wives or husbands, nervous children, paranoid business partners were all common clients of Xavier. It was rare that I was called to assassinate anybody who was living their day to day. Reducing travel to the bare minimum to stave off suspicion made a lot of sense.

Still, it sucked. Fae on this island were living in little more than a cage, unable to leave their towns without interrogation, and bound to the island by monsters.

"When this is over, you'll be able to visit the south again."

Hatter's lips curled up. "I hope so."

"So, what are we going to do today? Make a plan of attack? Map out the city?" Xavier often did this work for me. Then he'd give me a few options I could select from to execute the mission.

But there was no vampire overlord here, presenting options. We'd have to do that groundwork ourselves.

"Today, I want to assess you."

I blinked. "I'm sorry, I thought you said you were going to assess me? As in, see if I'm up to snuff?"

No one had tested me since I'd passed Xavier's elite-level assassin exam with flying colors. The best score he'd ever seen, in fact.

"We don't know your magical abilities, nor you ours. If we plan on working together, it would be smart to witness some demonstrations, maybe spar a little."

My shoulders slumped. Today, I wouldn't be getting anywhere near my goal. It would be another day in Faerie, another day wasted on someone else's agenda before I took control over my own life. Another day before finding the sister I'd dreamed about last night.

Again, an image of Elise, chained and in a dank cell, rose in my mind, and I heaved a sigh. I wanted to act now, but I knew preparation was key. For her, I could wait a few more days to make sure that my mission succeeded.

***

Sweat dripped down my face as I dodged one of Henri's well-aimed punches, and exploded off the ground to kick him in the chest. He slithered away with the grace of a snake and winked at me.

I snorted. *Look at Mr. 'I'm not an athlete' showing off.*

We'd been sparring for hours. Learning how the other attacked, and identifying our own weak spots. It was a common methodology for people who worked in teams, a fate I'd resigned myself to.

Well, kinda. When this mission finally got underway, I planned on calling the shots. Although I had yet to let Hatter in on that fact.

He'd nearly punctured me with a practice sword, when someone knocked on the door to the great room.

Hatter stopped and raised a hand. "Hold up a moment." He twisted to face the door. "Come in!"

March Hare poked his head in, demonstrating that he knew better than to stride into a room during an active sparring session. "Henri? Might I have a word, please?"

"Sure, March, what's going on?"

March Hare shot a glance at me. "Perhaps we should discuss this in private?"

Hatter shook his head. "Alice is with us, and I don't want to keep secrets from her any longer. Whatever you have to say, she may hear it."

That got my attention. Just yesterday, I'd been in the dark about everything. I'd expected that sort of shielding to continue, and to learn only what was necessary to get the job done. Xavier worked that way; as a matter of fact, a lot of leaders where I came from took that approach.

But not Hatter.

Interesting . . .

March didn't seem pleased, but he did as Henri said, entering the room with his strange half-hop, half-walk gait.

"It's Alran. He's reported an increase of soldiers leaving the castle today and marching out of the city. I thought it prudent to send a force to follow?"

"Absolutely. Five should do. Thanks, March." Henri was about to turn back to me when the hare spoke up again. "There are two more things."

Hatter nodded. "Okay, shoot."

"Herald made contact. He's being kept at the castle past his shift times for reasons unknown. However, he wanted to apologize for leaving the princess at the tower." March darted a glance at me. "He said he was frantic and late for duty. He didn't want to lose his head."

Henri sighed and shook his head. "I expected as much." He moved over to an armchair in front of the hearth, collapsed into it, and laid his forehead on pressed together palms. I watched Henri, wondering what he would say.

I'd been upset at Herald for leaving me, but when presented with the information that he could have been killed for being late, my frustration fizzled. How could you blame someone for wanting to avoid execution? Plus, Dee and Dum had gotten me here fine. They'd probably been more entertaining, too.

I was about to say just that, when Henri lifted his head from his hands. "In times like this, I think it's best that we show mercy and kindness where we can. Get a message to Herald that he's forgiven. There will be no repercussions."

March's chest fell, and a relieved look came across his face. "Will do, sir."

"And the last matter?" Henri prompted.

"The Habernail family is in need. Pete got taken to jail two days ago for mild disobedience. He'll be in for three weeks. The mother is out of work at the moment, and there are five children. I was hoping that we might dip into the coffers and provide them with food until Pete is released?"

"You needn't have asked," Henri said right away. "Give them whatever they require. If the coffers run low after they've been taken care of, I'll search for a new commission to replenish them. Make them your personal priority."

March nodded. "With pleasure. I'll do it right now." He left the room.

In the last minutes, I'd learned so much about the rebellion, how embroiled they were in people's daily lives, and how essential Henri was. It sort of blew my mind.

Only three years older than me, and he's a real leader.

I shook my head. In the human world, many twenty-one-year-olds wasted their time, but here, Henri looked out for dozens of people.

"I'm sorry if my decision displeases you, Alice."

I blinked. "What? Why would they?"

"You're shaking your head. And you do have some reason to be displeased with Herald."

"I guess so, but to be honest, I don't feel bitter toward him. He did what he thought he had to do to save his neck. I'm used to that kind of thinking." I gazed out the window. The great room was on the same side of the house as my quarters and had the same view of the castle. "I thought you handled that perfectly. Like a real leader. Better than I could have done."

"I don't believe that," Henri said.

Silence hung between us, heavy and thick. I was sure that we were both thinking about my bloodline and the responsibility that came with it. Hatter was probably wondering how he could help me grow into leadership, whereas I wanted to ditch that responsibility as soon as possible. Not only did I not want others relying on me, I didn't understand Faerie. Little felt homey or right here, and I still had no plans to stay.

Aware that Henri was waiting, I cleared my throat. "Can I ask you a question?"

"Of course."

"What's up with how March Hare walks? I've studied a lot of people, analyzed their gaits for weaknesses or concealed weapons, but I've never seen anything like how he moves."

Henri snorted. "Looks like I owe March five crowns."

I turned to face him. "What?"

Hatter stood and crossed the room. "March made me

bet when you'd ask about that. I said you wouldn't, but he disagreed. Obviously, I should learn not to question others' lived experiences."

I tilted my head. "Now I'm even more intrigued."

He stopped in front of a covered easel on the far side of the room. "How you see March now isn't a representation of his true form." He pulled the covering off the painting.

I walked toward the portrait. The subject was an umber-skinned man wearing a military uniform. He was tall and powerful-looking, with dark, intelligent eyes. I'd never seen him before, but something about him was familiar.

"Who is that?"

"This is March Hare, or as he was known years ago, Lieutenant Augustus March. He served your parents in their army."

My lips parted in shock. "But . . . why is he a hare now?"

"March was one of the first rebels to speak against the Red Queen, so she had him transformed. Of course, she saw fit to maim him before transforming a once proud soldier into a hare. Weakness of any sort is frowned upon here, and she wanted to ensure that no one would take him seriously again." Hatter shook his head. "His strange gait is partially a result of the injury, and partially because there's still an elf inside that hare body, trying to fight its way out."

If there had been any question that my aunt was a

monster, this story erased it. I hated her more than ever, and my resolve to do something about her rule increased tenfold.

"Well then, we'd better keep training so we can help break him free."

CHAPTER 10

I pulled on a pair of loose, black trousers with a sigh. Hatter had confiscated my leggings because spandex stood out too much in Faerie. I understood his reasoning, but I missed them. I wasn't sure if I'd ever get used to the easy, breezy feel of linen.

I crinkled the fabric between my fingers wistfully. *At least they're black.*

My gaze trailed to my selection of shirts, which succeeded in lifting my spirits. While I hated the new loose pants, the tops here were a different story. I loved that I could wear shirts with holes in the back that allowed my gold-veined wings more freedom to stretch and feel the air flow around them. Back home, they rarely got time to breathe, let alone fly. Due to the restrictions that went along with living in the human world, I was sort of a poor flier. Hopefully, with practice, my flying would improve while I was here.

Once dressed and ready, I made my way to the kitchen, where I found Dee and Dum arguing at the end of a table big enough for fifteen.

"Morning, girls." I ignored their bickering and placed the kettle atop a burner before flipping it on.

"Morning, Alice!" they chimed in unison, and extended their fists to me.

"You know that the act of waking up isn't really grounds for a fist-bump, right?"

I'd taught the girls the gesture yesterday, and they hadn't stopped wanting to blow it up since.

"Maybe not for you," Dum said and gave an exaggerated stretch.

I laughed and gave in, fist-bumping both of them, before proceeding to peruse the tea selection.

I'd been sad to learn that coffee didn't exist in Wonderland. Yet another reason to finish the job of killing the Red Queen and hightail it back to the human world.

I plucked what Dum had informed me was the most caffeinated tea in the stash, and prepared a bag. When the kettle screamed, I poured boiling water over the tea, savoring the nutty, malty scent that rose from my cup.

"What's the plan for today?" I joined the twins.

"Not sure," Dum said, shooting Dee a look that said 'keep quiet'.

I sniggered. These girls would never make it as assassins. They wore their expressions too openly.

"Hatter didn't mention anything after I went to bed last night?"

"Everyone turned in after you," Dee piped up.

I rolled my eyes at their sweet fae attempts to lie by omission. I'd separated from the group right after dinner, needing alone time. But thanks to the creaking floors of the house, I always heard when Henri returned to his room. Last night, that had been hours after me. Clearly, the sisters, who lived under the stairs, didn't realize how noisy the halls were upstairs.

"I'm not sure that's—"

"Biscuits incoming!" March Hare burst into the room holding a tray of steaming rolls that made my mouth water.

"Isadora's daughter dropped them off. Scoot over!" he commanded the twins, who fluttered two seats away in a huff.

March Hare deposited the tray onto the table with a clatter, and fell into the chair. "I hope that's enough!"

"For what? And can I have one?" I asked, unable to stop sniffing the air. Was there anything better than freshly baked bread?

March Hare's eyes narrowed, and he moved the tray a few feet away. "No, no, no! These are for the meeting today. No one touch!"

Yeesh, and Xavier thought I was testy.

"A meeting?" My gaze swung to Dee and Dum. "So that's what's happening?"

"Not for you." The door swung open again, and

Henri appeared, looking as handsome as ever. "We're going on a journey."

"A journey? As in . . . outside this shack? What about the bandersnatch herd?"

"I'm sorry that headquarters isn't to your liking, Your Highness." Hatter moved to the tea stash and started preparing his own cup.

I scowled. "Don't call me that. Or 'Princess'."

I was interested in avenging my parents and meeting my sister, but I still had no desire to take the crown—a position that made everyone in headquarters nervous.

"As you wish." He twisted around, mug in hand. "But yes, you, Dee, Dum, and myself will leave today."

"Why?"

"I spoke with Sansu, who you haven't met yet. He had what I thought was a brilliant idea. Since we've been training, it's clear to me that you're strong with four elements. I can't help but think that it would be doing you a great disservice by not trying to relearn how to use your aether magic." I shook my head, annoyed, but Henri didn't even blink. "I want to find an aether-blessed fae who can teach you to use the fifth element."

My lips pursed, but Henri steamrolled right over what was about to be my adamant protest.

"I know you don't believe that you have it, but I *know* you do. The power to manipulate the fifth element doesn't just disappear. And after seeing how strong you are with the other four elements, I bet that once you find your aether magic again, it won't take long until you remember how to use it."

Tension creeped up my neck. He seemed so positive, but I felt the exact opposite, and wished he'd drop the whole aether-blessed thing.

"I really think I should get on with scoping out the bandersnatch herd, or maybe the castle. Recon is key."

"If you want to drastically increase the chances of losing your head, that sounds like a great plan," Hatter replied as the kettle began to whistle at his back.

My fists balled. "I wouldn't—"

"Yes," Henri cut me off. "If you proceed unprepared, someone would notice and suspect something. If they told the queen, you'd be toast. As far as I'm concerned, freeing your aether magic is the *best* preparation."

Dum piped up. "She definitely would cut off your head, Alice. She's horrible." The pixie shuddered.

"Let's compromise," Henri said. Taking his sweet time, he poured the water into his cup before turning back to me. "We go on this journey. If you're really not aether-blessed, it will take four days tops. Once we return, I will personally oversee reconnaissance of the castle, and put together teams to help you achieve your goals. If you *are* aether-blessed, the first part will take longer, but you'll have a much better chance of defeating the Red Queen." He paused and a small smile grew on his face. "You might even thank me."

I'd never rolled my eyes harder.

I was sure that if I could use aether, I would have

done so by now. It would have made my job as an assassin a hell of a lot easier. Why would I resist that?

Then again, to have another skill and teams behind me when I met my parents' murderer *would* be useful. I might consider myself a lone wolf, but I wasn't idiotic or proud enough to think I could take on the queen and the soldiers she commanded all by myself. At least not after seeing just how many of them there were the other night.

Four days tops . . .

I hated that I'd have to wait longer to avenge my family, but the payoff was worth it.

"Fine. I'll take that deal."

"That's what I like to hear," Hatter said with a grin that made my stomach flutter. "I'd like to get started soon. What do you say we eat on the run?"

"Yes, let's get this over with," I replied.

"Great." Henri sipped his tea. "Pack a small bag of clothes and whatever else you'll need to travel for a couple of days, and meet me in the entryway."

I stood. Even if I didn't want to go on this side venture, at least we weren't wasting any time in starting it.

When I met him in the entryway thirty minutes later, Henri had a cloak in one hand and a travel bag slung over his shoulder. The cloak was embellished with gems on the hems, and was much heavier looking than the one he'd insisted I wear the night of my breakout.

"Put this on," he said, extending the garment to me.

"And hide this inside the pocket." He produced a dagger with the other hand.

I took the weapon happily, but gestured out the window where the sun streamed in. "It's really warm out there, and this looks thick. Can I use the other one? It's more lightweight."

"You could," Hatter replied. "But I'll need an alibi for vanishing, and I figured you'd want to see the city. If you're playing the part of one of my clients, this cloak is a better costume."

My ears perked up. Hell yes, I wanted to see more of the city.

I snatched up the cloak, and threw it over my head, careful to keep my white-blonde hair tucked behind my ears, and the braid trailing down my back. "Let's go."

Hatter's eyes swept over me. "Perfect. No one will be able to tell who you are."

He opened the door, and for the first time since I tried to escape, I stepped outside.

Heat engulfed me, and the varied sensations of the city filled my ears. Vendors yelled out deals, rickety street stalls roasted small animals—probably rats—on sticks, and down the street, skinny children, who were only a few missed meals away from starving, laughed and kicked a ball around.

I hadn't been outside in two days, but in the hours I wasn't training, eating, or sleeping, I did have time to sit by my window and watch the people of Heartstown walk on by.

As far as I could tell, Henri's neighborhood was poor, but the fae were mostly happy. I'd often wondered how much of that was due to him helping others whenever he could.

"Stick close to me so people will think you're a client visiting from a village. Fulfilling a custom order should give me an alibi for not being seen for a few days." Hatter gestured to the embellished cloak. "We'll stop by the fabric stalls in the central market too, just in case, so no one can question what I'm doing."

I had no idea what he did for money, but since Hatter didn't bother expanding, I didn't bother asking. Instead, I focused on memorizing every twist and turn of the city that I could.

As we walked through the streets, people called to Hatter like he was some kind of hometown hero. He waved and smiled at each of them, accepting the attention with ease and grace. He was so *good* that it made me almost feel uncomfortable, so aware of my many flaws. The kicker came when a young girl dressed in little more than rags ran up to us, he beamed so hard that my heart clenched.

"Henri! Henri!"

"Yes, Gila?" he asked, peering down at the girl.

"Will you sing us a song?"

"I'm a little busy right now, but—"

"Oh, pleeease!" the girl batted her little eyelashes in a way that gave Dee and Dum a run for their money, and I watched as Hatter's defenses crumbled.

"Sure. A short one." He looked at me. "You don't mind?"

"I'll be over there." I pointed to the side, because a crowd was already gathering to listen. I didn't do crowds, but the girl looked so happy that I was content to loiter on the outskirts.

"Actually, wait up," Hatter smiled, and though that sight usually sent my blood rushing through my veins, there was something naughty to this grin. Something—

"Sheeee walked into town, a maiden fair!" The line boomed from Hatter as he extended his hand for mine.

Heat flooded my cheeks. Oh my god. No way. I was not about to be serenaded here, with all these people watching!

"With rosebud lips, and long teal hair!" Hatter continued, a devastatingly wicked grin on his face. He had to be loving this.

"No." I pinned him with a glare, doing my best to scare him off. "Just *no*."

Finally, he let it go, dropping his hand and strutting through the overjoyed crowd, still belting a tune about a maiden fair coming to town and stealing his heart.

Taking my out, I tried to scurry backward, to put space between me and the songbird embarrassing me to death, but more fae had gathered behind me to eat up Henri's performance. I was stuck.

"How romantic!" a female fae swooned. "You should dance with him!"

"Bad feet," I lied. "You take my spot."

"Oh no! I couldn't. I—oh! He's back!"

Noooooo. I turned and found that she was right. Hatter was coming back this way, stopping only to spin little Gila, before continuing on.

"Dance with him!" the same nosy woman yelled, pushing me forward so I jostled slightly into circle that had formed around the entertainer.

There was nothing to it. I had nowhere to go. And yet, despite my cheeks being heated to lava levels, revealing my embarrassment, I put on my most ferocious, un-maiden-like face just in time for Hatter to come to stand in front of me again.

"She walked into town, the maiden fair, and when she left." He paused dramatically, his green eyes burning into mine, and for a moment, I thought I might actually die, "no lady could ever compaaare!"

The last note ended with a boom and Hatter bowed before me.

The crowd burst into applause. Hell, the woman behind me actually wailed she was so moved. Good grief.

I'm going to kill him, I thought, hiding my face.

"Thank you! Thank you!" Henri faced the crowd and gave another bow. "Now, if you'll excuse us, we must be getting on with business." He grabbed my arm, which sent an annoying burst of tingles down my spine, and led me away from his fans.

"What was all that about?" I hissed, trying my best to ignore the warmth in my belly from his touch. "I thought I was supposed to be incognito?"

"You are, but I spotted a golden opportunity, and had to take it." He gestured back to the group he'd performed for. They were all watching us leave and gossiping. "None of those fae are soldiers, so they're relatively safe. For the next few days, they'll be talking about the maiden I tried to woo in the street. Between that, and you being my supposed new client, I've ensured a perfect cover for my absence."

Well, shit. I couldn't really argue with that, could I?

Still, I wrenched my arm away, and put space between us. "Fine." I glared at him so he knew I meant business. "But don't do that again. It was humiliating."

Henri laughed. "Are you kidding? I thought you were going to gut me back there. I wouldn't dare try that again."

Someone called out to him, and Hatter gave me a casual wink before turning his attention to the fae.

I fell a pace behind and shook my head.

It blew my mind that everyone in the city seemed to want to speak with Henri. There was no way that most of them knew he was a rebellion leader. In fact, most probably didn't know about the rebellion at all. Some were undoubtedly Red Queen supporters, whether through the enchantment or them just being shitty people.

And yet, *everyone* we passed seemed to love Hatter.

What must that be like?

The thought had no sooner entered my mind than Hatter came to an abrupt stop, and I ran directly into his rock-hard backside.

"You okay?" he asked.

I stepped back. "Of course." Although, from the way my heart was pounding from his nearness, I wasn't sure.

"Good," his face softened. "This is the stall I was telling you about." He gestured to a table in front of him, on which a spread of cloth lay. "Which material would you like me to purchase for your fascinator?"

Fascinator? As in the hat that British royals wear?

My eyebrows knitted together, but Hatter gave me a look that said I should know what he was talking about, so I pulled myself together and played along, glancing down at the wares.

Crushed velvet and felts of every color imaginable presented themselves to me. I ran my hand over them one by one, enjoying the softness. I made a show of picking them up to determine the weights. To be positive I was playing it up enough, I even sniffed the bolts of fabric. And all that while, the vendor smiled and nodded and presented other options, until I revealed the one fabric I would've chosen all along. It was a deep teal velvet. A color I knew that would look perfect with my eyes.

"Your favorite color," Hatter remarked.

The chair in my room flashed in my mind, almost the same color as the fabric, and only slightly darker than the wallpaper.

My chest tightened. Had Hatter decorated that room for me?

"We'll take this much, please," Hatter said, holding up

his hands to indicate over a yard of fabric. The vendor clapped his hands and packaged it up.

Once our cover was complete, we continued on, occasionally stopping at other booths to speak to vendors. Nearly everyone focused on Hatter, although one woman, a brownie if I wasn't mistaken, zeroed in on me.

When after some time she didn't break her stare, unease began to trickle through me like ink in water.

"Henri," I whispered, and gestured to the brownie's stall some twenty feet away. "That person over there is staring at me."

Hatter's lips lifted. "It's okay. She's on our team. She just hasn't been able to stop by headquarters yet to meet you. Let's go say hi."

Feeling silly for making something out of what was apparently nothing, I followed him to the brownie's table. Once there, Hatter hugged the woman and then gestured to me.

"Isadora, I see that you've already noticed Alice Queenly?"

Isadora gripped my hand, and for the first time, I got a good look at her.

Like most brownies, she was on the chubby side, dark-skinned, and had lots of dark hair, although luckily for Isadora, her abundant tresses seemed to have grown mostly on her head. I'd never seen such a full head of hair.

"I've been dying to come by Henri's place and meet you, Princess. You look so much like your mother, who I just adored." She squeezed my hand tighter. "How are you finding Wonderland?"

"It's . . . interesting." The urge to pull my hand back was as strong as my desire to ask how she knew my mother. But considering the gleam in Isadora's eyes, I thought the latter might make her emotional. I didn't want a weepy fae on my hands, so I did neither, and instead asked a safe question. "Are you the one who sent the buns this morning?"

"Yes!" She brightened. "Did you like them?"

"March wouldn't let her have one," Hatter said. "You know how he is."

Isadora broke our connection and placed her hand on her hips. "I'm going to have a talk with him! We've been waiting for you to return for *so long*, and he can't hand over a single roll!? That hare!" She huffed and turned to the pastry-laden table behind her. "Please, take these hand pies."

"Thank you," I said, liking her spunk, but also intensely uncomfortable that others had been waiting for me to return to Faerie when I had no intention of staying.

My eyes shifted to Hatter. "Don't we have somewhere to be?"

He nodded. "You're right. Sorry for the brief meeting, Isadora, but we must go."

"May the aether light your way," she said.

My breath hitched at her words. Did she, too, believe that I could use the aether?

Before my discomfort could deepen, Hatter led me away from her booth. We'd turned onto a quiet street when he spoke next.

"It's a respectful salutation. Isadora didn't mean anything by it."

"Oh, okay," I said, relieved that a stranger wouldn't be counting on me to accomplish the impossible.

"Let's go back toward the house. Now that I've made an appearance with a client, no one will expect to see me in public until the hat is done. But still . . . it's best to be careful."

I nodded and followed him to the hole in the city wall that the pixies and I had entered through. Because Henri was a large man, it took some maneuvering for him to fit through, but he managed.

"So, are we going back toward the tower?" I asked after a furious dash down the path and into the forest.

"Only for a bit, then we'll divert north." Hatter's hands formed a circle. "If Wonderland Island is this circle, then Heartstown is where my thumbs meet, and the tower where you entered Faerie is the point where my middle fingers meet. We'll go to the center of the island and then north. From there, I hope we can find an old fae named Coleti. Besides the Red Queen, she's the only aether-blessed fae on the whole island."

"*Hope* you can find her? No one called ahead or anything?"

Phones and the internet didn't exist in Faerie, but

there should be some way to send a message. Perhaps by bird or rider?

Thinking of birds brought to mind Dee and Dum. They were supposed to be with us, but I hadn't seen them since that morning.

"Where are the pixies?"

Hatter chuckled. "Don't worry about the twins. They'll catch up. And Coleti isn't expecting us, although because you're here, perhaps she feels someone approaching. Sometimes the strongest aether-blessed fae can do that, and she's the strongest in all of Wonderland."

"Is Coleti of my line?"

Hatter shook his head. "A refugee from the Dark Court."

"So, she must be of the Dark Court's royal line. Or a very genetically blessed fae."

"She's never claimed royal lineage." Hatter shrugged. "She's one of the few whose gifts survived the cullings."

Historically, being able to use and manipulate the aether was a way the ruling families of Faerie had asserted their dominance. For a while, they killed those outside the family line who cropped up with the same power. And while they'd continued to do so for centuries, the ability kept popping up—albeit rarely.

We fell silent, and I took the moment to mull over that information as I devoured my savory hand pie. It was spiced to perfection and filled with a meat and three types of vegetable that I couldn't place, but liked.

"How long until we reach Coleti?" I asked once I was done with the delicious pastry.

Hatter twisted his lips to the side. "It'll be almost a two-day journey. That's with stops along the way to eat and sleep and continue your training. I'm hoping we might even run into a wild herd of bandersnatch, so that you can study them up close. That would be helpful for when you go after the queen's herd around the city."

"Seeing a wild one would be cool."

Hatter gave me a soft smile. "You'll likely hear it before you see it. Until then, why don't we get some cardio in?"

I groaned, but didn't have time to argue, because Henri set off at a run.

"I'm timing you!" he called back over his shoulder. "Loser owes the winner an ale when we return."

Oh no, he didn't. I sprinted after him.

CHAPTER 11

The sun had almost dipped below the horizon when we finally stopped to make camp. Well, Hatter called it making camp. In my opinion, throwing our bags on the ground and sitting next to them hardly qualified as making *anything*.

"You didn't bring a tent?" I asked.

Hatter pulled something that resembled a bar of food out of his bag. "Nope. If any of the queen's men realize you're here, you'll become the top fugitive in Wonderland Court. It's best not to have things like a tent attracting attention or hindering us from running away."

"Right." I glanced up at the sky. At least if I had to sleep without cover, it didn't look like it was about to rain.

I started to shrug off my cloak, but Hatter shook his head.

"Leave your hood up. If the wrong person catches sight of your hair—"

"Look around, Henri." I gestured to the wider woods. "We haven't seen anyone all day."

"Just because you haven't seen anybody, doesn't mean they're not around." Hatter arched his brows. "Have you seen Dee and Dum since we started on our journey?"

He knew I hadn't. I'd commented on it many times because the pixies were supposed to be traveling with us.

"No," I admitted.

"That's because we don't want you to see us!" Dee's high-pitched voice sang out.

I twisted my neck from side to side, trying to spot the pixies.

Dum let out a tinkle of a laugh. "You'll never find us if we don't want you to."

As if to drive the point home, both pixies flew toward me out of nowhere and erupted into a fit of giggles as they landed on my shoulders.

Although I should've been annoyed because people were making fun of me, I snorted. Staying mad at the twins was difficult. "Where have you been all day?"

Dee wiped her forehead dramatically. "Flying our wings off to keep up."

"And staying out of sight in case you needed any help," Dum added.

"Help? What are you two going to do if the woods are full of dangerous creatures?"

"Remember the venom?" Dee tapped her tooth.

"How could I forget? But you said that you would need a swarm of pixies to take someone down. There are only two of you."

"Wild hordes of pixies live everywhere. All we'd have to do is send out the call, and they'd come flying."

I blinked. "And what would happen if Henri or I were to stumble upon them?"

Dum's eyes popped open wide. "They wouldn't do anything to you if you were just running through the woods! We're not monsters, Alice!"

"Good to know," I teased and sat down next to Hatter. "So, is anyone keeping watch?"

"I'll set up an alarm," Dee said. "It should be enough to alert us if someone's approaching." She gestured to Hatter and me. "I assume you two can take it from there?"

I shrugged and laid my head down on the bag as I wrapped my cloak around me. I supposed that would have to do.

My group fell quiet, but the forest was still alive with sound. In the dark, creatures shuffled and squeaked. Within seconds, their sounds were joined by the gentle snores of Henri, and the much louder, truck-driveresque snores of a pixie.

I'll have to remember that tomorrow . . . tease them a little, I thought, closing my eyes and letting the noises of the woods, so different from what I was used to, roll over me.

Soon enough, the fluttering of the leaves became a meditation, and sleep began to drag me under.

Whoop! Whoop! Whoop!

I jolted up from the ground, grabbing for my dagger as the unnatural whooping shattered my trancelike state. "What the hell is that?"

At my side, a disoriented yet still devilishly handsome Hatter shot up, and looked from side to side. "It's the alarm. There's something—"

"A Cheshire cat!" Dum screeched, her eyes large and pinned on something directly behind me.

I whirled around and found, to my great surprise and bewilderment, a disembodied pair of glowing, amber eyes and a wide smile.

I leapt back and held my dagger at the ready, prepared to attack whatever this bodiless thing might be.

"I mean you no harm. I merely saw visitors in my part of the woods, and came to see who you were." The eyes turned their full radiance on me. "Now I see who you are indeed."

Hatter swore beneath his breath. The next thing I knew, his hands were pulling the hood of my cloak up over my head.

"I cannot unsee what I've already seen. Nor can I forget." The mouth without a body spoke in a slow, dreamlike manner that made me shudder.

"If you're going to sneak up on us like that," Dee's hands flew to her hips, "the least you can do is show us your body."

"Fair point," the mouth said, and the form of a cat materialized to frame the eyes and lips.

He was striped, but not like cats I'd seen in the human world. No, this cat looked like he was wearing a prison jumpsuit, with horizontal lines going all around him, and alternating dark and light purple. He was the oddest-looking feline I'd ever seen, and with human-like teeth filling his mouth, he was also the creepiest.

"Please don't tell anybody who you've seen," Dum's voice sounded much more worried than her sister's as she leapt off a leaf to hover in front of me. "You know what will happen if you do."

"My allegiances lie where my allegiances lie." The cat grinned wider.

"Oberon's ears, Cheshire cats! Always talking in riddles," Hatter growled, his fists tightly clenched as though he wanted to punch the creature.

The cat must have spotted the blooming aggression, because he disappeared and then reappeared five feet to the left, away from Henri.

"I've never had a problem with them," the Cheshire cat remarked and then began to hum and sway from side to side.

"Should we be worried?" I asked Hatter and covertly gestured to my dagger. "Or should we . . . do something about this? Ask who sent him."

"There's nothing to do," Hatter spat. "You won't catch him, and even if you did, Cheshire cats answer to one fae and one fae alone. But he'll never tell who it is." His eyes darted to the purple-striped cat. "He could be an envoy for the queen, or someone else."

"Or I could be *free*," the cat piped. "You fae always seem to forget that some of us are free." His glowing amber eyes locked onto me. "We owe our thanks for that to this one's mother."

My breath hitched in my throat. "My mother? Did you know her?"

The cat hummed again.

My lips pressed together hard. Obviously, I would need to take a different tack with this creature. If he had known my mother, and if she had been kind to the Cheshire cats, I could leverage that.

"Well, you're lucky if you did. I've heard a lot of good things about her."

"The current queen of the island would not agree," the cat retorted.

That made my spine straighten. I hadn't heard a concrete reason as to why the Red Queen would dislike my mother. Only vague assertions that as girls they hadn't gotten along well. However, if this cat had known my mother, maybe he was better informed.

"Why do you say that?"

The cat stopped humming and transported himself in front of me.

Hatter tried to pull me back, but I shook my head and waved him off. "He won't hurt me."

I didn't know how I knew that, felt certainty . . . this cat was interested in me, but didn't want to hurt me.

The cat arched his eyebrows at my presumption, but spoke anyway. "The sisters had a tumultuous relationship from the start. But it only got worse when your father arrived in Wonderland."

"Why? Did he say something to one of them?"

"More like he couldn't make up his mind!"

My throat grew tight. "You mean he liked my mother *and* my aunt?"

"Who he liked was obvious from the start. Who he was *supposed* to like was the problem." The cat laughed.

"What do you mean?"

He didn't answer, only continued to laugh.

This went on for what felt like hours before I stomped my foot and swiped at him. "I demand that you tell me."

The cat let out a hiss. "No one demands anything of me. I'm free. I work only for the betterment of this island —and that involves no fae." He disappeared and reappeared, this time up in the tree, far above our heads. "And as for you . . . well, it remains to be seen which princess *you'll* turn out to be most like."

There was a pop, and the next second, he disappeared.

Everyone in our camp waited for him to reappear, for the cat's dreamy voice to cut through the calm of the night.

But he didn't return.

"We should move," Henri said.

I spun to face him. "Move? But it's night, and we've been traveling for hours!"

"Doesn't matter," Dum said, her tone soft and

worried. "You upset the cat by threatening him. We don't know who he belongs to."

"He said he was a free cat." I put my hands on my hips, not about to start traipsing through the woods if I didn't have to.

"He might be free, but that doesn't mean he doesn't have friends or alliances." Dum leapt into the air. "I'll be above, watching."

Dee joined her sister, and Henri bent to gather his things.

Although the last thing I wanted to do was begin hiking again, I also didn't want to be left alone in the woods. If fae rebels were worried about the cat, I should be too.

Trying to keep my grumbling to a minimum, I picked up my bag, readjusted my cloak, and resigned myself to continuing our journey.

CHAPTER 12

We traveled through the night at a pace that didn't allow for chatter or questions. We didn't even stop for water and food, taking sustenance as we went. Whenever I suggested that perhaps we'd gone far enough, the others insisted that we hadn't and we needed to continue hiking.

Only when the sun broke over the horizon and seeped through the dense forest did Hatter stop and throw down his bag. He breathed a sigh of relief and began stretching.

"What's going on?" I grumbled. I was fit, but after what had to be at least twenty miles of walking, my legs ached something fierce, and skipping a night of sleep had made me grumpy as hell. "Did you hear something?"

"The only thing that changed was the Cheshire cat's ability to find us."

"What?"

"Cheshire cats can appear and reappear at any time of the day or night, but their magic is strongest in the moonlight. He'll no longer be able to track us through the forest, like he could have during the night."

"What about tomorrow? Will he be able to find us again as soon as the sun sets?"

"Thank the aether, no," Dee exclaimed from where she was standing on a branch, her hands on her knees as she tried to catch her breath. "Tomorrow, he'll have to start fresh, if he wants to find us at all."

And that was the question, wasn't it? Was that Cheshire cat a free cat who I'd offended, or did he work for someone—an enemy?

"Are there lots of those? Cheshire cats?"

Hatter shrugged. "No one knows. Unless you can capture one, which is tricky, you rarely ever see Cheshire cats."

"Capture one?"

"That's how they are bound to a fae," Dum explained. "Kind of like a familiar, except they never come willingly."

"That's not true," Hatter said.

"I stand corrected," Dum retorted, her lips pursed. Clearly she needed some sleep too. "They rarely come willingly—and even then, only to an aether-blessed fae."

I'd have to think about that.

"Well, there's no point in worrying about him tonight —or today, as it is," I said. "Should we rest?"

Hatter shook his head. "We're actually close to Coleti's cottage. It should be only ten minutes or so that way." He waved vaguely to our right. "Once we get to the cottage, we'll be safe. She'll have enchantments up, so we can rest then."

"I guess we should be on our way—" I stopped to sniff the air.

My eyes opened wide, and a rush of adrenaline flew through me, making me feel more awake than I had in hours. There was a scent of smoke on the air, light, but definitely present. And it was coming from the direction that Henri had indicated.

Blood froze in my veins. "Henri, do you smell—"

But he was already on the move, sprinting through the woods.

Without thinking, I followed, noting with each step that more smoke was filtering through the trees. I caught sight of an orange glow not far in the distance, and my stomach clenched as I pushed my legs harder.

When we burst into a clearing, I gasped.

My hunch had been right. It wasn't just a fire—the cottage before us was engulfed in flames.

"Coleti!" Henri yelled, and dashed into the blaze.

The aether-blessed fae . . . shit!

Calling on my powers of air, I created a buffer of fresh, breathable oxygen around my face before dashing into the cottage. It wouldn't last forever, but I only needed to get Henri and Coleti out.

"Alice!" Henri's voice boomed through the crackling flames and thick smoke.

I squinted and spotted a white flash in the far-left corner.

"Over here!"

I charged through the thatch-roof cottage, basically a tinderbox, pushing aside what flames I could with my fire magic.

"Is she alive?" I asked as I approached him.

"There's a pulse, but it's weak." He gestured to the fae's feet.

Squatting, I grabbed her feet and, using my legs, pushed up with a grunt. Breathing was becoming more difficult as the buffer of air around my nose was being eaten up by the flames. We needed to get out of there fast.

We shuffled through the path I'd created, and where the fire had overtaken it once more, I tried to fight back as best I could, switching between water and fire magic. Once, the aether-blessed fae's hair caught flame, and I had to drop her legs to squirt water at her head.

After what felt like hours later, we stumbled out of the cottage, hacking and coughing. Dee and Dum were floating at the boundary of the clearing that the cottage had been built in. We brought the aether-blessed fae over there and set her down.

"Oberon's ears!" Dee exclaimed. "Is she dead?"

I knelt down to check. She wasn't breathing or responsive, and I couldn't feel a pulse. "I'll do CPR."

Confusion flashed across everyone's faces. I took that as a sign that CPR probably wasn't a thing in Faerie. My belief was confirmed when, after the chest compressions, I pressed my mouth to the fae's lips.

Dee announced her skepticism. "I won't even ask, but I will say that this human tradition seems *weird*."

I ignored her and continued performing CPR. Henri hovered around me, spouting suggestions that wouldn't help at all. I was about to tell him to shut it, when Coleti sucked in a breath, and her eyelids fluttered.

I leaned back and waited.

The fae drew in another massive breath and, sooner than I would have anticipated, her eyes opened wide. They were a bright, crystalline violet that glowed with an otherworldly light.

The aether, I realized, as the fae locked eyes with me.

"You. I knew you'd come."

I blinked. "How?"

"No time." Coleti coughed. Blood stained the front of her shirt, and I winced.

She was alive now, but she wouldn't be for long.

She lifted her trembling fingers slightly, and bright white light poured from them. It flew into the cottage and disappeared. "Follow the aether. The book will tell you what to do."

She coughed again, this time more violently, and her body began to spasm.

"No! No! You can't—"

My words died on my lips as the fae fell silent and still, her eyes open and staring at the sun high in the sky.

"She just . . . she—"

Henri grabbed my shoulder. "There's nothing we can do about it right now. But, Alice, we have to go back and get the book . . ."

I shook my head. This was insane, stupid even. Why was I here? Was her death because of me? Did the Cheshire cat guess that we would come here and do this?

I'd caused many deaths in my life, done it willingly. At first, to feel love that never came. Later, to pay off the debts I owed Xavier, and earn my freedom the right way, so I wouldn't have to fear being hunted by magical creditors. But this death was different. I knew in my heart that Coleti had died because I had been coming to see her.

And even seconds from death, she still tried to help me.

My breath hitched. Hatter was right.

I can't let her die in vain.

I shot to my feet and ran back into the burning cottage, sucking air as I crossed the threshold of Coleti's home. In the few minutes I'd been trying to save her, the fire had grown out of control. I could no longer push it back with my fire magic. My only chance was to douse the areas where I wanted to walk.

I conjured water and flung it on the ground, trying to create a direct path that followed the white light flickering in a sea of orange and red. Ten paces into the home, a *crack* rang through the roar of blood in my ears.

My eyes snapped up to find the ceiling caving in—falling right above me.

"Oh shi—"

A hand yanked me back just as the roof landed right where I'd stood.

"Alice! Change of plans! We have to get out of here!" A sleeve placed over his nose and mouth muffled Hatter's voice.

As my lungs were burning hotter by the second, I copied him and covered my nose and mouth too. "No! We need the book!'

"We can find another way! It's not safe. We—"

But I wasn't having it. Coleti wanted me to have the book. She said she'd been *expecting* me, so I would damn well find it.

I whirled around, doused the flames from the caved-in ceiling, and charged forward before he finished his sentence.

I'd lost the flickering aether light when Hatter saved me, but it didn't take too long to find it again. It flashed brilliant white in the back left corner of the home.

Right where he found Coleti.

I shook my head. She'd probably been trying to get to it when she passed out from smoke inhalation.

The flames grew hotter and brighter the further I went, but I fought them as best I could. Thankfully, despite his pleas for me to turn around, Henri was following me. His power over water was stronger than mine, and together, we created a trail until I could no longer spot a flash of white light ahead of us.

"The book has to be somewhere in there!" I screamed, pointing to a hutch that seemed to be built into the wall.

The fire licked its wood sides with gusto, making me hope that we weren't too late.

Henri and I tag-teamed the hutch, drenching the flames with water. The moment my hands touched the wet wood, the door fell away, like it had barely been holding on.

I scanned the inside. Coleti had filled the cupboard to the brim with ceramics and jars overflowing with crystals and rocks, but there was no sign of a book.

"I don't see it!" I called back to Hatter.

We rifled through opposite sides of the hutch, pulling everything out, examining the objects, and throwing them behind us. And still nothing.

My stinging eyes filled with tears. What the actual hell? Where had Coleti hidden the book, and why didn't the aether lend another hand?

Henri was running his hands over the inside of the cupboards when he started coughing and couldn't stop. He bent at the waist, his palms bracing him against the cupboard wall as coughs wracked his body.

I laid a hand on his shoulder, and he bent lower, moving his hands to the next shelf for support.

"I can't carry you out of here if you pass out," I told him. "Go. I promise I'll only be a few more—"

Hatter rose suddenly, his bloodshot eyes wide as he felt the back wall of the shelf that had been supporting him.

"What? What is it?" I pressed.

"A secret compartment," he replied, and then punched through the wood of the hutch.

A hole leading to the innards of the cottage appeared, and inside rested a single book.

I grabbed the tome and whirled around. "Let's go!"

Henri followed, and faster than I dared to hope, we were bursting out the front door of the cottage, gasping for breath.

I made it about halfway to Dee and Dum, who were in hysterics on the edge of the lawn, before I collapsed on the ground and began hacking up my lungs. Hatter fell next to me, also coughing.

"By the aether, you two gave us such a scare!" Dum soared over. "What can we do to help?"

I pounded the ground with my free hand, trying to get my breathing under control.

"Just let them breathe, idiot," Dee said.

The pixies backed off, waiting for us to catch our breath. When Hatter recovered first, he leaned close and began rubbing my back in calming circular motions. "Easy, Alice. Try to breathe in and out of your nose."

Normally, I would tell someone who touched me without permission to take a hike, but his touch felt so good, grounding. Plus, I couldn't breathe, so a mini lecture was out of the question anyway.

Eventually, the coughing stopped, and my eyes quit stinging. After what felt like forever, I sat up. The moment I did, Dum flew at my face and hugged my nose.

"Ummm." I squirmed because her hug was constricting, and my breaths were just starting to come freely again.

"Dum, get away from her!" Dee hissed, pulling her sister back. "Can't you see you're making her uncomfortable?"

Dum unlatched herself. Her blue eyes brimmed with tears. "Sorry, I—"

"Don't apologize. It's fine," I said. Even though Dee was right, and I had been uncomfortable, I didn't think Dum should feel bad for wearing her heart on her sleeve.

"How's the book?" Hatter asked.

The book!

My eyes shot to the small tome I'd risked my life for. It lay on the ground, right where I'd collapsed on top of it. I snatched it up, my fingers feeling the stitched bindings, and the symbols etched into the leather cover.

"Seems fine." I glanced at the spine. "It's in English?" I hadn't thought about it until I read the title, *Properties of the Aether*, but shouldn't a fae book be written in some other language?

"I suspect there's a translation spell on it," Hatter said. "Either from a witch or an aether-blessed fae. After all, the aether-blessed exist in your world, too. Not just Faerie."

He had a point.

I opened the book. "It looks very . . . in-depth."

That was an understatement. The scrawled text was tiny and packed tightly.

Hatter chuckled. "Those types of books usually are. They—"

A loud *boom* sounded as the cottage, or what was left of it, collapsed.

My eyebrows shot up. "You know what? We should probably move. Even if that fire doesn't spread, whoever set it might still be around."

Dum gasped, and Hatter's eyes widened.

"You're right," he whispered. "I can't believe I didn't think of that earlier."

"You were preoccupied with trying to breathe," I made an excuse for him.

And rubbing my back.

I still wasn't sure how I felt about that.

"What are we going to do with Coleti?" Dee asked.

Oh snap. My attention fell on the old fae at the edge of the wood, her body eerily still in death.

"We'll take her with us," Hatter announced in a tone that brooked no argument. "Give her a proper burial."

I nodded. I had no idea what a proper burial would entail here, but it was the right thing to do.

I rose and stuffed the book into the pocket of my cloak. "I'll take her legs."

Our group walked for miles through the overgrown woods until we came across a trickling stream. We lowered her onto a bit of earth that looked softer than the rest, and Hatter laid the old fae's head down on a mound of moss before standing and wiping the sweat from his face.

I did the same, although it seemed pointless. It was probably around noon, and the sun had gone from warm to blazing. Sweat drenched my clothes, but I tried my best to ignore it.

There had been no deodorant in the market, so other than bathing, an activity I planned on bringing up after we dug a grave, there was nothing I could do about the smell or the revolting way my clothes clung to my skin.

"We didn't see or hear anyone around," Dee said after briefly scouting for whoever started the fire. "Specifically, no cats."

"Good," Henri looked relieved not to have to hike through the thick vegetation any longer. "This place seems nice, and it's not so far from her cottage. She might have actually come out here and liked it. What do you think about burying her there?" Hatter tipped his head at a plant-free area behind a large tree.

"Looks perfect." I wiped the sweat and grime from my hands. "Together?"

"Together," Henri confirmed, pressing his palms out.

I rarely used earth magic, preferring air and fire, but as it flowed from me, a sense of relief overcame me.

Earth, more than any of the other elements, was grounding, calming. And after the events of last night and this morning, I needed that right now.

As our power flowed from us, digging a hole in the

ground bit by bit, it became clear that using earth magic calmed Hatter too. His face, which had been previously lined and hard, loosened, and his shoulders lowered.

"So, is earth your primary element? You were strong with it when we sparred, too," I commented when the grave was about three feet deep.

"Water and earth are about equal," Hatter replied. "You?"

"Air, followed closely by fire. Earth is my weakest."

"Doesn't seem weak at all to me." He gestured to the piles we were moving. Mine were equal to his, and our paces matched.

"Guess I'm competitive."

He chuckled. "You don't say?"

Once the grave was deep enough, I used a bed of air to lower Coleti into it. The pixies placed a bouquet of wildflowers on the old fae's chest, and then we covered her up. When a mound of unsettled dirt concealed the body, I turned to Hatter.

"Should we say a few words?"

"I suppose so. I'll do the honors," Henri stepped forward to stand at the base of the grave. "Coleti, I knew of you only from the lips of others, but by all accounts, you were an astounding fae. Strong with each element, and willing to help a traveler should they be in need."

Hatter gulped. "I worry that it was our need for your knowledge that caused your demise."

I bit my lip. The same anxiety had been resonating

through me, and although it didn't make things better, it felt good to know I wasn't alone in that fear.

"And if that is the case, I'm sorry. I hope you'll forgive us." He bowed his head. "May the aether light your way."

"May the aether light your way," everyone else murmured, their heads bowed in reverence.

CHAPTER 13

After the funeral, Hatter and the pixies went to scout the surrounding area. Less familiar with Faerie woods, I stayed at our temporary camp with the book and supplies.

No one wanted to be asleep if the Cheshire cat returned and brought enemies with him, so we decided to remain by the stream and rest for the afternoon. When night fell, we'd leave.

I couldn't say I minded the break or the alone time. The past four days had been a whirlwind of change and people and revelations. No matter how thoroughly Xavier had trained me to take in new information and assimilate it quickly, when it was personal, it took longer to digest. I still hadn't completely managed it.

Not to mention that, while the others explored, I was able to sneak in a bath without worry that Hatter would see. My clothes still stank to high heaven, but at least I was clean.

Now that I was refreshed, and no pixies were around to chat my ears off, I leaned up against the trunk of a tree to examine *Properties of the Aether*. My fingers brushed the green leather, dipping into the embossed runes on the cover. But even though I was ignorant to their meaning, I had no doubt that these symbols denoted power.

I flipped open the book, and got lost in the pages. All of this was truly astounding, and a few times I even gasped out loud. I stayed like that, riveted to the page, until a splash cut through my focus.

My eyes shot up to find Hatter had returned. And he was in his undies, bathing in the stream.

My breath hitched in my throat. *Damn, boy . . .*

Clothed, Hatter was easy on the eyes, but when the shirt and pants came off—oh buddy.

He bent to wash his long, black hair in the stream, and my eyes trailed over his back, which rippled with coiled muscles, all the way down to the tight balls of asscheek, which, now that his underwear was wet, and he was bent over, were *highly* visible.

My mouth went dry as I thought about what might be on the other side of that peach.

Old gods, I know I haven't spoken to you much—okay, ever— but if you're listening now, pleeeease make Hatter turn around.

"Creeping much?" a high-pitched voice whispered in my ear.

I let out a yelp and jerked to the side.

Hatter twisted at my noise, and his eyes widened. "Sorry. I—I didn't know you were awake," he bumbled, clearly embarrassed. "I didn't mean to be inappropriate, princess—err—Alice. I'll get dressed."

"Uh, it's fine." I felt my cheeks warm. "I actually just woke up from a nap. Gonna start . . . reading now!" I picked up the book and waved it in the air.

Dee, who was now sitting on my shoulder, chuckled. "Yeah, reading some *body language*." She held out her fist so that I could bump it and blow it up.

These pixies definitely did not understand the concept of a fist bump.

"No way! Get away from me," I hissed and batted her away.

The pixie soared off, giggling as she disappeared through the trees.

Trying to pretend that nothing had happened, I stuck my nose in the book, where it determinedly stayed as Hatter emerged from the stream.

"Find anything good in there?" His voice was higher than normal as he approached.

"If by good you mean strangely intriguing, yes."

He sat across from me and wrapped his arms around his thick legs. "What caught your eye?"

I'd devoured ten pages of the book already, and so far, what I'd read explained so much about my life.

"You were right. I'm pretty sure I'm aether-blessed."

Hatter's lips curled up. "I like hearing you say that first part."

"Don't get used to it." I handed him the book, open to the page I'd been reading. "Second paragraph on the right page. Read it."

"'The aether is not only a powerful force that an aether-blessed can manipulate, it protects the fae too. Particularly in the case of trauma, mental or physical, the aether might—'" He paused and his eyes lifted to meet mine. They were filled with shock.

"Keep reading."

"'The aether might muffle or encase the fae's recollection of the distressing period. When this happens, the fae's aether magic—the magic given by the old gods—is often locked up tight with their memories and unusable. This occurrence is rare, but has mostly been observed in aether-blessed children' . . ."

"Sound familiar?"

Hatter looked up from the book to lock eyes with me. "Your memory loss is the aether's way of protecting you."

"Exactly."

Tears pricked my eyes, and I was relieved when Hatter resumed scanning the book so I could wipe them away without his notice.

"I think it's safe to say that they never involved a mind witch," I mused. "My parents leaving me with a vampire was traumatic enough to kick the aether into overdrive." A humorless laugh escaped me. "This sucks . . . I wish I could remember them."

Hatter scoured the words, and he turned the page

once, twice, three times, before he stopped. "There might be a way."

I leaned forward, waiting for him to bestow the answer on me.

"An aether-blessed person who has lost recollection of a period of their life can recover it," Hatter read. "When they break the protective hold of the aether, their memories will be freed."

"Ugh!" I threw up my hands. "How does it expect me to do that? This book better have amazing instructions, 'cause this is some real chicken and the egg shit!"

"It suggests that you find another aether-blessed fae who can help pry the aether out of you. Or . . ."

"What?"

"There's also the chance that someone telling you about your past might break a few memories free. But the book warns that this method is more painful, can take weeks or months, and the person has to know you and your past very well."

All the times Henri had told me about my childhood came roaring back.

"Can you do it?"

Hatter seemed to anticipate the question, because his response came out quickly. "We were friends, but I don't think so. Your trauma is associated with your parents leaving, and the book details that the most potent memories will be the ones most likely to release the aether's hold completely. So I might help you loosen the binds on your aether magic, but I wasn't around for the most traumatic times. It wouldn't break your memories free."

He gulped, probably relieved that he wouldn't have to be the one to put me through pain. "Unfortunately, now that Coleti is dead, the only other aether-blessed fae on Wonderland Island is the Red Queen."

"I'm sure waltzing up to her and asking would go over swimmingly."

A soft chuckle left Hatter's throat. "Likely not."

"And we can't get off the island because of the kraken, right?"

"It's extremely dangerous. The kraken has orders to stop anyone from leaving, and the queen's dragon—the jabberwocky—patrols the skies. Herald was able to get off our island by transforming into a small bug and flying to mainland Faerie. But even then, we weren't sure he'd make it. It's a long journey."

"And I don't have the option of transforming."

"There might be one other person on the island who can help," Dum piped up and shot Henri a nervous glance. "In the Enchanted Forest."

His spine straightened. "I forgot about him. You're so right, Dum! That's an option."

My eyebrows knitted together. "I thought you said there weren't any other aether-blessed fae—"

"He's not a fae. He's one of a kind, and one of the oldest magicals in Faerie. If anyone else knows anything about the aether, it's him. The trouble is, he lives in a place where most don't dare to go because it's basically haunted and overrun with monsters—the Enchanted Forest."

"Sounds cozy."

Hatter smirked. "Try dangerous and terrifying, but I think it's our best shot." His eyes traveled to the book. "Or we could rely on this?"

"Both. Tonight, we move." I gestured to the book. "Until then, I'll be devouring that thing cover to cover. Others should too, even those who aren't aether-blessed. This knowledge was dangerously close to dying on this island. That should never happen."

"You need to sleep, too," Hatter said. "At least for a few hours."

"Good point." I shimmied to lie flat on the ground. "And since you're already in study mode, I'll take the first napping rotation."

Hatter chuckled. "But of course. Sleep well, Alice."

The sun was setting as we continued our travels north. I'd surprised myself by sleeping for hours on end, while Hatter and the pixies took turns resting and keeping watch.

They insisted it was fine that I'd slept so long, that out of everyone, I needed the rest most because I'd soon be trying to unlock my aether magic. Still, my guilt grew as the pixies snored loudly on my shoulders.

"So, how long until we find this guy?" I asked, trying to block out my guilt.

"Two days at a slow pace." Hatter glanced up at the stars, now just beginning to blink in the night sky. "Once we get to the forest, it could take weeks to find him."

"We don't have enough supplies."

The hope had been that we'd be able to stay with Coleti and pay her for whatever supplies we used. Obviously, that hadn't worked out. As a result, we had only a couple more meals' worth of food in our bags.

"I know," Hatter replied. "But we have money, and there are a number of villages along the way. We'll stop and resupply. We'll just have to be careful that no one sees your hair."

My hand flew to my braid, hidden beneath the cloak. It still stunned me that the shade gave me away so easily. The Red Queen was truly crazy.

"Too bad you don't have like a super strong, magical fae hair dye here," I muttered. "Maybe this wouldn't be an issue then."

"What is that?"

"Coloring for your hair. People do it all the time in the human world. Although their's is just regular dye. Not magical."

Hatter's eyebrows pulled together. "That is the strangest thing I've ever heard."

"Fae don't color their hair?"

"By the aether, why would they?"

His tone was so incredulous that I had to laugh. "A lot

of humans do it just for fun. Come to think of it, some of the most popular shades are found naturally on fae. Maybe that's why——"

Hatter's hand slapped over my mouth, but I jerked away quickly, jostling awake the pixies, who let out high-pitched yelps as they woke.

"Hey!" I hissed. "Don't you——"

He jumped in front of me and gestured for us to kneel. "Someone's coming."

My spine straightened, and I listened hard. A few seconds later, I caught it too, the sounds of people talking as they tramped through the woods.

I shot to the ground next to Hatter, who was already crouched and peering over a downed log.

"Who are they?" I whispered.

Instead of answering me, Hatter sought Dee and Dum with his gaze. "Go check it out."

The girls leapt off my shoulder and soared out of sight.

I tapped my fingers on my knee as unease rushed through me. I hated doing nothing. It made me feel like such a sitting duck—just waiting for something terrible to happen.

Still in a squat, I shifted from side to side, and felt the book bump up against my right hip. I inched closer to Hatter.

"Do you think it's the people who set Coleti's house on fire?" I asked, trying to ignore Henri's alluring, spicy scent.

"Maybe," Hatter replied unhelpfully.

Thankfully, we didn't have to wait too long for proper answers; five minutes later, the pixies returned, their eyes wide, and wings trembling.

"Queen's men, lots of them, marching this way," Dum said. "They're wearing the battalion suits. Spades."

Dee nodded. "I heard one talking about being on the lookout for a white-haired girl."

"Oberon's ears," Hatter cursed.

"Spades?" I asked, trying to ignore the way my stomach twisted into knots.

"The queen's army is divided into suits, Clubs, Spades, Diamonds, and Hearts. They wear the symbols of their battalion on their chests," Hatter explained. "They each do different jobs. Clubs and Spades are usually sent out to keep the peace, while Diamonds guard the castle."

An image came to mind, from the night he'd shown me the castle, hundreds of guards standing at the ready. I hadn't noticed any symbols then, but it had been dark.

"And Hearts?"

"Hearts are a small, elite order," Hatter whispered. "They only guard the queen."

Special ops. Got it.

"These are Spades. What does that mean?"

"They're better trained than Clubs. More powerful. Some are shifter-fae and have excellent senses, too," Dum interjected. "It's best if we just lie low until they pass. Less of a chance anyone will hear or see us."

Hatter nodded and repositioned himself so that his back was against the log we'd been peering over. "Everyone, come close. If this is a normal-sized battalion, this could take hours, and we don't want anyone to freeze when the temperature drops. We'll use Alice's cloak for a blanket. Alice, you can use one of my shirts to cover your hair."

Dee and Dum didn't need any convincing. They gleefully zoomed over to Hatter, and sat on his lap.

"Alice?" Henri gestured to the spot next to him. "I know you're not exactly cuddly, but the further north we go, the colder it will get at night. Body heat will help us all."

Hell's balls.

Tonight was already chilly, and it wasn't even full dark. Why did I have to be a weak-skinned Cali girl?

"Come on, Alice," Dee smiled to expose her fangs. "We won't bite . . . hard."

I snorted, grateful for her humor, which lessened my tension. "Try to bite me, and I'll knock your block off, pixie."

I plopped down next to Hatter, and tried to ignore the butterflies swarming in my stomach as he threw the cloak over us.

CHAPTER 14

I woke to bright sunlight searing my eyes, and Hatter's arm draped over my shoulders. Beneath the cloak, his body was pressed tightly against mine. In the night our fingers had found each other's and intertwined, making my nerves tingle and my heart race.

"Have a nice sleep, Alice?" Dee asked.

I glanced around Hatter to find the pixies sitting by a pile of freshly picked berries, and smiling at me suggestively. Dee lifted her fist, and Dum joined her in a fist bump. They both squealed as they blew it up.

I should never have taught them that, I thought rolling my eyes.

I tried to wriggle out from Hatter's arm without waking him, and after succeeding, crawled toward the pixies. "What are we still doing here? We were supposed to leave as soon as the Spade Battalion passed!"

Dee shrugged. "We've been walking for forever, so everyone just crashed." Her eyes darted over to Hatter, who was still snoozing with his head resting on the log. "Plus, you two looked so cute—"

"Oh, stop it!" I swatted at her. "We have to get moving!"

I crawled back to Hatter and crouched. Feeling hypocritical, since I despised being woken up more than anything, I shook him.

"Hey. We have to go."

His eyes fluttered open, and when he caught sight of me, his lips softened into a sleepy smile that clenched my heart. However, the moment fizzled as quickly as it came when a bird called out.

"What the—" Henri's head swiveled to take in his surroundings. "Oh no! We lost a day!"

"I know," I frowned. "The twins have been awake for who-knows-how long, watching us slumber."

"Sorry. But you two looked so tired!" Dum's lips lifted into a mischievous grin. "And cute."

"All right, let's move." I sprang up from my squat and began gathering my things while Hatter and the pixies squabbled over timelines.

"I know my opinion will probably be shot down, because apparently Dum and I don't make good choices." Dee glared accusingly at me as we began trekking through the woods again. "But we'll have to stock up on food in the next town."

Hatter stayed quiet for a long moment before replying. "Alice already considered that, and you're all right to be concerned over rations. Once we hit the Enchanted Forest, there's no chance for food, and who knows how long it will take us to find the caterpillar."

I stopped in my tracks. "I'm sorry, did you just say we're looking for a *caterpillar*?"

As Hatter turned to me, a deep line formed between his eyebrows. "Didn't I mention that?"

"Yeah, no. You called him a legend, but you failed to mention that the person we're looking for is this tall!" I brought my fingers about an inch apart.

The others burst out into laughter.

I crossed my arms over my chest and waited for the clowns to stop. "What's so funny?"

"He's not your normal caterpillar," Dum answered. "The stories claim he's as tall as you."

"Oh . . . well, I guess that will make him easier to find."

"Don't speak too soon," Hatter said. "The Enchanted Forest is like a maze. All races of fae have gotten lost in there, sometimes for weeks. Many emerge as nervous wrecks."

"Why?"

"Because the forest tests you," Dum said. "Each test is different, so the best we can do is lean on each other for support, and work as a team."

Wonderful. Because those are two things I'm so great at.

Hatter gripped my shoulder, and bent down to look deep in my eyes. "It's okay, Alice," he said as if he could read my mind. "We'll worry about it when we get there. For now, let's walk and be on the lookout for a town where we can find provisions."

I merely shook my head, and we continued on.

We didn't come across a town until the sun set, which, considering we'd slept past midday, wasn't that long. Still, the timing was fortunate. After hearing that the queen's soldiers were searching for me, I was keen to avoid contact with anyone but other rebels.

"Should I go too?" I asked as my group assessed the quiet village from the outskirts of town. "Are we going to rob a store?"

"Rob it?! We're leaving crowns!" Dum looked offended.

I had no idea why she was hanging out with *me*, an *assassin*, if the idea of stealing some bread offended her, but some people were odd like that.

"Sorry." I replied, feeling a little bad when the pixie continued to glare at me. "It's just that it's getting late. I wasn't sure if anything would be open."

"I'm not sure if you should come or not," Hatter said. "All the buildings on the outskirts look like homes, and usually shops are centralized. Going into a shop means walking through the town, which means more chances that someone will spot your hair. The pixies and I can get the food. But honestly, after learning that soldiers are after you," he gestured around to the wider woods, "I don't feel comfortable leaving you alone. Even if you are capable, there were so many of them."

I didn't take it as an insult. There was no way in hell I'd be able to fight off the number of soldiers we'd seen trekking through the forest. "If only I could use aether to mask my stupid hair."

"Actually . . . maybe we can make that happen."

I turned to Hatter, incredulous. "Excuse me? You said the memories you had of me wouldn't be enough to free the aether."

"We can't free all of your aether magic, but it wouldn't take much to change your hair color. Perhaps I can loosen a bit, and you can try?"

I chewed on my bottom lip. "But I have no idea how I'd go about it. And the book said that this would be painful . . ."

"I'd only talk about casual things. Like when we used to play as kids. If they don't lead to trauma, they probably won't hurt. And if it does, we'll stop right away. It's worth a shot."

More than anything, I wanted to recall my past on my own, to be able to mull over those early memories in private. But it *would* be handy to have my hair a different color—masked by a glamour that only the aether could create.

I sighed. "Fine. Just let me review this first." I opened the book to the page where it explained how to manipulate aether, and read it again.

Strong visualization is key. Okay, got it.

"All right, I'm ready."

The pixies sat on a branch as if this was story time.

Hatter gave me a soft smile. "One of my favorite memories of you was from your fifth birthday. Everyone at the castle wanted to celebrate."

A lump rose in my throat. Few people had ever celebrated my birthday. Jax and a girl I befriended when I was eleven were the two exceptions.

"But Elise and I wanted to do something different. Something that you'd been dying to experience, but your parents deemed age-inappropriate."

"What was it?" The words popped out before I could stop them, so great was my curiosity.

"You wanted a ball, one to celebrate you."

I jerked back. "No way!"

"Yes, way. I know it's hard to believe, but all little Alice wanted when she was five was a handsome prince to sweep her off her feet and dance with her at a ball."

"I was so basic!"

Everyone except me laughed. I was too mortified to think anything about that memory was funny.

"I wouldn't say that," Henri said after he stopped laughing at my expense. "You were just a young girl who wanted the world."

Huh, okay, I could live with that version.

I nodded. "Continue."

His lips quirked up. "Elise and I put together a ball—"

I arched my eyebrows. "You told me Elise was two

years younger than me. I highly doubt that at three, anyone has ever arranged a ball."

His cheeks colored. "You're right. But she did help . . . a little. Now, no more questions. Concentrate on trying to remember."

Oops. He had me there.

I closed my eyes, because as embarrassing as the memory he'd chosen to share was, I needed to try to unlock my aether-magic.

"You wore cornflower blue, and I escorted you to the Grand Hall, where a harpist was playing music."

As if by magic, a song played in my mind, something that resembled Clair de Lune, but more lively—it had to be fae.

"Elise was there already, sitting on the throne and instructing us to dance."

My sister's image filled my mind. Even though I'd only just remembered her, it was easy to picture Elise sitting on a throne, playing queen. Watching a young Henri and me holding each other.

A soft hand landed on mine—Hatter's.

"I wanted to impress you, so I'd learned the latest court dances. If you want, I can show you now?"

My breath hitched, and although I knew it would be smarter to say no, I couldn't stop myself. "Yes," I whispered, keeping my eyes closed. "That might help."

He pulled me up, wrapped an arm around my waist and took my hand in the other.

"Whoa, eight-year-old Henri, getting fresh," I said, trying to lessen the tension in my chest.

"Get to visualizing, Princess," Hatter whispered back.

I brushed off the 'princess' comment as he led me in a dance. Thankfully, the surrounding ground was flat, and the dance was contained, because otherwise I would have fallen flat on my ass.

"The harpist played, and Elise sang, and—"

I sucked in a breath as something odd happened.

I *remembered.*

I remembered how young Hatter and I spoke to one another, happy and sweet. How Elise had sang her heart out from the throne, and eventually came to join us in a dance. How I'd loved every moment of my personal ball.

"I—it was perfect. The best gift." I opened my eyes to find Hatter watching me as if I was the most beautiful thing in the world.

But something was distracting me—something deep inside my core had unlocked and was bubbling up inside of me.

I winced. The sensation wasn't pleasant, kind of like gas pains, but at least the pain gave me an indication that our tactics were working.

I dropped his hand and took a step back, just in time for it to burst.

There was a brilliant flash, and then aether, in the form of a bright white light, hovered in front of me. Instinctively, I latched on to it, cupping the power that I'd called in my hands. The essence of the old gods swirled above my palms as I stared, mesmerized.

"Use it," Dee urged with a squeal. "Change your hair!"

I closed my eyes again and visualized hard, picturing what I wanted done. Although I felt nothing, I didn't let up, and when I heard Dum gasp, I knew *something* had happened.

My eyes popped open. "Did it work?"

I scanned my friends, all of whom looked gobsmacked and had apparently been rendered mute.

Needing an answer, I reached for the braid trailing down my back, pulled it over my shoulder. A smile bloomed on my face.

Gone was the moon-white hair I'd rocked all my life, and in its place were vibrant teal locks.

Our laughter filled the air as Henri, Dee, Dum, and I sprinted away from the village, our arms laden with as much bread, cheese, dried meats, and apples we'd been able to grab before the pajama-clad store owner descended the stairs and sounded the alarm.

That we'd chosen to strike in early evening had worked in our favor. The shops were closed and the streets empty, reducing the chance that I was recognized even more. People were settling down in their homes, and by the time most of the fae poked their heads out their front doors to see what all the commotion was about, we were already disappearing into the trees.

"Think they'll follow?" I asked once we were deep into the forest.

"Why?" Dee remarked, still giggling. "You changed your hair, so there's no suspicion on that end. They don't know what's going on. And as soon as the market owner notices we left money on the table, people won't have a reason to chase us."

That was true. We'd left more than enough coin to cover the food we'd snatched. I only hoped that we had grabbed an ample amount for the rest of our journey. Even if the little break in was kind of fun, I didn't want to get caught over something stupid.

"I hear a river," Henri remarked. "Let's break for dinner there."

Following our ears, we found the river only a short distance away. Once there, we sat down on the banks, and divided the food for a meal, storing the rest in our bags. My stomach growled as I put together my sandwich, and we'd just dug in when a strange sound cut through the calm of the forest.

"Did you hear—" Dum flung a hand over her mouth.

Everyone stiffened as the trees rustled about thirty feet away.

Had somebody followed us from the town? Perhaps a shifter fae with a keen sense of smell? And what would they do if they caught us?

I tensed, and we all rose slowly, waiting, preparing to run.

The grunting hit my ear first, followed by a softer, younger whine. Then an animal with the face of a dog, but the body of a large, powerful feline, bounded out of the trees. It was a baby, and right behind it, the mother emerged, her head swinging watchfully side to side.

She stopped when she saw us, and bared her long, sharp teeth. As a low growl rang from her throat, we all lifted our hands and slowly sat back down, not wanting to alarm the animal that looked so powerful and fast.

After she concluded we weren't a threat, the mama followed her youngling, who hadn't noticed us in the slightest. They approached the river and drank.

Henri let out an exhale. "A bandersnatch. Thank the gods we're far enough away to not be a threat. The mothers can be very aggressive in protecting their young ones."

"So that's a bandersnatch . . ." I trailed off, watching the mom and her cub. I'd heard them before, and seen a painting of the creatures, but seeing them in real life was different.

She did what any parent would do, shielding her child from us as the small one drank. The moment the baby had its fill, it began to romp around the riverbank until the mother herded it back to the river and then gently pushed it in.

Bath time. I grinned as the young one rolled around and yowled in the water.

"The Red Queen has a herd of these patrolling the city?" I asked.

"That she does. She used the aether to bind them to her," Henri said. "Don't let the wee one's cute demeanor fool you. They can be ferocious, intuitive, and very fast. Even in flight, most fae can't outpace them."

As I watched the baby traipse around in the stream, I realized just how wrong it was that my aunt enchanted these creatures to do her bidding. These animals should be wild, living in the forests of Faerie. They should be enjoying life, just like this pair. Being forced to serve someone else was something that I was all too familiar with, and it stunk.

"Are you getting all misty-eyed, Alice?" Hatter's tone was light and teasing and immediately brought me back to reality.

He'd caught me. How embarrassing.

I took a hard bite of my apple, thankful for the juicy fruit. Even if the bars of food Henri packed had kept hunger at bay, I preferred fresh produce. "No way. Let's talk strategy. I have a lot of questions about this caterpillar," I said, trying to distract from my softness. "You claimed that he was a legend, and old, but really what *is* he?"

"No one knows," Dum replied with a few crumbs hanging off her face. "He's been on Wonderland Island since before the fae came. He's not of any fae race, and not a pure animal or shifter. He's his own type of creature."

He'd been here since before the fae inhabited the islands? That was a hell of a long time. Fae had lived in Faerie for thousands of years. And before the fae arrived, other creatures had lived here—the gods of old.

"Is he a god?" The question sounded stupid even to my own ears, but it was the best I had to go on.

"He denies it," Dee said. "And I'm not sure why anybody would deny being a god. Particularly in times such as these."

She was probably right, so I dropped the subject, and everyone finished their meals in silence.

"We should walk a little longer, find a place to hunker down, and then rest for a few hours tonight," Hatter advised once he'd swallowed his last bite.

"I thought you said that we didn't want to sleep at night because the Cheshire cat might be following us?" My eyebrows furrowed at this change in opinion.

"I don't want to," Henri replied. "But entering the forest at night would be foolhardy in the extreme. I'd prefer for us to get our bearings first—or at least try to."

"Plus, we're far away from where the Cheshire cat first found us," Dee added. "More than likely, he's lost our trail, and we're out of his jurisdiction."

"Jurisdiction? Do you mean that another cat could live in this area?"

Dee nodded, which I didn't find reassuring.

"What if we come across another Cheshire cat?"

"We'll deal with that then," Henri cut in. "Once we're

closer to the Enchanted Forest, it's likely that no one will claim that territory. It's simply too—"

"Creepy." Dee shuddered.

With that, everyone stood, and we resumed our hike.

Although I knew the least about where we were going, I could tell by the somber expressions on my friends' faces that I wasn't the only one anxious about entering the Enchanted Forest.

CHAPTER 15

"That's where we're going?" I stared out into the sea of crimson leaves and bone-white trunks. Thin trails of red ran down the trunks, as if the leaves were bleeding. "Why do the trees look like that?"

"Legend has it that millennia ago, a battle was fought here," Hatter said, his tone low. "A great aether-blessed general placed the forest under an enchantment. One that forced his opponents to relive their greatest fear and deepest shame over and over. No one on the opposing side could leave. They got trapped here."

He shot me a sidelong look. "The red foliage of the trees came from their blood—the white, from their bones. When you get closer, you'll be able to see images of eyes in the bark, too."

"Oh, just wonderful."

"Yes, it's disturbing," Henri agreed. "Some say the

enchantment is still in place and draws all sorts of monsters."

I shivered. "I don't suppose there's a different Enchanted Forest? Maybe we can try that one first?"

"Or perhaps you can think of a better way to free your power?" Henri looked hopeful.

"I can't." I sighed, knowing in my heart that was a fact. "Let's go find this caterpillar."

We were silent as we trudged across the expanse of meadow leading into the woods. Actually, since we'd seen the bandersnatch, our group had been quieter than normal. If I was trying to be optimistic, I would say it was because we were exhausted. But I was neither a natural optimist, nor delusional.

We were terrified, every single one of us. And for good reason.

The moment I stepped through the tree line, the cold seeped into my skin as a foreign magic weaved through my hair, into my lungs, flooding my veins. To top it all off, the midday sunlight diminished, leaving us in darkness that only appeared to deepen as I stared into the woods.

The general who'd enchanted this forest had been strong—very strong.

"Stick together," Hatter warned, as if anyone needed a reminder.

If nothing else, the disturbingly accurate images of a thousand eyeballs staring at us as we walked through the woods would keep me from straying. The pixies clearly felt similarly. They were flying so close to my face that their wings acted like fans. Henri walked in front of me only far enough so I wouldn't trip him by stepping on his heels.

"Any idea when we can expect the first . . . experience?" I asked.

Hatter shrugged. "No two people have left the Enchanted Forest with the same story."

"You sure know how to make a girl feel better," I muttered under my breath.

Carefully, we proceeded onward, everyone so silent that I swore I could hear Hatter's heartbeat. Soft sounds of the forest surrounded us, but nothing strange or abnormal. Just animals and the passing of wind through leaves. Still, the trees themselves were so unnerving, and the unnatural darkness so all-encompassing, that I jerked and startled with each noise, until about a mile or two in, when I finally relaxed a little.

Maybe people were just being dramatic? Perhaps the legends of this place were worse than actually being here. It wouldn't be the first time—

A figure side-swiped Hatter to the ground and released an eerie screech.

Dee let out a scream, and Dum buried her face into my teal braid. I fell upon Hatter's assailant, only to find it was no longer there. He'd disappeared, as if made of air.

I scanned our surroundings and found we were utterly alone. There was not even the slightest movement of trees or leaves to indicate someone was nearby.

I inhaled a steadying breath. "Henri? Are you okay?"

His face turned to me, white as a sheet. Hatter was most definitely not okay.

"What did you see?" I extended my hand to help him up.

"Nothing . . ." he replied cagily. "Let's get going."

So we did. We kept weaving our way through the forest filled with tree trunks that glowed like ghosts. The story Hatter told rang through my mind over and over. I couldn't help but feel like each tree wasn't just grown from the bodies of the soldiers, but that they were the *actual* soldiers. Troops reincarnated to stand strong and tall in the place of their death. The idea alone raised goosebumps on my arms.

Why I insisted on creeping myself out when there was no way to know if my theory was true was beyond me. But I knew one thing was for sure. Faerie felt different from the human world. Magic was in the bones of this place, the air, the soil, and every inhabitant. While the same sensation permeated the Enchanted Forest there was also something *more*. Some strange, artificially dark, and unexplainable force.

Unexplainable, but also vaguely familiar.

The trees thinned, and we found ourselves in a large clearing with two paths stemming from it, one tracking right, and the other, left.

I gestured to the trails. "Which way?"

If there were footpaths, there had to be a reason. Perhaps the caterpillar had a walking routine—or crawling routine. Whatever a caterpillars' locomotion was called.

Hatter diverted to the right trail. I went left to check out the other side. Dee and Dum were in the air, scanning every which way from their heightened position.

I peered down the trail before me. "I don't see anything—"

My words died on my lips as a tall, slender woman dressed in red appeared out of thin air. On her head sat a gold crown, each tip ending in a heart, leaving me one guess as to who this was. The woman, my aunt, I was sure, glared down her aquiline nose at someone I couldn't see, as if she was ready to tear them apart.

"You guys . . . I see—"

Hatter let out a cry, which was followed by identical screeches from Dee and Dum.

I whirled about. Henri was transfixed by something that, from my position, I couldn't see. Between us, the pixies gestured in opposite directions, their eyes wide with fear as they took in the woods.

What the hell is going on?

I raced across the clearing, dead-set on grabbing Hatter and getting out of there, and ran smack into an invisible wall. I swayed, and it took a second to reorient myself, but when I did, I noticed that the air in front of me shimmered.

My hands began tracing the line of shimmer, searching for where it started and ended. Wherever that was, it wasn't within the clearing.

"No!" Henri screamed, his voice brimming with pain. "Leave him alone! Leave my father alone! Please, I beg you!"

My heart lodged in my throat as, finally, I understood what was happening. The forest had divided us into four quadrants. Each of us in a box where we would experience our own private terrors—just like the soldiers who had died here.

A sob choked out of Henri, and unable to stop myself, I craned my neck to the point of pain, so that I could finally see what he was witnessing. In front of Hatter, a man with long, black hair was placing his neck over a box as another fae, a soldier, wielded an axe. A beheading. His *father's* beheading.

Dee and Dum were too hidden by the leaves for me to see what they were experiencing, but from the sounds of their screams, I knew it was terrible too.

And then there was the woman behind me— undoubtedly the Red Queen—who was still walking toward me.

"You think you can get away, sister?" the queen asked, yanking my attention away from the others and into my own nightmare.

Sister? I whirled around to find that another person had materialized.

Moon-white hair glistened back at me. The tresses were so like my own, and Hatter had drilled into my head how dangerous that was, that I had no question who this person was. My mother stood with her back to me, arms extended in self-defense, as her sister, the Red Queen, marched forward menacingly.

"You don't want to do this, Sela," my mother screamed out my enemy's given name, her voice a swirl of anger, sadness, and fear. "Think of my girls. They'll grow up without parents, they'll despise you."

My fists clenched for but a moment before I hurled my dagger at the Red Queen. I watched furiously as the blade flew right through her without harm. Realization set in, and along with it, the terror that I didn't know how to handle this situation.

The Red Queen wasn't real. This was a vision meant to break me down—and I had no idea how to stop it.

"They'll never know," the Red Queen barked back. Her long, black hair billowed behind her as if being blown by an otherworldly wind. "Just like the entire court doesn't know that you have what should have been mine. They don't know that you stole my future, but now I'm stealing yours."

"Isabel! My darling, Isabel!"

A gasp escaped me as a male fae, surely my own father, appeared at the Red Queen's back. He ran toward her bravely, determination to save his wife glinting in his eyes and a sword in hand.

The Red Queen turned on him, and without hesitation, shot a blast of aether straight at his heart.

My father crumpled to the ground, his eyes open wide, unblinking, unseeing—dead.

A sob wrenched from my mother's throat. "You loved him! How could you?"

"He never returned my love. He spurned it! Why should I have spared him?"

On the ground, my mother burst into tears. "He didn't mean to love me. Nor I him, it just—"

"Happened? You should've thought that through."

The Red Queen hurled aether at my mother, and slammed her magic into her again and again and again, never letting up, not for a second.

With each attack, my fingernails dug deeper into my palms, until I couldn't take it anymore. I had to act.

My dagger was too far out of reach, but on the ground lay a few rocks. I picked one up, barely noticing that its jagged edge scraped my skin. I hurled it at the Red Queen.

Of course, she didn't let up in her attacks, but neither did I. I couldn't.

The next stone I grabbed was particularly jagged. Its edges cut into my skin, drawing blood, but I didn't care. Hell, I could barely think straight through my fury. I was pissed not just at this vision, but for the others. At my back, they screamed and cried, tormented. I couldn't take it anymore.

A roar ripping from my throat, I charged the Red Queen, mercilessly slashing the rock at the vision.

And she disappeared.

I took a step back, gasping. "What the hell just happened . . .?"

I stared down at the rock in my hand and noticed that the cut had been deeper than I had realized. Blood dripped from my palm down my wrist.

All of a sudden, I understood.

I whirled around to find the pixies still screaming and crying, and Hatter curled into a ball, his arms over his head.

"Blood!" I yelled to them. "The visions stop with blood!"

Something in my tone must have gotten their attention, because everyone turned to me.

I held up my injured hand. "Cut yourself, apply blood!"

Dee and Dum bit into their hands without hesitation and zoomed straight for their offending visions. Hatter, however, seemed frozen in fear. His arms trembled so violently, that it broken my heart. Had I been able to breach the walls that separated us, I would've done it for him. But I could not. He had to do this, had to break the magic so we could move on.

"Henri! Use your sword! Cut your hand! It will go away! I promise!"

Trembling, Henri rose from his crouch, drew his blade, and dragged it across his palm. That was enough for his vision of the executioner to pause.

"Run through them with your blood," I instructed. "It's a sacrifice! The forest wants to weaken us!"

Henri did as I said, and in the next moment, his tormentor vanished, along with the shimmering walls.

He fell to the ground with a sob, and I dashed over to him and knelt next him, sliding my arm around his shoulder.

"It's okay, they're gone," I whispered. "They're not real."

"Yes, they were," Dum said as she lowered herself to the ground next to me, her body trembling. "They were our past, horrors that already happened. What's more real than that?"

I couldn't argue with her, but something told me we couldn't stay here either. The visions could come back, or new ones might appear.

"Guys, we need to move. Can you do that?"

In answer, the others rose.

"Let's go this way," I gestured to the trail I'd watched my parents die on, if only because I didn't want Henri to have to approach where he'd seen his father die.

I picked up the dagger I'd hurled, and wordlessly, my friends followed me down the path. It didn't take long until I was certain that I'd unwittingly chosen the right way. I felt like I was following the aether once again, like at Coleti's cottage.

If the caterpillar is aether-blessed, maybe I'm sensing him?

I hoped so, but kept the thought to myself for now.

"I can't wait to get out of here," Dum croaked, clearly about ready to break down.

Feeling sorry for the pixie, I tapped my shoulder. She flew into my hood and nestled within its folds, hopefully experiencing some relief.

Henri was still quiet, dutifully watching the woods as we passed through. Dee was helping him, probably needing the distraction.

"As long as we stick together, we should be okay," I said, trying to reassure my friends.

"Stick together and work together," Henri broke his silence. "Alice, if—"

A rumbling growl cut him off, and everyone stopped in their tracks. Dum burst out of my hood, her body shaking once again.

"Where did that come from?" I asked, my words tight.

Turning on the spot, I found a monster standing on the path behind us. It was the size of two full-grown grizzly bears, with teeth six inches long, and claws the length of my hand. The beast snarled and stomped at the ground like an enraged bull.

While we might have been able to defeat the claws and teeth and size of this creature, something else caught my eye that killed all the hope within me.

Its fur shimmered with magic, making my throat tighten. I'd seen protections like this on people who knew they were being trailed by those of my former profession. Such magical barriers were difficult to break, and we had none of the proper tools at our disposal. Whatever we threw at this creature simply wouldn't penetrate its hide. Or worse, the beast might absorb it and be able to use it against us. In short, we had no freaking chance against this thing.

"Run!" I spun and broke into a sprint.

Behind me, Hatter's heavy footsteps slammed into the ground, and above, the pixies' fluttering wings sounded like a whistle screaming through the night.

The beast released a roar and charged.

I darted glances from side to side, trying to find an escape route. Would it be best if we dove into the woods? It would be harder to stick together. But if we stayed on this trail, the beast would have a direct shot at us, and I had little doubt that it would win.

Hatter and I could try flying, but I wasn't very agile, and the trees in these woods grew freakishly close together. Plus, I was wearing the damn cloak, and the process of shrugging that off would slow me down.

My muscles burned, and my lungs spasmed as I pushed my body. Second by second, the animal grew closer, its bellowing cries and labored breaths resonating in my ears.

"Arghhh!"

My heart seized at Hatter's cry, and I checked on him, only to find him gripping his shoulder.

"Henri! What—"

"Keep running and watch for the trees! They attack with fire!"

This can't be real.

Impossibly, we pushed harder and gained some ground. Still, if we didn't do something, it was inevitable the monster would catch us.

Taking my chances, I shot a ball of fire back at it. The

attack struck, and just as I suspected, the beast's fur glittered, and the fire dissipated all around it.

So elements couldn't defeat it. The best we could hope for was to hold it back until we found a clear enough area to take off.

"Henri! Fling rocks at it!" I screamed.

I knew the instant Henri complied, because the beast whined and then growled louder.

Joining in the fight, I scanned the trail ahead, and directed the rocks in front of us to fly at the monster. I dared a glance back.

Oh no . . .

My stomach pitted ever deeper to find the creature's eyes bulging and glowing red. All my tactics had done was piss him off more.

"Henri! We need to fly!" I flung my bag of food at the beast so I could unclasp my cloak, but was interrupted as a tree somewhere in the woods hurled a ball of fire at me.

I leapt to the side, barely avoiding it.

"Dammit!" I screamed as I nearly collided with another tree, and my cloak went askew again.

"I'll buy you time!"

Hatter's wings snapped out to lift him into the air. More agile than I could ever dream of being, he wove through the trees and soared back toward the monster.

"No!" I yelled, but didn't stop running because, at that exact moment, another tree launched a ball of flame at me.

I dodged it, and a stream of expletives left my mouth.

Roars from the beast and yelps from Henri flew up behind me. Knowing I needed to hurry before another tree attacked, I wriggled out of my cloak and gripped it tight, hoping the book wouldn't fall out of the pocket. I stretched out my wings, and without a second's hesitation, I lifted into the sky.

And through an invisible wall of magic that sent tingles up and down my spine.

Above, the pixies let out astonished gasps. They'd felt it too, the shift. I was certain that we'd dashed through a ward of sorts. An enchantment to protect someone in these woods. And as the beast ran into the ward like a dog barreling into a sliding glass door, it seemed he wasn't allowed within the protection.

I let out a relieved breath as the creature growled and swiped at the barrier but could go no further.

Above the monster, Henri was still pummeling him with rocks. He hadn't even noticed that we'd stopped running.

"Henri! Fly toward me," I screamed, not about to risk the beast leaping up and injuring Hatter when he was mere inches from safety.

Henri's head snapped up. Confusion flashed across his beautiful features when he saw us standing still.

"There's a ward," I explained. "Fly over here!"

Thank the gods the fae hunk listened without question and flew past the barrier. He joined us as the monster continued to snarl and rage just out of reach.

"That was lucky," Henri said, looking anything but lucky with the gash in his shoulder and disheveled appearance. "I wonder who put that up?"

"I bet we'll find them right up there." Dee pointed further down the path.

We turned as one. Not only was something glowing up ahead, but something deep inside me acknowledged the glow. It had to be aether.

"Guys," I said. "I think we've found the caterpillar's lair."

"Well, what are we waiting for?" Henri asked. "Let's go talk to him."

CHAPTER 16

The caterpillar was as advertised: massive, with blue skin and horizontal yellow stripes ringing his round body. He sat atop a large, white-capped mushroom, his antennae standing at attention like a watchful dog's ears.

And he was smoking a hookah.

"Ummm, hi," I said, because the creature was glaring down at me with large, black eyes.

Despite his obvious annoyance, he continued to make rings with the smoke. Astonishingly enough, they exited his mouth in all different colors.

Wonderland was so strange.

"Who are you?" the caterpillar asked.

"Me?"

"Yes."

I threw my shoulders back. "Alice. Alice Queenly. I'm—"

"No. Truly, who *are* you?"

"Alice," I repeated, more loudly this time because maybe he had crappy hearing? "I'm from the human world. I—"

"I asked, whooooo *are* you?" He pinned me with a stare, and annoyed that he'd cut me off twice now, I glared back.

"I just told you." My hands landed on my hips. "I'm Alice."

Was this a joke? We'd risked insanity walking through these woods, and this guy was going to ask me the same question again and again?

Henri, ever the calm one, stepped forward to stand next to me. "Princess Alice White of the Wonderland Court begs an audience with you, sir."

I cocked my head. Alice White? Huh, I'd have to ask him about that later.

"The princess . . . Is it?" The caterpillar's bushy blue eyebrows pulled together. "She doesn't look like much of a princess to me. Especially not of the White line."

"Her hair is aether-altered," Hatter explained.

Although I found the caterpillar's assumption absurd, at least bashing me was an improvement over him obnoxiously repeating the same question.

I placed a hand on Hatter's shoulder, silently telling him I had this.

"To be honest, I don't feel like much of a princess either," I admitted, "but that's what they tell me. Actually,

I identify much more with the warriors whose ghosts fill this forest."

The caterpillar stared at me, took a huge puff of his hookah, and then blew the smoke right in my face.

What an asshole.

"I see that you're more astute than you appear. Because of that, I will hear your request. *Now.*"

When the caterpillar says jump, I guess I'm supposed to say how high?

"It's come to my attention that I'm aether-blessed. The issue is that my magic is locked up tight inside me, with traumatic memories. I've been told only another aether-blessed fae or you can release them?"

He took a puff of the hookah before sending another plume of smoke into my face. "You are correct." He looked down at me, offering me nothing more.

"Well, will you help me? Will you release my aether so I have a chance at fighting the Red Queen?"

Belatedly, I realized that it was probably idiotic to tell this guy why I wanted the aether released. Then again, he might already know.

Though, as I studied him, and he assessed me in return, I got the sense he didn't give a damn about the Red Queen. No, this caterpillar, with his eyes narrowed and lips pressed firmly together, was considering my offer in a way I recognized.

He looks like Xavier when he's negotiating an offer.

"I will help you," the caterpillar said.

Behind me, Dee let out a cheer.

"But first," the caterpillar continued, "I require payment."

"We don't have any—"

"Of the sort that only a warrior can provide."

A pit formed in my stomach; whatever this caterpillar wanted, I knew I wouldn't like it.

"What do you need done?"

"There's a creature in these woods. One who has stalked me for centuries. I wish for you to kill him. Bring me his eyes as proof that the job is complete."

"Do you have any other specifics? What kind of creature? A furry monster chased us earlier . . . Is it that? What kills them?"

"Not the beast, something else. My enemy is unnamable, a shadow. He has kept me trapped here, behind my own protections, for centuries. Physically, I am no match. However, I have a weapon that will slay him."

The caterpillar picked up a tobacco tin, and twisted the lid. Slowly, he pulled out an object and held it up.

A single claw?

"Is that going to be sufficient?" I asked.

"Absolutely," the caterpillar replied, his antennae sticking up as if I'd offended him with the question. "This weapon has been dipped in the blood of the creature's enemies. As such, it is very powerful. He will be drawn to it—want to kill you for possessing it."

"And what about the other monsters? What if we can't find this shadow because of everything else in the forest?"

"Impossible. Where the shadow goes, others shun." He turned his small eyes on me. "Do you accept?"

I didn't trust those beady, black eyes, but if I wanted to free my aether magic sooner rather than later, I didn't have much of a choice.

I reached for the claw. "We'll do it."

CHAPTER 17

"How can we be sure we can trust him?" Dee's voice was even more high-pitched than normal, riddled with fear and tension.

"We can't. We just have to hope he stands by his word."

I thought about Xavier, how he only gave people the information that they needed and nothing more, but always kept his promise. The caterpillar reminded me so much of my vampire overlord.

"Creatures like him usually do," I assured her. "It's one of the few reasons others trust them."

"Still, Dee's right," Hatter said. "I can't help but think there's something off about this scenario. He's trapped himself in the forest. If he's so powerful, couldn't he magic his way out?"

"Just keep your eyes open." My fingers grazed the

claw in my cloak pocket. "He said that the shadow would seek the claw, so there's no telling when he'll show up."

Hatter came up beside me. "I bet that means that the barrier around the caterpillar, the one that stopped the other monster, is the only thing keeping it out of the shadow's hands."

Although the stipulations of the barrier were unknown to us, I figured Henri was probably right. I suspected that it had only let us past because we bore no ill will toward the caterpillar.

We walked through the ward that the caterpillar had up. As we went deeper into the woods everyone took careful, quiet steps. My gaze pierced the darkness, searching. A part of me hoped the shadow monster would appear so we could get this over with. Another part, however, dreaded meeting the creature. If the caterpillar, one of the most powerful beings on the island, couldn't deal with the shadow, then how would we?

A twig cracked.

"Did you hear that?" Dee squeaked.

"Yeah," Hatter said. "Ready your weapons."

My dagger was already out, and I pulled the claw from my pocket with my other hand. The pixies' fangs descended, and Hatter unsheathed his short sword.

I turned inch by inch to examine our surroundings. I'd almost made a full revolution when I spotted something that made my hands tighten around my weapons.

Red eyes glowed in the darkness. The shadow creature had already found us.

I extended my dagger to point at the creature. "I know you're out there. And you know what I have, what I mean to do with it." I wasn't privy to the details between the monster and the caterpillar's hostilities, but I'd been involved in enough deadly feuds to be sure that each party was aware of the hate simmering between them. "So if you don't mind, I'd like to get out of here. Let's finish this."

At my invitation, the beast flew into motion, red eyes barreling closer. Snarls ripped from the beast's throat, and dozens of trees fell as he neared.

I lowered into a fighting stance. I could only see his eyes, but judging by the size of the glowing white trees that hit the ground, he must be massive. When he appeared, I needed to be ready.

"Oberon's ears," Dum moaned. "This was a terrible idea."

"Don't think like that." In moments of danger, there was nothing more dangerous than negative thinking. "We've already killed the beast. We're already victorious. Tell yourself that."

Henri's eyes glittered, and he gave a stiff nod.

Before anyone could attempt to bolster morale further, the monster was upon us, bursting through the trees to land in front of us.

I gaped. I could see how someone might think this beast was made of shadows, especially in this bleak forest. He looked a bit like a werewolf, although with a human nose. Save for the creature's eyes, which glimmered like red jewels, it was black and necrotic. Even its clothes, little more than rags, were black. It reminded me very much of a zombie.

Like he's dead, or close to it . . .

Dee let out a war cry, shattering my blossoming thought. The pixie then soared toward the fifteen-foot-tall creature.

"Dee! No—"

My scream died in my throat as the shadow swatted her to the side and straight into a tree, before lunging at me.

"Flank him!" I screamed.

Hatter and Dum followed through, each attacking the beast from the side, and buying me time to position myself to sink the claw into his skin. Hatter's sword slashed the shadow monster, and shimmering aether spilled out of his hide.

My brows pulled together. I'd fought many ferocious magicals before, but this creature was a total mystery. I didn't know a single race of fae that could be killed by a claw doused in the blood of their enemies.

Or one that bled aether.

I dodged backward a step as a hand with overgrown claws lashed out at me. As soon as the hand fell, I pivoted and returned the attack with the claw.

The beast caught sight of my weapon and reared back, away from me, spraying aether everywhere, including splattering on my face. I gasped. As if the aether had forced a revelation into me, I suddenly understood.

This thing, this horrible monster, was aether-blessed. He had to be the general Henri had mentioned. The one who'd fought the war and created this forest of terror. Somehow, he was still alive, haunting the woods—and had it out for the caterpillar.

And now us, I thought as the beast released a resounding roar that made the hairs on my arms stand on end.

Dum had been sinking her tiny teeth into the creature's back every chance she got, and was about to do so again, when the monster pivoted away from me to round on the pixie. My heart lodged in my throat as large jaws snapped in the pixie's direction, and Dum disappeared.

"Alice! Now!" Henri screamed.

I lifted the claw high overhead and leapt. Time slowed as, with each passing millisecond, I expected the beast to turn and sink his teeth into me next.

But he didn't.

Instead, he was cringing and whining, thrashing his head about. When I was close enough, I took advantage of his distraction, and slammed the claw hard into his back.

The bastard exploded into a cloud of smoke as the aether that had been holding him together soared away through the forest.

I gasped, collapsing to the ground where the monster

had stood. Two rubies, his eyes, fell beside me as a slight weight landed on top of me.

I scrambled away, only to stop when I realized who the weight belonged to.

"Dum!" I yelped. "Are you okay? Did it bite you?"

What a stupid question. The pixie had been in the monster's mouth! Of course, it bit her!

"It tried, but I attacked its tongue." Dum smiled proudly. Her fangs were longer than I'd ever seen them.

"Oh . . . Damn, girl, that's vicious," I replied, impressed by her bravery.

"Thank you. Can I borrow your cloak to dry off? That thing had horrid breath, and I don't want to stink."

"Here." Hatter handed her a shirt from his bag. "Use this. We'll check on Dee."

Dee!

I rose and darted over to where the other pixie lay on the ground. She was breathing, and my heart rate slowed in relief.

"She's still passed out, but alive," I said as Hatter joined me.

I picked up the pixie, who stirred as her eyelids fluttered halfway open.

"Thank the gods," he replied, looking relieved.

I didn't answer, only began stroking Dee's tiny head, pushing her red hair out of her face.

Her eyes fluttered again and then opened all the way. They focused first on me, then Hatter. "Did you get that monster?"

"We did. How do you feel?"

"Like hell," the pixie gripped her head. "But ready to get out of here."

"You and me both, sister. What do you say you travel in my cloak until you're able to fly?"

The pixie nodded, and I pulled my hood up to set her inside.

Once she was nestled in with her sister at her side to make sure she didn't lose consciousness again, I went to scoop up the rubies. Gems secured, I turned to Henri. "Ready?"

"As ever."

We marched through the woods side by side, this time not bothering to remain on the lookout for any other creatures. Instinctively, I knew that our battle with the shadow monster had made every other creature in the forest scamper far away. Only one would want to see us, and as we trekked back to him, I steadied myself for what was to come.

The minute we emerged in the caterpillar's clearing, I threw the rubies on his mushroom. "We did it. Now pay up."

With one of his many hands, the caterpillar picked up the rubies, and for the first time since I'd met him, he smiled. "So you have. You, the warrior princess, have done what many have sought to accomplish, yet none have achieved. You truly are of the aether, then." He took a puff of his hookah. "I'll say, that might be the biggest shock of my life."

I rolled my eyes. "Just release my aether magic."

The caterpillar tucked the jewels into a space where one of his thorax segments met another. "Would you like to go about this the fast way? Or more slowly?"

"What's the difference?"

"One hurts much more."

"Which one?"

"Fast."

I cocked my head. "How much faster is it, though?"

"Hours."

"Both hurt anyway, right?" The book had told me as much.

He nodded.

My options were to be in excruciating pain for a short burst of time, or experience duller pain for hours longer. There was no question as to which I'd choose.

"The fast way."

"Very well."

The caterpillar gestured for me to stand directly before him, which I did.

"Now, stay still."

He extended his hands, and they glowed brilliant white. I shot one last glance back at my friends before the caterpillar's magic struck me.

A sensation of hot metal slicing through my core wrenched a scream out of my throat, and I fell to the ground, unable to hold myself up.

"Stay still!" the caterpillar screamed, as light—aether—streamed from his hands to me.

Had I been able to scream back, I would. As it was, inhaling a single breath took too much effort.

The caterpillar's magic plowed through my body like a truck, knocking over everything in its wake and then crushing it. My eyes spasmed, and blood pounded in my ears as sensations became too much to bear. I released a cry, and heard a rush of footsteps behind me, closing in.

"Do not touch her!" the caterpillar commanded.

Someone, Hatter, retorted, "Do you want her to die?"

Why not? It already felt like I was. My bones felt as if they would disintegrate to dust, and my head . . . by the old gods, my head pounded as if it would explode at any moment.

"Hold on!" the caterpillar yelled.

I screamed as pressure so intense enveloped my skull until it threatened to crack open, and then . . .

A dam burst, and memories flooded me, threatening to overwhelm me.

My mother, heavy with child—Elise—explaining to me that soon I would be a big sister.

The day I met my baby sister, and the way her full head of dark hair glistened in the light shining down upon the castle gardens.

The first time my father thought me mature enough to join him on his rounds through the city.

Henri knocking on my bedroom door, asking if I wanted to play.

Me, Henri, and Elise, running through the castle hallways, our laughter making servants smile.

A flag bearing a white rose on a field of teal, waving high above the castle.

A scream wrenched up my throat as, one by one, more memories tumbled out of me. Some were darker, and only now, through the eyes of an adult, would I have noticed the threatening current in them.

My aunt, the Red Queen, watching me and my mother during the feast, her eyes narrowed and hard.

My aunt whispering to some guards, and once, sneaking back into the castle under the veil of night.

I gritted my teeth as each beautiful and dark moment spun out of me.

The aether magic was unraveling, allowing the memories to come forth. The pain built, and I was sure that soon enough, when it had completely released, the most pain would consume me.

And while I was mentally preparing for it, I wasn't ready when it hit me only seconds later.

The searing energy sliced through my body, cutting it in half as if it were an actual sword. I curled in on myself and squeezed my eyes shut, unable to take it.

"Kill me!" I yelled. But instead of a blade falling and slicing my neck to put my misery to an end, soft murmurs of assurance met my ears.

Hatter . . .

His words slowed my heart rate for a moment, before another hot bolt of pain cut through me. I cringed. "No! Kill me! End it!"

The caterpillar let out a maniacal laugh. "I told you it would hurt."

My teeth gnashed together. The bastard was taking

pleasure in this. He was happy that I had chosen this, that I was experiencing pain . . . but why? Even through the near madness the pain brought on, I could comprehend that the caterpillar didn't seem like a sadist. Strange and haughty, yes. But crazy? No.

Is he getting something from this?

I forced my eyes to open, and glanced up.

The gleam in the caterpillar's eyes, and the slight upturn of his lips answered my question. And though my limbs felt as if they were being ripped from my torso, I resolved not to take my eyes off him. The others were watching me, but I had to watch *him*.

The unraveling continued, faster and faster and faster as the magic released. The tipping point was subtle but welcome, and finally, the pain began to decrease. Keeping my eyes open was no longer a struggle. My body didn't need to be curled in. I sat up, and Hatter mumbled something encouraging.

But my attention wasn't on him. I was still focused on the caterpillar, who looked all too pleased at this whole arrangement.

And then, suddenly, everything stopped, and a white ball of light burst from my heart.

My aether magic . . .

I released a sigh and watched as the aether burned brightly, hovering in the air before dissipating. It flowed back into me, filling me, making me whole once more.

Except part of it didn't. A small part flew toward the caterpillar, and he gulped it down quickly—so quickly that someone could have convinced themselves that it didn't happen.

But it had. I was sure of it.

"It's complete," the caterpillar said, his voice louder, stronger than before. "Your powers of aether are free."

Yes. My body vibrated on a new frequency, one that the aether was responsible for.

And yet, appreciating it was impossible.

When I'd killed the shadow monster, a white light had bloomed out of it and soared through the woods. A very similar thing to what had just occurred. I hadn't understood why that would happen before, but now I did.

"You've been living off the aether of these woods, haven't you? You *and* the shadow monster."

The caterpillar's beady eyes widened for a moment before he caught himself. "Excuse me?"

"You are . . . were . . . both powerful because you lived off the aether that came from the souls who died here. The souls who created the forest." I gestured to the white-barked trees. "But you knew it couldn't last forever. Your supply was finite, especially with someone sharing the old gods' energy. You needed him killed."

"I needed him killed because he was a monster threatening my life."

"Yes," I agreed. "He wanted your ability to manipulate and siphon aether too. Which makes sense. He was here first." I shook my head as it all came together. "But you won. You called the aether magic from him as it left his body, like you did with some of my power. Not all of it, just enough that you thought I wouldn't notice while I was suffering."

His segmented body stiffened.

"I want it back," I demanded. "I risked my life for this, and gave you what you wanted. We had a deal, and this wasn't part of it. So give my magic back to me."

"That's impossible," the caterpillar replied.

I glared at him. He wasn't fae, so he could lie, but it seemed like he was telling the truth.

"Then you owe me, and I'm not leaving until you pay up." I crossed my arms over my chest. "After all, you just took my *aether magic*. Surely you can conjure up something amazing with it?"

Behind me, I could feel my friends vibrating with anxiety and fear, but I didn't dare break the caterpillar's stare. We were in a standoff for power.

"Fine," the caterpillar said after a few long moments. He bent over and pulled a chunk out of one side of his mushroom, and then an equal-sized chunk from the other side. "I have a feeling you might be needing to sneak around in the future. Of course, when you learn to fully control your aether magic and the surrounding aether, you might be able to manipulate your size yourself. However, I doubt that will be any time soon."

He extended the mushroom chunk in his right hand. "This bit will make you bigger. And this," he waved the left hand's chunk, "will make you smaller. Everything you can carry on your person will be affected—including weapons." He arched a knowing eyebrow. "Only a nibble is necessary."

Careful to keep them separate, I took the hunks of mushroom from him, and after committing to memory which did what, placed them in the pockets of my cloak.

"Thank y—" Henri started to say, but I held up a hand, cutting him off.

"It's a good start, but not enough."

"I beg your pardon?" The caterpillar's cheeks turned purple with fury. "I've given you something of very high value. Not just anyone can enchant food."

I knew that. Dee and Dum had mentioned the same thing when I asked about the 'drink me' liquid and the 'eat me' cake. Apparently, they'd had to hire a witch from the human realm to make those, and at great cost to the rebels. And yet, I wasn't about to agree so easily.

"I am aware. But that's my magical life force you sucked down. A gift from the old gods. Something that will allow you to keep taking aether from the forest. And while you might love your mushroom bits, I *know* that my life force is more valuable." My fingers skimmed the dagger at my side. "If you don't agree, we might have to settle this another way."

The caterpillar's beady eyes latched onto the dagger, and he gulped. "Fine. What do you want?"

"A trip back to Heartstown." I pointed to Henri. "His house, if you can swing it."

"B—but that's—" the caterpillar stammered.

"Still not as valuable as my life force, I know. I'm cutting you quite the deal." I gripped the dagger, waiting.

The creature scowled. "As long as you agree to never return, I'll do anything to get you out of here."

My lips curled up. "It seems that we have a deal."

The caterpillar thrust out four of his hands. "Hold on tight."

I was about to ask if this would hurt as much as releasing my aether magic had, but the scoundrel didn't give me a second.

His power bloomed out of his fingertips. The aether swirled around us, blinding me.

"Grab my hand!" I screamed, and flung my arm around for Hatter.

A dry, warm palm gripped mine at the same time as the pixies flung themselves inside my hood. Suddenly, the ground ceased to exist under me, and everything disappeared.

CHAPTER 18

When I regained consciousness, my entire body ached something fierce, and even more disturbingly, I had unexpected company.

March Hare had pulled a gold armchair up next to my bed, and was slumped over in it, his black ears flopped forward as he snoozed. On his lap, the resident mice, Dormouse and Tim, napped with him.

"What happened?" I whisper-moaned, and eased myself up off the bed.

March's big ears caught the sound of my voice, and he leapt out of the chair, throwing Tim and Dormouse to the floor with a cry as he scurried over. "Princess! Lie down this instant!"

"But I have to pee," I said, my brows furrowed. "Why are you guys in here? Was I sick?"

I didn't feel sick, but then again, with my aether magic swirling about inside me, and the kink in . . . well, all my joints, I didn't feel like myself either. Even my wings ached; a new sensation for me.

"In a manner of speaking. You really should lie down," March Hare said, and twisted to the mice. "And you two, go inform Hatter that she's awake."

They scurried out of the room as fast as their little legs could carry them.

I had no idea what was going on, but I knew one thing: the longer I stood there, the more I felt like my bladder would burst.

I took two steps toward the restroom.

"Oberon's ears! Let me help you." The hare assisted me inside my personal bath, and then just stood in the doorway, waiting.

"Umm, some privacy?"

His dark eyes popped open. "Oh! Of course. So sorry."

He shut the door, and I shook my head before going about my business.

Something had totally happened, and I needed to figure out what.

After relieving myself, I freshened up. Splashing some water on my face and brushing my teeth made me feel almost like new. For good measure, I did a few stretches and air squats to get the blood moving and wake my brain up.

When I was prepared to face March again, I exited the bathroom to find him standing inches from the door.

"Were you there the whole time?"

March nodded. "What if you fell?"

Why was he treating me like I was some breakable object?

"Why would I fall?"

In response, March Hare grabbed my hand and pulled me over to the gold armchairs. While I'd been in the bathroom, someone had brought a platter of bread, meats, cheeses, and fruit. "Please, Princess, sit and eat."

"I wish people would stop calling me that," I replied, but acquiesced to his wishes, because now that I'd taken care of one bodily need, another had arisen. I was ravenous. "Thanks for sending for the grub."

"My pleasure," the brown rabbit replied. "I must say, you look rather better than I thought you would."

"Do I usually wake up looking like hell?"

"No, but when the four of you arrived two days ago—plopped unceremoniously in the great room, I might add—you all looked awful. The pixies were limp as dishrags."

My hand stopped, poised over a bunch of grapes. "I'm sorry . . . did you say we got back two *days* ago?"

March Hare nodded. "Aether travel is notoriously tricky. Those who can't control the aether usually lose consciousness. You were out for a long time, but considering the distance you traveled, it's not unreasonable."

"You know where we were?"

"Henri woke yesterday. He filled us in on everything."

"And the pixies?"

"They've been stirring. We expect they should wake at any time."

I exhaled a long breath, trying to get my bearings. I'd been unconscious for two days, and traveling for . . .

My spine straightened. *Tomorrow is my eighteenth birthday.*

"I guess I'm glad I woke up now. Turning eighteen while passed out would have sucked."

March Hare's ears drooped, and he looked away.

"What? What else happened?"

"Nothing happened, per se," the hare said. "It's just that you lost more time in the Enchanted Forest than you think—which is not unusual, if the tales of those woods are to be believed. Today is actually your birthday. You're eighteen."

I dropped the piece of cheese I'd been holding. *Today is my birthday?!*

I'd waited so long for this day. The day when I'd be free of Xavier. And even though I'd shattered that contract already, it still felt momentous. By the law of my world, I was an adult, able to do whatever I wanted. When I completed my mission and left Faerie, I'd truly be free.

Today is my birthday. Holy shit!

I leapt out of my seat began shaking my ass to a hyped up, Doru-basing, version of 'Happy Birthday' complete with beat drops and all.

Happy birthday to me! Suck it vamp, I hate thee! Happy birthday to meeeeee!

Right away, March was at my side. "Princess! Are you all right? Maybe you should sit—"

I grabbed his paws and swung the hare around in a circle. A laugh burst out of my throat as we spun, but I seemed to be the only one enjoying myself. For the first time since I'd woken, the hare's expression of concern melted into a more familiar one of annoyance.

I laughed again and put him down. "Sorry, I'm fine. You have no idea how long I've waited for this day."

"We're happy you're here to share it with us," a deep voice said. "Happy birthday, Alice."

I spun to find Hatter, leaning against the doorframe, his dark hair tumbling past his shoulders and eyes bright as they raked over me. He looked like a mother effing model, and my heart rate kicked up a notch.

"How do you feel?" He extended a piping hot cup of tea.

"Fine," I said, ignoring the dull ache in my joints as I took the mug and tried to act freaking normal, not like a boycrazy teen. "You?"

"Better by the minute." Henri smiled wider, and his green eyes crinkled at the corners. "Do you think you'll be up for a celebration tonight? Something quiet and intimate? I've asked a few of the rebels to come over."

"Celebrate?"

Girlish excitement rose inside me. I hadn't had a birthday party since I was five—and I'd only recently been reminded of that one.

"Of course," he said. "We couldn't let your day go unnoticed."

"But . . . what about the mission?" My goal sprang back into my mind, alongside the guilt that I'd momentarily forgotten about it.

Hatter shrugged. "Half the day is lost, so we'll get to it tomorrow. Besides, preparations are already underway for a party. Of course, you can call it off, but I hope that you won't. So many people want to celebrate you."

I chewed on my bottom lip. Assassinating the Red Queen and finding Elise were my top priorities. Should I be partying?

As if sensing my indecision, Henri spoke again. "I don't know about you, but my muscles and bones need time to recover after aether travel. And speaking of aether, you'll need to practice with yours before we take on the queen's herd. Perhaps take the afternoon to practice, and tonight we'll feast?"

I tilted my head, and tellingly, my neck popped.

I have been go, go, go since the night I killed the mafia alpha wolf. A rest and some time to practice aether magic without stakes would be nice.

My lips curled up as the idea that I was getting an actual birthday party thrown for me set in. "Sounds like a great idea."

As it turned out, it wasn't just a *nice* idea to delay the start of our mission. If I wanted to control my aether magic when I confronted the Red Queen, a delay was necessary.

Because damn, that shit was wild.

I practiced for hours on end with variable results. About half the time, the aether did what I wanted. The rest of the time, it would cater to its own whims, or simply float out the window, away from me and dissolve into the air.

Those moments were infuriating, but Henri insisted that they were also to be expected.

"I remember you practicing with aether as a girl. You hated when it didn't do what you wanted," he said after stopping by my room to check on me.

"That's not really what I want to hear right now." I pushed past him to storm out of my room. I'd been there all day because the great room was being set up for my party, and Henri wanted to keep that a surprise. I'd honor his wish, but in that moment, I really needed a change of scene.

I huffed as I made my way down the dark hallways, very aware that his footsteps followed. When I got to the kitchen, I grabbed an apple, took a savage bite, and collapsed into a chair.

Hatter entered the room behind me, an amused smirk on his face. "You know, fifty percent isn't too bad. When you were younger, the aether only did as you wished maybe twenty percent of the time." He moved to the counter and began preparing a drink.

I gaped. *What is he smoking?! Is he kidding?*

When no indication to a joke came, I had to press the fact. "Twenty percent?! That's a terrible average!"

"Yeah, so half the time is a major improvement." He paused, a thoughtful expression crossing his face. "Now that I think about it, your mother had seemed pretty impressed by your achievements. She said you were more advanced than her at the same age. And that aether is an extension to the old gods powers, and therefore you must earn control over it. I think you're being too hard on yourself."

An image of the woman he spoke of filtered through my thoughts. I could remember her now, her red lips that she always kept painted, her white hair, so like mine. It was a pleasure to be able to see her, though, if I tried too hard, the memories tended to assault me. It was simply too much, too fast. I found it best to dip in and out of them leisurely. To learn bits at a time.

"Speaking of my mother," I started with the question that had arisen a few times since we'd returned. "When we were in the Enchanted Forest, you introduced me to the caterpillar as Alice White."

Surprise flitted across Henri's face at the abrupt change of topic, but he rolled with it. "I did. Because I knew he'd recognize and respect the royal name."

"It was my mother's familial name?" I felt dumb

asking because I should probably remember this, but I didn't. Not yet, anyhow.

He nodded.

I leaned back, mulling that over. "What was my father's house name?"

"Torna. You have family on his side in the Riverland Court. As your mother was the higher ranked royal, you and Elise took her name when you were born."

I supposed I shouldn't be surprised that Queenly, the last name I'd known my whole life, was a lie. My parents had probably made it up when they handed me over to Xavier as another means of protection. But now that I knew the truth . . .

"That's what I'm going by from now on, Alice White."

Henri's lips quirked up, and he handed me a mug. "Good choice, the name suits you."

I looked in the cup. The concoction smelled sweet and alcoholic—a welcome distraction at this point.

"What is this?"

"Cider. Take it upstairs, and get ready for your party. Friends will be arriving in an hour. I'll have March bring you a dress you might like in a few minutes. If you hate it, he can bring you others."

I leapt up from my chair. "An hour?! Why didn't you say so?! I have no idea how to apply fae cosmetics!"

I darted out of the kitchen, not even stopping to shoot back some sass when Henri burst into laughter.

CHAPTER 19

"Alice?" Dee's voice came through the door. "Are you ready? Everyone's waiting."

I glanced in the mirror, almost unable to believe that the girl staring back at me was the same one who'd worked for Xavier Doru just days ago. So much had changed.

Back then, I wouldn't have been attending a party for fun, but to off a mark. I'd still be counting down the days until I earned my freedom. I'd be hiding my wings with straps, instead of exposing them in all their glimmering, gold-tinted glory. And I wouldn't have met the pixies, or Hatter . . . Three people who had weaseled their way into my heart surprisingly quickly.

And still, something was missing.

I leaned closer to the mirror, trying to suss out what I needed to add to my outfit.

Dee knocked again, this time faster, making me grin. Such an impatient thing.

"I'll be right there," I called.

"Okay, but hurry up! You're missing out."

A faint flutter of her wings told me she'd left, and I applied a coat of lip rouge before looking in the mirror again.

There. Perfect. Much more powerful looking—not at all nervous, I lied internally, and without giving myself another moment to debate, left the room.

My breath was tight in my chest as I descended the stairs to the faint sounds of music and fae. I was excited to have a party thrown in my honor, but nerves riddled me more than I cared to consider. A party felt like an enormous step, like ingraining myself into society.

Even though I didn't plan on sticking around, I wanted to impress the fae. To assure them I could rid them of the Red Queen.

In a few days, my mission had transformed from a purely personal vendetta into something else, something more. I couldn't deny that I liked the idea of being able to make a positive difference in others' lives for once.

After all, I'd killed many. And even though they were routinely the worst kind of people, I'd never had any proof that I'd left things better.

I had a lot to make up for. Changing thousands of lives in one fell swoop would be a good start.

But first, to meet a few of Henri's friends.

I stopped in front of the bright green door that separated the great room from the hallway. Music poured through the wood, chords of harp and piano and some unnameable string instruments wiggled into my ears, easing my nerves.

Although I couldn't name the song, somehow, I knew I'd heard it before. And that, once upon a time, I'd liked it.

I wouldn't be surprised if Hatter had chosen to play it for me because he remembered that I liked it. He was that kind of guy.

My hand had landed on the doorknob, and I was about to turn it, when it opened from the inside. My heart skipped a beat as I locked eyes with Hatter's twinkling emerald ones.

"I was about to come get you." He winked, and my stomach erupted in a swarm of butterflies. "Thought maybe you'd changed your mind, and wanted to hermit up in your room again."

"Why would I do that?" I retorted, completely aware that, back in the human world, that was exactly what I would've done if I wasn't paid to go to a party.

"Because you're scared?" A hint of teasing in his voice made all this—the nerves, the attraction, the expectations —easier.

"I'll show you scared." I strode forward, making it three steps before my feet stopped working.

I'd expected the constant fixtures in Henri's home— the pixies, Dormouse, Tim, March Hare, and maybe ten more fae max, but at least fifty people filled the room, all of them smiling at me.

I took in the people standing among what had to be hundreds of white roses sitting in gold vases. Like in my room, teal was a prominent color too, which was nice. It helped settle me, somewhat. I gulped, as my gaze shifted from the decor back to the faces. "I thought you said this would be intimate? Who are all these people?"

His hand landed on my lower back. "Rebels you have yet to meet. Well, actually, you have met a few."

A pair waved from somewhere in the middle.

I squinted to find Isadora and a younger version of the brownie—probably her daughter—who'd dropped off the biscuits.

"There are so many of them. Is this everyone?"

"Less than half. But we can't have everyone showing up here on the same night. It would look too suspicious."

I was relieved that not everyone was present. Sometimes, I'd had to be social when I worked an assassination, but in those instances, I was never playing myself—I was Alice the Dagger, and had a veil of steel to protect me. Here, all I had was black silk and a few pieces of gold jewelry that Hatter had given me to wear for the occasion.

I ran my hand over the silk, reveling in how it clung to my curves but still breathed. "How did you pick out this dress, anyway? And the jewelry? I particularly love the earrings, they're perfect."

Hatter's cheeks darkened as his eyes followed my

roaming hands. "It's been here for a while. You seem like the right size, and I thought it might suit you."

"What do you mean by 'it's been here for a while'?"

He glanced away. "That was my mother's dress. She actually wore it to your parents' wedding, years ago. The earrings too."

His mother's dress. He didn't speak about his mother much, even less than he talked about his father. Although I was curious what had happened to her, I knew better than to dig into open wounds.

I cleared my throat. "Well, she had excellent taste. Classic, and her color palette is on point."

Hatter chuckled and offered his arm. "Would you like me to make some introductions?"

Once more, my eyes scanned the crowd in front of us. Everyone was still smiling kindly, waiting. I didn't know if I would make it through all of them, or even half, but something in me wanted to try.

Hatter's friendly ways must be rubbing off.

"Yes, I'd love that."

I put on my brightest smile as Henri led me into the crowd and introduced me to others. After a bit, he had to take his leave to see to the food, but by then, I was fine. Everyone was kind and, to my shock, genuinely pleased to be celebrating my birthday.

It felt odd that strangers cared more about my special day than those I'd been raised with. Odd, but admittedly nice.

I was finishing up a conversation with Isadora and her

daughter, Circe, when the music took a turn, and a cry of delight rippled through the crowd.

I tilted my head. "Why is everyone so excited?" I asked Circe, who looked ready to burst with excitement.

"This is the latest song by that composer Hani! Everyone's talking about him and this song at court. The dance that goes with it is so fun!"

A grin broke on my face. Her exuberance was infectious. "Show me?"

Circe shook her head. "Sorry, Princess, but I have my eye on a certain blue-haired someone, and this dance is meant to be done with a partner."

A partner, huh? I guessed I was out then. People had wanted to talk to me all night, but none seemed inclined to get too close. I hadn't stepped a toe on the dance floor.

"All right, then, go find your partner." I winked, and Circe squealed as she ran off into the crowd.

"Sansu had better be ready, 'cause here comes a steamroller." Isadora sighed and shook her head. "He seems interested, but it's hard to tell what she's thinking. Circe has been unusually quiet about him. She acts the same when she's hunting something. It's the only time that she's quiet, actually."

I let out a laugh. "I don't see that he has any reason to complain. She's very pretty, so young and vibrant. Wish I had that bubbly energy."

I watched the girl two years my junior skip through the crowd in search of her guy.

"Oh please, Princess Alice, you and Circe are about

the same age. You're not telling me you feel old and beaten down already?"

I wouldn't have said that, although mentally, I identified as older than my years. I'd seen a lot of shit, and that tended to wear a person down.

"Not at all. I'm just not as vivacious, I guess."

"Come to think of it, I haven't seen you on the dance floor yet. That's a shame."

"I would dance, but no one has asked." I shrugged because it was true and I actually liked dancing. Here though, dances seemed to be done with partners. There hadn't been a single solo act, and I wasn't trying to start a trend. "I don't know any of the routines."

"Happy to help with that." Hatter's deep voice ran through me, raising the hair on the nape of my neck.

I turned to find him smiling at me, hand extended.

"May I have this dance?"

"Are you sure?" I gestured around. At least four females were eyeing him. "It looks like you can take your pick, and I'll only step on your toes. You'll have to teach me even the most basic steps."

"That's all right. I'm a patient teacher. And you of all people should learn the courtly dances."

My lips pressed together. I'd told him that I didn't intend to stay.

"After you dethrone the Red Queen, there will be a celebration," Hatter continued, reading my facial expression. "Everyone will want to thank you."

My lips softened. *Good save.*

"Go on, Princess Alice. It'll be fun." Isadora pushed me toward Hatter.

"I don't know . . ."

He released a chuckle. "I've never had such a reluctant dance partner."

"That's because you've never met someone quite like me."

"That much is obvious," Henri replied in a way that made my stomach twist.

I tried to force down the reaction, tried to put up my mask of hardened-lone-wolf again, but one look into his eyes and I failed. He smiled, and a wave of ease washed over me, making my shoulders loosen. I drew in his aroma and the rest of me softened too. Why was I making this difficult, anyway?

It's only a bit of fun. You remember what that is, right, Alice?

Sometimes I wasn't so sure.

"Fine." I took his hand, still out there, waiting for me.

Henri led me out onto a makeshift dance floor, where six or seven other couples swayed and twirled to the music.

"Give me your other hand." Hatter offered his right hand to me, and then placed the left on his hip. "Mimic my posture."

I did as he said.

"Now, let me lead. Don't fight it."

"I've never been very good at that."

"Now's the time to give it a shot. You might find you enjoy relinquishing control every now and again."

I was about to retort when Hatter swung me in time to the music.

The dance resembled a strange mix of a refrained waltz and a spicy tango. Elegant and sensual all at once.

Hatter was a remarkable dancer. He led with strength and grace. Even though I stepped on his toes half a dozen times, he never lost his patience with me. In fact, as I picked up the moves, he only challenged me more, once grabbing me by the hips and twirling me through the air as if I weighed no more than a feather.

When he caught me, I became breathless, his face inches from mine, and the spicy scent of him filling my nostrils, lighting my blood on fire.

"You all right, Princess?" Henri whispered.

"All right? I'm buzzing, I'm so alive," I said, ignoring his use of my title so as not to break the spell between us.

Hatter's lips spread in a heart-stopping smile. "Excellent."

He pulled me so close that our chests touched, and his hips swayed sinfully as our eyes locked together—the center of our own world.

Blood thrummed in my ears.

I was inches away from crossing a dangerous line. Part of me desperately wanted to rush over it, to see what would happen if I gave myself to Henri. What would he do if I pressed his lips against mine and ran my fingers through his long, black hair? The other part, the girl who planned to go home, screamed at me to step back.

To guard my heart.

When the song ended, we swayed gently to a stop, still pressed together, our eyes locked and pulses pounding. Though I didn't dare tear my eyes from Hatter, I knew that dozens of eyes were on us—burning into my back. It felt as if the whole room was holding their breath, until someone started clapping, and the rest of the crowd burst out in applause.

Circe and her blue-haired crush sidled up to us. The girl gripped my forearm excitedly. "You were a natural! We might have to ask the band to play that song again so I can watch you from the beginning."

"Please, no," I laughed breathlessly. Hatter's eyes burned like emerald fire, and my heart was still beating like I'd run a marathon. I needed to separate from him. He was too intoxicating. "As a matter of fact, I think it's time for me to get a snack and some air."

I dropped Hatter's hand before anyone could force us to dance again. "Thanks for the lesson."

I sashayed through the crowd, pausing briefly to talk to an elderly elf who wore a military uniform, and a middle-aged faerie with the most beautiful rainbow-colored wings.

When I reached the refreshment table, I piled bread, cheeses, a few raw veggies, and meats onto a plate before grabbing a glass of wine. When I was sure that I had all the sustenance and distraction I needed, I turned to face the rest of the party, and found who else, but *Hatter*.

"Are you following me?"

"It appears I might be." He poured himself a full

glass of wine. "I hope you'll excuse that. It seems I can't help myself."

A blush crept up my neck, and I combated it the best way I knew how. With sass. "Most men can't."

Hatter arched his eyebrows. "Probably because you're so humble."

I snorted a laugh, and the heady sexual tension that had built as we danced dissipated.

We went on like that for some length of time, teasing and vaguely flirting, until finally, the crowd began to thin. I breathed my first full breath since entering the great room.

My birthday party was coming to an end.

"Would you like them to leave?" Henri asked, attuned to my mood, as he always seemed to be.

"Kind of, although I don't want the *feel* of the party to end." The longing in my voice was plain. I hoped that I didn't sound pathetic, but if I did, I couldn't help it. I might be tired and ready to retreat, but the party was marvelous.

Hatter gave me an understanding smile. "There will be more parties. But I do think it's for the best that tonight comes to an end. It's late, and we have work to do tomorrow."

Right. Work.

Tomorrow we would hunt the queen's herd of bandersnatch in hopes of drawing my aunt from her castle. I wasn't sure how many we would have to injure or kill, but I hoped it wasn't a lot. I might be an assassin, but unless it was life or death, I didn't like killing animals. And especially not for sport.

My motto was you shouldn't kill the beast if no one would eat the meat, and I doubted that anyone would be eating these bandersnatch.

But I couldn't deny that in this circumstance, things were different. The reasoning behind the attack made perfect sense. We needed to draw the queen out from behind her strong castle walls. This one act of protest might save a lot of lives—fae lives—and rid the Wonderland Court of a tyrant. Those goals were worthy, even if the methods were distasteful.

After Henri announced that the party was over, each attendee stopped by to wish me a happy birthday before they left. Finally, after what felt like years, only Henri, the pixies, the mice, and March Hare remained.

Dee stretched her little arms wide and yawned. "What a shindig! I am pooped. Off to bed!"

Before she soared off, March grabbed her by a wing. "Oh no you don't. You snuck out of preparing for this, and made your sister and me do all the work. You're on clean-up duty with the mice."

"There's not a bigger person on clean-up duty with me? This will take all night!" Dee wailed.

While March Hare and Dee continued arguing, I decided to leave them to their own devices, and made my way to bed. As the door to the great room swung closed behind me, Hatter opened it once more.

"You're skipping out on clean-up too?" I teased.

"Absolutely," he said. "March gets paid for running the household and making sure people are in line. I get paid to make art and hats. That allows me time to ensure everything in rebel-land falls into place."

"And here I was under the impression that March was your right-hand man."

"Who says a housekeeper can't be a right-hand man?" Henri arched his eyebrows at me. "March is indispensable. A tidy home makes a tidy mind, and all that."

My thoughts flitted back to the disorderly easels that normally dotted the great room, all in various stages of completeness. The rest of the house, however, was always spick and span—March's work. It was a relief to realize that Hatter needed help keeping the ship running, that he wasn't totally perfect.

"Is there an official time we'll begin the mission tomorrow?" I waited at the top of the stairs, so we could walk side-by-side.

"I'm waking up early to prepare, although most people won't be here until late morning. We're supposed to strike early in the afternoon. The herd migrates through various areas of the city. We'll be timing the attack to their movements, so it'll be easier for us to retreat when guards storm the streets. When they find no one, hopefully the Red Queen will make an appearance to find the culprit. I believe she will. She values her herd greatly."

Our footsteps sounded loud in the empty hallway,

striking the wood and emitting a dozen creaks as we walked.

"They migrate to catch criminals, right? Because they can sense if someone is not loyal to the queen? So the routes must change to keep people on their toes."

"They can sense wavering loyalty or a criminal's guilt only if the subject in question was enchanted by the mist the Red Queen's witches unleashed on the land. None of the rebels are enchanted, thank the aether. And yes, the herd migrates, and those migrations rotate daily. Herald was able to get this week's rotations. We know they'll be near the main market after noon. "

We reached my room and came to a stop. All the sounds of the hallway vanished. I was instantly aware of the sound of my breathing, and the heat coming off Hatter in the drafty old house.

I twisted to face him, and the air between us grew thick. It would be easy enough to continue talking about the mission, easy enough to brush off our simmering attraction, but I had a feeling that neither of us wanted to.

But then, what *did* we want to do?

After I killed the Red Queen and found Elise, I planned on going home, and Hatter was very much a part of the Wonderland Court. People loved him here, and he loved his homeland. I couldn't see him coming back to the human realm with me. Nor was I sure that I wanted to be the reason he left Faerie.

After all, just because I wasn't staying didn't mean I

wanted Wonderland in chaos. This place was in my blood, and I wanted the fae here to live full, rich lives. Hatter had already proven that he was a leader among the fae. I had faith that he could give that to them.

Henri gulped, the nerves showing on his face. "I hope you had a fun party."

"The best." I resisted the urge to reach out and caress his face.

"Good, then I guess this is goodnight."

Hatter made to turn, but unable to stop myself, I reached out for him, my hand landing on his rock-hard bicep.

My mouth went dry, and I gulped to wet it. "Henri?"

His cheeks darkened. "Yes?"

My toes curled in my shoes at his husky tone. "I want to thank you for everything. For bringing me here, for telling me the truth, and for resisting my desire to go after the queen right away—even if I was snotty about it."

He let out a thin laugh, which made me smile.

"And especially for your friendship. I haven't had many friends in my life, and if I were to remain here," I paused because his face fell so drastically it almost ripped out my heart, "I know we would be close."

"I'm happy to hear you say that," he replied, although his tone was more wistful than happy.

My insides churned with emotions. With sadness, lust, fear of doing what I wanted, and most of all the fear of regret.

I leaned forward and planted my lips on his cheek.

Inches away, his lips called me, tempted me like no other lips had. But this was as far as I could go.

I might be hardened, all steel and sass, but I'd had my heart broken once, and Jax was a much lesser man than Henri. I couldn't do that again.

If I fell all the way for this fae, I wouldn't survive a separation.

"Goodnight, Hatter," I said, committing to memory the sensation of his warm skin pressed against mine.

The brief, sweet moment that would have to last me for the rest of my life.

CHAPTER 20

Sunlight streamed into my room as I emerged from the bathroom, a towel wrapped around my long, teal hair, prepared to seize the day. Not even Henri was up yet. The old house remained quiet and still, exactly what I needed.

I'd always done my best work alone, in silence. And before we left to take on the queen's herd, I needed to practice with my aether magic.

Perching on my bed, I began flipping through the pages of *Properties of the Aether*. All types of aether manipulation, from conjuring objects to putting magical creatures in a fae's thrall—even creating a glamour—had to do with visualization and willpower. However, in the book, the various uses were detailed individually. It made me wonder if not all aether-blessed had the ability to perform every single aspect of aether magic.

I'd never asked the aether-blessed fae who Xavier had

periodically hired to glamour my ears so I appeared human if there were limits to her power. And although many of my memories had returned, I still couldn't recall my parents using aether. Since they were royals, I knew that they must have been able to, so the lack of recollection was annoying. Perhaps they hadn't done it often. Or maybe their use of the aether had seemed mundane to me. Like the everyday stuff that people forget over time.

In the end, it didn't really matter. Whatever the limitations of others, I planned on working my way through every chapter of this book, mastering each lesson as best I could to increase my chances of defeating the Red Queen.

Starting with the magical discipline of conjuring.

I skimmed the pages for the fifth time, committing them to memory. Once I finished, I scanned my room. The book suggested starting with an object that I could see and touch—preferably hold—and then duplicating it. On the vanity next to my bed, the earrings Henri lent me the day before glinted in the early morning sunlight.

I picked them up, cupping the elegant studs in my hand and examining them closely. They were fairly small, about the size of a pencil eraser. In their center, a bright aquamarine stone glittered, surrounded by a wreath of golden roses.

Teal and gold.

I glanced around the room, taking in the familiar color scheme, a combination that I now knew was of my mother's royal house.

My heart squeezed. Henri's mother had once worn these earrings to my parents' wedding.

Besides my terrible aunt, Henri was the one person, in all of Faerie and the human world, who had known me the longest. There was a familiarity there—a weight that was obvious whenever Hatter did certain things, like make sure I wore my house colors to my birthday party. Our families were so intertwined, like our pasts, that sometimes, it overwhelmed me.

I sighed, wishing things were simpler. That I wanted to be a princess. Why was it so hard to commit to something I'd been born into?

My gaze shot up as a sound came from the room next door. Low singing. Henri was up too.

I needed to begin my practice.

Allowing my fingers to run over the textured gold roses and the smooth stone, I committed the feel of the earrings to memory before closing them in my fist. Then I called on my aether magic.

The surrounding air warmed a few degrees, a subtle sign that aether was at work. Keeping the vision of the earrings in my mind's eye, I stared down at my other, open, palm, and imagined a replica appearing there.

The change rolled out slowly—a glint of gold, a faint weight falling into my hand, the cold of metal settling against my skin—but it picked up steam the harder I pushed.

To my surprise, less than a minute later, the earrings simply winked into existence in my hand.

My lips quirked up as I studied them. Even without opening my other fist to examine the real pair, I could spot differences. The shade of aquamarine was off, too dark, and the earrings were smaller.

But still, the replicas were close. Damn close. And it hadn't been as difficult to work with the aether as it had the day before.

My hope spun up. And for the first time in years, I allowed that feeling to simmer before I tossed the imitation earrings on the vanity, and tried again.

Many hours and more successes than failures with the aether later, it was time for our mission. My fingers trembled as I pulled on an elegant, dark navy cloak embroidered on the edges. As I did so, I was careful to fit my wings through the holes without bending them, a new practice for me.

Now that we no longer had to worry about my hair giving me away, Henri had gifted me a less restrictive cloak. Probably another of his mother's garments.

I stretched my wings out, grateful that I could walk around the city with them free. They gave me another means of escape, should I need one. In that way, they acted like a security blanket, almost as comforting as the dagger on my hip and the magical mushroom bits in my pockets.

After one last glance around my room to make sure I

didn't leave anything necessary behind, I made my way to the entryway.

Henri already stood in front of the door. The pixies hovered on either side of him, and eight rebels, including Circe and March Hare, waited in the hall. Like me, everyone else wore cloaks to hide their weapons.

"Ready?" Hatter asked me. As he spoke, I tried hard not to focus on his lips. Lips that I'd had to force myself not to kiss last night. Lips that I *still* wanted to kiss.

I cursed my restraint.

"Alice? Are you okay?" Henri asked, his brows knitted together.

Oh shit, I hadn't answered him.

"I'm fine and ready as I'll ever be," I said, straightening my shoulders.

Quickly, we established two teams and then left headquarters. Hatter led the way through the streets. As we walked, no one paid much attention to us. It seemed that, despite the warm weather, cloaks were a reasonable fashion choice for all seasons in the Wonderland Court.

I shook my head, and was wondering what that said about the place, when Hatter came to a stop and held his hand out to hold back those behind him.

"Do you hear them?" he asked, gesturing left. "I think they're on the street up ahead."

My ears strained, and I cupped one as I tilted my head in the direction Henri had indicated. The strange growling yowls sounded garbled, as if the bandersnatch were eating.

"You're right."

"Let's separate," Hatter said.

Everyone split, Henri leading one group, while March Hare led the other. I was in Hatter's group.

"We'll take this side. March's group: flank the other side of the herd from the next block. Pixies, be on the lookout for the queen's men. Use the signal if you see them. Everyone else, attack inward, and remember to watch out for any kicking. Their legs are powerful."

Personally, the creatures' jaws worried me more, but I'd take advice from someone who knew better.

"Once we've killed or injured as many as possible, split and meet back at headquarters. Any questions?"

A knot wound in my stomach as a stab of unease hit me. Every time I considered attacking the herd, I remembered the mother and baby animal I'd seen in the woods. All the bandersnatch probably wanted to live that way. They hadn't chosen to be controlled by my aunt.

And yet, the rebels assured me that going after the herd was the only way to draw the Red Queen from her castle. I couldn't just brush off their beliefs. They'd been around much longer, put up with my aunt's shit for years. They knew this land far better than me, and this was their lived experience. I needed to *trust* them.

"All right, let's move," Henri said when no one posed a question.

We split off, and slowly made our way down the street. There was no way we'd sneak up on the beasts, which had incredible hearing, so we weren't even about to try. We only moved slowly to give March's team time to catch up. Attacking simultaneously was key.

Now that we waited at the end of the street, I could hear the herd clearly. They were eating, taking a break from their search for dissenters.

Hatter had mentioned that the bandersnatch's ability to sense a lack of loyalty was tied to the enchanted fog that the Red Queen had blanketed her subjects with. Apparently, the creatures couldn't sense disloyalty in those who *hadn't* been enchanted. Fae who ran when they saw the mist crawling over the land—like the rebels. Hence, the bandersnatch only created a fuss when the enchantment wore off on someone who had been affected. Such a scenario had only happened five times in thirteen years.

Using animals to detect untrustworthy subjects among those specifically enchanted to be loyal, made little sense. That is until you took into account the Red Queen's history.

She'd killed her sister, the only family she had left. She'd erased her subjects' memories. Currently, she starved and mistreated many of them. The Red Queen didn't deserve her subjects' trust and she knew it.

I bet my aunt is paranoid as hell.

I huddled behind Hatter to wait for the signal. It came quickly, in the sound of a hawk's screech.

Adrenaline flooded me as we exploded into the main street and sprinted toward the herd.

The animals stood grouped together, at least fifty of them. Many drank from a fountain that featured a stone, stern-faced faerie holding a bouquet of roses. My horrible aunt. One of the creatures splashed inside the fountain, more carefree than the others. My heart lurched as a memory of the baby bandersnatch in the river flitted through my mind.

My teeth gnashed together as I recalled all the assurances of the rebels that this was the only way, and surged ahead to be the first in my group to burst into the herd.

I dodged one creature's powerful hindquarters as they popped up at me, and slammed my dagger into its underbelly. The bandersnatch fell with a horrible yowl as the rest of the herd erupted into chaos.

Trying not to think or feel, I made my way through the creatures, my dagger moving efficiently with every slash and stab. I experimented with aether magic too, and it came easier than ever before.

By my third attempt at using it, I recognized the aether as the most effective weapon we had, and much more humane than my blade. It smothered the bandersnatch's snouts, forcing the beasts to collapse within seconds. After one collapsed, I'd make a cut in their leg so that the queen would be unable to use the beast to do her bidding anytime soon. But at least this way they'd live and could heal.

I switched to striking exclusively with aether first, moving through the herd and downing the beasts that others were aiming to kill. I was at the fountain when someone cried out for help.

Pivoting, I found March Hare pinned up against the wall, slashing his blade at a bandersnatch's snout.

I couldn't help but admire the beast. It didn't give a damn about the glint of metal, only about defending its herd. But when the bandersnatch slammed its body into the wall, nearly crushing March, I acted against it, smothering the beast's nostrils until the creature passed out. Once the bandersnatch was down, I slashed its leg with a blade to restrict its mobility.

I'd just rushed over to help March back on his feet when the oddest sensation came over me. I gasped and spun on the spot.

No onlookers hung around; they'd all run off to alert the authorities, or remain safe from the fighting animals. Four rebels stood on the sidelines, injured or on the lookout for the authorities.

None of them watched me, but I swore someone somewhere was. Their eyes burned through me—assessing me.

"Alice! We need to finish this!" Hatter's scream rang in my ear, yanking me back into the moment.

Only five creatures were left, the largest and most ferocious, and they were fighting tooth and nail against the remaining rebels.

I waved someone over to take March, and leapt back into the fray.

Moving on autopilot, I used aether to smother the beasts' noses and send them into slumber. Within minutes, all five were on the ground, passed out.

I took a step back, taking in the destruction. A dozen animals were dead, and the rebels who were still able to move were sorting through the rest, injuring them just enough so they wouldn't be able to patrol the streets. One such creature released a moan when a rebel cut through the muscle of its hind quarter.

I winced, and the guilt that the battle had pushed back rushed forth, stronger than before.

Tears filled my eyes. "I can't stand this. It's so wrong."

"I know," Hatter said, his voice thick with emotion as he took in the scene. "I know, but—"

The sound of an alarm, much more high-pitched than alarms of the human world, pierced the air, and the rebels stiffened.

"We have to get out of here." Hatter grabbed my arm, and pulled me behind him. "Disband! Back to head-quarters!"

We made it only two streets when I heard screams flying from behind us. Shouts of men, and at least two cries for help.

I pulled my arm out of Hatter's grip. "Some of our people are in trouble!"

"Don't turn back!" He gripped my arm again and pulled me forward.

"You can't leave them!"

Henri whirled me around to face him. "We have to! They knew the risk. *You're* the most valuable person in this force, and you can't be seen until the queen is out in the open."

I opened my mouth to argue, but Hatter didn't let me get a word in. "If I have to drag you back to headquarters kicking and screaming, I will," he growled. "I won't let anything happen to you, Alice. Because if you fall, all of Wonderland falls with you."

I sucked in a shuddering breath. He was right. Aside from my aunt, I was the only fae in Wonderland who had aether magic. The only one with the power to stand up to her.

"Fine." I gestured back the way we'd come. "But I expect you to send help. You can't leave them—"

"I would never leave them high and dry." His eyes burned through me. "Once we regroup, we'll figure out who's missing. The soldiers will keep them in jail until the queen delivers a mandate. That will likely be after she checks on her precious herd. Long before that happens, a rebel faction will extract them. But for now, we must leave."

If this were anyone else, I wouldn't have believed them, but I trusted Henri. These people were his family. He'd keep his word.

So once again, I ignored my gut, and together, we sprinted back toward headquarters.

CHAPTER 21

We weren't the first people to return to headquarters, nor were we the last. Two others with injuries had somehow beat us back. The four rebels who'd remained at Hatter's, one of them being Isadora, had already started tending to the injured in the middle of the narrow hallway.

Henri and I stayed out of their way and took turns glancing out the window to look for the others.

When four more bounded up the stairs and burst through the door, unharmed, they came bearing bad news.

"Soldiers went after March," Alran, a massive elf, reported. "Circe tried to defend him, and they grabbed her too. We tried to get them back, but there were so many soldiers."

Isadora's hands clapped over her mouth. Although I'd

never been much for comforting others, I felt the urge to go to her.

I crossed the hallway, and wrapped an arm around her. "We'll get her back."

"Of course we will, Princess," she said weakly. "I believe in us—in you."

My stomach twisted, but thankfully, I didn't have to respond because Hatter took control.

"Move into the great room. We can talk more comfortably in there."

The rebels filed out of the hall. Before I could join them, Henri wrapped his big hand around my wrist, stopping me. "You don't have to be party to discussing the rescue mission. You did your part. Actually, you're probably the only reason we all got out of there before those last five bandersnatch took us out. It would be best if you began preparing to meet the Red Queen."

I tilted my chin up. "I want to be present, and I don't need alone time to be prepared to fight my aunt. I'm ready."

Hatter gave a slow nod. "Okay. But stand in the back. Otherwise, everyone will be watching you, assessing your leadership style. I know that's not what you want."

It wasn't, so I did as he said, posting up near the door, while he stood in front of the fireplace, and called the gathering to order.

"It appears that two members of our ranks are in need of extraction as soon as possible. Everyone here knows that the queen prefers not to take criminals behind castle walls."

Called it, paranoid.

"That works in our favor. March and Circe are likely being kept at the jailhouse, which is much more accessible than Heart Castle."

Hatter's gaze found Isadora. "Correct me if I'm wrong, but your daughter doesn't have a previous record, does she?"

Isadora shook her head. "It's her first offense."

"Good. It's only March's second, and the first offense wasn't nearly so large. We can work with that. Where's Tully?"

A hand shot up, and a faun with extra long horns who had stayed behind to wait for our return stepped forward.

"You have familial connections with the jailer, right? And they don't know about the rebellion?"

Tully nodded.

"Can you go to the jailhouse and state that you were at the scene of the crime? That the bandersnatch attacked first, and the riot started as self-defense? They'll keep you there for questioning, which is what we want. Keep them busy. In the meantime, we'll—"

An alarm, the same one we'd heard earlier, squealed, high and soul-shattering.

Hatter's mouth snapped shut, and everyone in the great room stared at each other, fear glinting in their eyes.

My stomach sank. *This can't be good.*

"Henri! You don't think . . ." Isadora's words died on her lips as she whipped around and tried to bolt through the door.

I pressed my arm across the doorframe, halting her. "Isadora, stop! Whatever it is, we have to think this through."

"It has to do with Circe, I know it! She's my only daughter, Princess!" A choked sob left her throat.

"And I would never expect you to let her fend for herself," I said, confused as to why Isadora would jump to the conclusion that the alarm meant Circe was in immediate danger. I chalked it up to maternal worry. "But we must coordinate and be smart. If you go out there looking for Circe before word has spread that they apprehended her, it puts everyone here at risk."

"She's right, Isadora. You need to stay here, where it's safe." Hatter's hand landed on the brownie's shoulder. "I'll search the streets and make sure the alarm has nothing to do with our attack." His gaze was pinned on Isadora, pointed and serious. I definitely didn't understand all the subtext flowing between them, but that didn't matter. I wanted to act.

"I'm coming too," I said.

"*Alice* . . ." Hatter's gaze leveled me.

"I'm going, *Henri*," I retorted. "And we need to leave now."

Tully was still sent to the jailhouse. Another troop of rebels would follow him there and break out Circe and

March. Henri, the pixies, four other rebels, and I were to investigate the alarm.

Strangely, since the alarm had started, it hadn't stopped. It continued to pierce the streets of Heartstown, almost like it was calling people to it. All the rebels in my group were on edge and very alert.

I pulled the cloak tight around my head. Something about this whole scenario felt off, and troubling. Why would Isadora assume that the alarm had been for Circe? Why hadn't I asked her, instead of jumping into action?

Henri took a sharp turn, and a sea of fae appeared at the mouth of our small side street. A square opened past the end of the road, and even more heads bobbed there, waiting for something.

"I can't get a clear view," Henri said, scowling at the ultra-tall fae—elves—who stood in front of us. "But only Dee and Dum should fly. I don't want to draw attention to the rest of us."

He darted a glance at me. "Are you okay to sit on my shoulders? Tell us what you see?"

I nodded, and our group approached the edge of the crowd. Dee and Dum fluttered up to the windows of someone's home, and perched in a flower box, while Hatter boosted me onto his shoulders.

As soon as I could see past the giants in front of us, all my breath escaped my lungs.

In the middle of hundreds of jeering fae, dotted with dozens of armed soldiers, was a rickety-looking platform. And on it knelt March Hare and Circe.

"What's going on?" Hatter asked.

"March and—what the hell?"

A fae who looked as though one of his parents might have been a troll, or some other gigantic creature, climbed the platform stairs. He lumbered past the soldiers that lined the back wall of the makeshift stage to stand right behind March and Circe, then the beast lifted his arms and roared.

All the hair on my arms lifted, but not only because of what was happening in the center of the square—though that was certainly enough to elicit such terror.

No. That *feeling* was back, the one that someone was watching me. Their attention burned through me like nothing I'd felt before, judging and calculating.

My gaze flitted down to the crowd. No one was looking my way, they were all staring at the stage. And I was too far back for the soldiers milling through the crowd to take any notice of me.

What the hell was going on here?

"*Alice!*" Hatter yelled, like it wasn't the first time he'd called my name. "What do you see?!"

I shook my head, pissed that I'd allowed myself to be distracted for even a moment. "March and Circe are kneeling on a platform. I think it's a trial or something."

Hatter swore, and his hands traveled from my calves to my hips. "Get down," he said and hoisted me off of him. "We have to do something, fast."

Even though I didn't know what was happening, Henri

seemed to have an idea. As much as I wanted to help retrieve March and Circe, I didn't see what we could do. There were six of us and two pixies against hundreds of fae who looked all too happy to watch our friends' precarious predicament.

"Alice . . . what I'm about to ask you to do is so dangerous, but I have to—for March and Circe."

Isadora's terrified expression, the way her hands trembled, rolled through my mind.

I nodded. "I'll do anything."

"I need you to use your aether magic. As much of it as you can. Make a spectacle. It's our only chance to stop this madness."

"And what are you going to do?"

"I'll fly to get them. *Alone.*"

I gaped. "Henri, that doesn't even make sense. They'll catch you in a second! We need you as much as we need them. There has to be another—"

A tinny voice pierced the air, and my gaze shot up to the platform. Although I could barely see it now that I was no longer on Henri's shoulders, long white ears and a pop of color from a blue waistcoat stood out above the crowd.

"Is that . . . Herald?"

"Yeah," Hatter's tone dipped, "and if he's here, Isadora was right to be terrified."

I was about to ask what he meant by that when Herald began reading from a scroll. "By order of the Queen of Hearts, the troublemakers Circe Blackthorn and March Hare are sentenced to immediate death for the crime of injuring Her Majesty's bandersnatch."

My throat closed up. *Immediate death?*

"Hatter!" I whisper-screamed. "We have to hurry!"

But it was no use, for as soon as Herald proclaimed the sentence, the monstrous troll pulled an axe out from behind him, and sliced through March's neck.

My hands flew to my mouth, and a strangled sound mixed with the cheers of the screwed-up, enchanted crowd.

"Circe! Hatter, we have to fly."

My wings snapped out, but Hatter's hand wrapped around my wrist, stopping me as the axe thunked against wood a second time.

"It's too late," Henri choked out. "We're too late."

CHAPTER 22

The mass exodus of the crowd, combined with our wish to avoid the soldiers clogging the streets, resulted in a delay in our return to headquarters. When we walked in the door, Isadora's eyes locked with mine.

My mouth went dry.

"Princess Alice?" Her voice trembled like a leaf in the wind. "My daughter?"

I went to her, and wrapped my arms around the brownie. "I'm so sorry, Isadora. The queen's men caught her . . . And the queen passed a judgment already."

I didn't have to say what the judgment was. According to the rebels, the queen had never acted so swiftly, but her punishment for dire crimes was *always* the same.

Off with their heads . . .

"We were too late." I gulped down the lump rising up my throat. "I'm so sorry. Really, I am."

The woman collapsed in my arms. The wail that escaped her pierced my heart, but knowing there was nothing I could do or say to make her situation better or even the tiniest bit brighter, I simply held her tight.

Hatter would deny it, but I felt responsible for both Circe's and March's deaths. Maybe for others too. As we'd fled the scene, the soldiers had picked off a few more people, those who didn't appear as jubilant about the beheading.

Perhaps they were dead by now too.

"Isadora?" Hatter's soft voice cut through my mounting guilt. "Can I get you something? Tea? Water? A place to lie down?"

The fae lifted her head. Tears streaked her face, and the whites around her dark brown irises were as red as the roses that decorated the city. "A—a—alone. I'd like to be alone."

"Dum?" Hatter waved the pixie forward. "Will you please show Isadora to an empty room? And stay nearby in case she needs anything?"

It was a good choice. Dum was sensitive, but she also knew when to be strong for someone who needed it.

Isadora released me, and allowed Dum to lead her up the stairs to a private space to grieve. When they disappeared at the top of the landing, my pretense of strength faltered, and my shoulders slumped.

Henri placed a steadying hand on me. "Thank you for that. Isadora won't be okay for some time, but I think your touch, your condolences, will help her—eventually."

"How?" I murmured, not even looking him in the face.

"You're her princess. She loves you and believes in you." He paused, as if deciding if he should continue, before adding, "When you were consoling her, you reminded me a lot of your mother. You have the comforting touch of the White line."

I shook my head. There was no way that was true. Me? An assassin by trade? I'd never known what to say to those in pain, just like I'd barely been able to say anything to Isadora. It felt so wrong when I tried. Fake and flat. I carried too much guilt around to be able to effectively comfort people.

And even if I had helped Isadora a little, I wouldn't settle for that.

"It's not enough." I lifted my face so that our eyes locked.

"Of course it's not," Hatter whispered. "But right now, giving her support and the space to grieve is the best we can do. I don't feel safe letting her go home. If the soldiers keep swarming the streets, they might be looking for Isadora because of her relation to Circe. In fact, it's probably smart if all of us lie low for a few days."

My heart raced. *A few days? Oh, hell no.*

I pushed past him to throw open the front door. "Look at this, Henri."

He didn't need to join me to see what I was talking about. Fae lined the run-down streets, all of them huddled close together, gossiping. Fear sparked in some of their eyes, confirming that the spontaneous, swift public execution wasn't a normal occurrence. What we'd done had sparked something that wouldn't be put out soon.

"This chaos, this fear, it isn't going to end in a few days," I said, as sure of that as I was of anything. "The Red Queen knows something is up. And she's paranoid, so she'll act out."

I thought back to the sensation I'd felt during the attack and execution—the sense that someone was watching me. I moved on, recalling the battalions in the woods, and finally, the fae I'd left injured on the floor at the Oyster House. Any of them could have told the queen about me. Or perhaps someone sighted me before I learned to hide my hair. It had been uncovered for hours before we reached Henri's father's house and a couple of times since then too.

I drew in a long breath. "Maybe she even knows I'm in the city."

"All the more reason to be careful."

"No. I'm done with the original plan." My spine straightened. "I'm not targeting others to get to the queen. Hurting those creatures was one of the worst things I've ever done—and I've done some shitty things." I glanced out the door again, watching the fae pass by, whispering of the beheadings. "And in the end, it didn't even matter. March and Circe are dead, and I'm partially to blame. The queen hasn't emerged from her castle, and probably doesn't plan to. I can't simply *wait* for her to come to me any longer. I have to make the first move." My tone hardened as I spoke, just like my resolve.

"Alice . . . What are you saying?"

My gaze turned on Hatter. "I want to infiltrate the castle. Soon."

"You've got to be joking."

"I'm dead serious."

"I'll admit my plan didn't pan out like I wanted it to, but you've seen how well guarded Heart Castle is. We can't go yet. We haven't even begun planning for a mission of that complexity."

"So what? You planned the bandersnatch attack for days, and look how that ended!" I thrust my finger toward the street, as if he could forget that he'd watched his friends die.

He gripped the sides of his head, looking as if he was about to rip his hair out. "That was unprecedented! I've never seen the queen act that way before. Her retribution is never so swift. Usually she throws people in cells and starves them for months before an execution. That was *insane*—even for her."

"I think we're seeing the tip of the iceberg."

We fought for hours, rounding on each other and going over the same points again and again. Eventually, others came to check on us, and got involved. Half wanted to act with me, the other half believed we should follow Henri's cautious plan.

But I wasn't having it, and in the end, I prevailed through sheer stubbornness. No matter how hard Henri argued, or how many excellent points he made, I didn't give a damn. I refused to let any more innocents die. If no one wanted to join me, I'd go it alone.

"When do you want to make a move?" Henri asked once we'd gathered everyone in the great room to discuss methods of infiltration.

"Tomorrow."

He groaned.

"Ohh, I don't know if that's brilliant, or a terrible choice, Alice," Dee said.

My eyebrows pulled together. "Why do you say that?"

"Tomorrow is the queen's unbirthday party," she replied.

I held up a finger. "I'm sorry, *un*birthday?"

The pixie nodded. "It's when someone wants another day to celebrate their existence. They choose a random day, and have a party! Not many people do it anymore, only nobles."

"Dee's right," Hatter said. "Preparations are already underway at the castle. That might be another reason why she was so quick to react today. She wants to remind people to stay in line. To not spoil her big day."

"Poor little queen, getting her unbirthday party spoiled." I rolled my eyes. My aunt was some absurd mix of ridiculous and cruel that I didn't understand. "Does that mean fae who frequent court will be there cele-brating?"

"Yes," Hatter said. "But it's invitation-only. Security

will be tighter than ever. I'm not sure how we'll sneak in."

I brought out my bits of mushroom the caterpillar had given me. Today I'd put them in my pocket, just in case our mission went wrong.

Most people looked confused at the morsels in my hands, but Henri and Dee drew in sharp breaths of recognition.

"One makes you shrink," Henri said.

"And the other makes you tall again," Dee finished for him. "This could work! Alice! You're a genius!"

"Definitely not." Someone smarter probably could have saved Circe and March. "But I can think on my feet." I held up the mushroom pieces. "There's enough of each that three others could take a nibble too."

Dee's hand shot up. "Pick me!"

"You're in. Dum too, if she wants. You're the best lookouts. But you won't need the mushroom."

"Being a pixie has *so* many advantages," Dee said seriously.

"I'm coming," Hatter said, as I knew he would. "I still remember parts of the castle well. That might come in handy. Of course, I look a lot like my father, so you'll have to glamour me . . ."

"No problem. I'll do it tonight."

Aside from my hair, I hadn't practiced glamouring yet, but I didn't care if I had to stay up all night trying to alter Henri's appearance. What I needed most were trustworthy people at my side. I'd do anything to have them join me.

Circe's love interest, the compact, blue-haired dwarf Sansu, volunteered in the name of avenging Isadora's daughter. Alran, the giant elf with long, flowing, gold hair, crystalline violet eyes, and muscles for days, volunteered too. Looks aside, which I knew from experience could get us far, Alran was Henri's primary sparring partner, and handy with a bow—an excellent choice for a mission.

"What can we do?" asked a small faerie near the back of the group, gesturing to those around her, who nodded in agreement.

"We'll need a distraction while we sneak inside," I said.

"Like what?" someone asked.

"Nothing that would get a rise out of the queen," I replied, not wanting to endanger them. "But it does have to be something that would get people talking—and preferably pull guards away from the castle."

"Why don't you capture a few of them and leave them in their underpants somewhere public," Alran offered, already demonstrating excellent critical thinking skills.

A few people laughed, and the corners of my lips inched up as the ethereal-looking elf continued.

"It would grab attention, but it's not so bad that the queen would call for heads to roll. The soldiers might not even tell her, if they're embarrassed enough."

"I like that," the faerie who posed the question of how to help chuckled. "Perhaps that'll be one tactic."

"I have faith that whatever the group comes up with

will be great," I said confidently. "That being said, I actually have a favor to ask."

"What's that?" Henri asked.

"Does anyone here have a stash of poisons I could peruse?"

Later that night, I stood at my bedroom window, fingering the travel-sized vials of poisons Sansu had given me. I hadn't known any of the rebels were actually poisoners when I'd asked, but it turned out that Sansu was one of the best on the island.

His concoctions were unique mixes of poisonous plants and venoms. None worked as quickly as Xavier's favored batrachotoxin, but Sansu assured me that if I tainted the queen's drink, she would only need to take a couple of sips for the tincture to take effect.

Truthfully, I'd much prefer to do the deed with my dagger. It was more satisfying, less sneaky, and more *me*. However, having the poisons on hand made me feel better. It was another tool in my arsenal.

The best assassins knew better than to be picky about methodology, and this was the most important mission of my life. I couldn't let pride impede getting shit done. If I failed, more lives would be at risk. The deaths of Circe and March already weighed on me, but if Hatter or the pixies died . . . I wasn't sure what I'd do.

Right on time, Henri knocked on my door. "Alice?

Are you ready?"

I crossed the room and let him in, giving him an über serious look as I did so. "I was born ready."

His brows furrowed. "All right . . . something tells me I'm missing something."

The seriousness fell from my face, and I laughed for the first time in hours. "Yeah, sorry. Couldn't resist, though." I gestured to one of the golden armchairs. "Have a seat."

He did as I said, squishing his hulking frame into the dainty chair. I took the opposite one, heaving a sigh as I sat down.

"Alice, I know that you feel guilty about Circe and March," Hatter's voice broke when he spoke his right-hand man's name. "So we don't have to go through with this tomorrow, if you're not ready. If you need—"

"I'm not changing my mind, Henri," I said. "You were right to stop me from charging into the castle the first day I got here. I would have been toast, but now . . . I've waited long enough. It's time to end this."

"But what about your aether magic? The Red Queen has used it all her life. She's more powerful than you."

I shrugged. "If it's a matter of time correlating to power, then she's always going to be better than me with the aether. But I don't think that's the case. Every time I practice with it, the aether comes much more easily—like it trusts me, and is willing to do my bidding. It's more a matter of bonding with it, and I have faith that when I need it most, it will be there for me."

Hatter inhaled deeply, and let it out slowly. "I respect that, but please understand I want you to be safe."

Safe? The idea was ludicrous. I'd grown up with a vampire, and even though I hadn't known it, a faerie queen had wanted me dead. I hadn't been safe for years. As the son of a known rebel, he probably hadn't been, either.

Still, his words were touching.

I placed a hand on his knee. "I don't want *anyone* else in the rebellion to die for this. They've suffered enough as it is." I swallowed the lump in my throat that formed as I thought of Isadora, crying a few rooms away. "What do you say we get started on your glamour?"

He nodded. "The Red Queen hasn't seen me in years, but I'm told all the time that I resemble my father. Still, I think changing my face will be enough."

"I have a few ideas."

I called on my aether magic, and allowed the shimmering light to dance around us. It came easier than ever before, heating up my fingertips—a sensation that I was still getting used to. When the aether washed over Henri's face, the element gave his already astounding beauty an ethereal glow.

The first thing I altered was his glossy, raven-wing black hair. It became an unassuming light brown. I softened his jawline next, wiped away his dimples, and made his full lips thinner. Lastly, and most difficult, I tweaked his strong nose.

When I was done, I sat back to examine my work. He

looked nothing like the Henri Hatter I knew, except for his eyes. Those burning emeralds, screamed *Hatter*. And yet, I didn't have the heart to change them.

"All done," I said, only then noticing that my throat had gone dry. I swallowed. "No one will recognize you. Check it out." I gestured to the mirror that hung above my vanity.

Hatter crossed the room and stopped in front of the mirror. "I hardly recognize myself. Nice work."

I performed a little bow. "All in a day's work."

"It seems so."

Hatter turned, and even though he looked nothing like himself, my breath still hitched. There was something about this guy, his charm, his ability to lead people, his kindness that radiated from his very being, that made me want him.

Judging by the way the air between us filled with electricity that danced on my skin, I was sure he wanted me too.

This is dangerous ground. Your heart will be broken when you leave.

I cleared my throat, thankful and also annoyed that my good sense had kicked in. "We should get some sleep before the big day."

Hatter gulped and tore his eyes from me as though it caused him physical pain. "Of course. Goodnight, Alice."

"Goodnight," I whispered as he left my room, taking my heart with him.

CHAPTER 23

I tightened my cloak, making sure that my dagger, the mushroom pieces, and the vials of poison I'd selected from Sansu's stash were all tucked in the bodice of my black gown. Once I confirmed that I had everything I needed, I slipped into a pair of flat, black boots. Finally, I glanced at my reflection, and like every other time I'd looked in the mirror that day, I reared back slightly.

That morning, Hatter had suggested that I again use the aether to alter my hair. Teal, which had always been my favorite color, was also a hue of my mother's royal line. While the Red Queen had never outright forbidden teal like she had white-blond hair, she *had* changed the colors to represent her reign. To wear teal might draw too much attention, so my locks were now a vibrant apple red. I was sure many others would be sporting the shade to butter up the queen, so red was safe, my best chance of blending in.

Satisfied that I looked the part of a noble fae going to a party, I made my way toward the great room. When I opened the door, my eyes widened.

As I expected, the guys and the pixies were present, all looking resplendent and dressed for a royal party. But other, unanticipated people milled around too. Everyone that had helped with our bandersnatch mission was there, plus many more.

Isadora stood out most, and when her eyes met mine, and her lips curled up in a small, sad smile, my heart nearly broke.

"What a surprise," I said, because people were staring, waiting.

"We wanted to see you off," the same little faerie from last night said. "Some of us are already in the streets, ready to create a diversion. The rest will join right after you go."

"Thank you. We appreciate your help so much." My voice grew thick, and I cleared it as heat crept into my cheeks.

What were these people doing to me? I was becoming an emotional mess!

It seemed that my verbal thanks wasn't enough. Everyone wanted to hug me and wish our party well. The emotion in their faces shone plainly. Though they hoped we'd return, they feared we would not.

I worked through the embraces and handshakes,

uncomfortable with so many touches, but recognizing their need for peace of mind. I wasn't sure if we'd succeed, but I'd do my best to give them what I could.

"I wish you the best of luck, Princess," Isadora said, clutching me tight. "Thank you for coming back, for taking the well-being of your people seriously. Many don't realize who you are or what happened, but they will—once she's gone, they'll remember the past."

She was the last to say goodbye, but the first person to sound so sure that we'd return.

"You deserve so much more than what you've been dealt," I replied. "Stay safe. We'll be back soon."

Isadora pulled away, her eyes brimming with unshed tears. "May the aether light your way."

The moment I stepped onto the uneven cobblestone streets of Heartstown, I breathed freer.

I'd never enjoyed being an assassin, but unlike my pitiful efforts to comfort others, it was something I knew. The start of a mission, how it felt to know that I was coming for my mark, was etched deep into my psyche. And already, my body was responding. I was ready to end the Red Queen, ready to take my vengeance, find Elise, and start living life on my own terms.

"Let's take the long way to the castle," I suggested. "Give the distraction team time to get into place."

The others agreed, and for a few minutes, we simply walked and watched city residents. The roses lining the street bloomed a bold red. Fae gossiped on every corner. Scents of fried meat filled my nostrils.

Life was going by as normal. No one even seemed to remember yesterday. Or they didn't care. I shook my head, hoping more than anything that this apathy resulted from the enchantment upon the citizens of Heartstown.

The sounds of shouting pierced the air, and my spine straightened as adrenaline pumped through me.

"Do you think that's them?" Sansu asked.

"Only one way to find out." I nodded for Hatter to lead us to the castle.

He did so, and minutes later, I found myself standing just across the street from Heart Castle. Soldiers stood on the drawbridge at the mouth of the castle, checking invitations, while others lined every entrance and wall, like when I'd seen the palace from the air.

But there were differences, too. A few soldiers were sprinting down the street, away from the fortress, hopefully to deal with the distraction our friends had cooked up.

Alran pointed to a darkened store. "There's a little alcove right in front of that shop. We can eat the mushroom there and won't be too far from the gate."

"We'll be on the lookout," Dee said, and as the larger fae jogged toward the alcove, the pixies got into position.

Once we were hidden, I pulled the chunk of mushroom that would make us smaller out of my right pocket. "Only a nibble. I'll go first—just in case."

It wasn't that I didn't trust the caterpillar; if he'd wanted to screw me over, he could have done so by simply sending me into the ocean where the kraken lived, instead of back to headquarters. My caution stemmed from the fact that I had no idea how much mushroom we would need to shrink. So it was only right that I play the guinea pig.

Carefully, I took a small bite, and passed the mushroom off to Hatter. A newly familiar sensation of shrinking came over me, slower this time, less jarring. Unlike in the tower, I didn't freak out, just waited for it to stop.

When it happened, I was two inches tall—half the size of the pixies. The mushroom was more potent than the 'drink me' liquid, then.

"Seriously! The tiniest nibble!" I squeaked.

The guys nodded, and soon enough, all three of them shrank to my size. As we emerged onto the street, soldiers began sprinting from the castle in droves. The distraction was working.

"This way!" Dum cried out over the sound of soldiers' boots hitting cobblestone. "We might have found another entrance!"

Only a dozen or so fae milled around outside the castle. Judging by their lavish attire, they were nobles attending the queen's party, and were busy watching the troops respond to disaster. We had a straight shot across the road and into the cover of grass that lined a walking path around the moat.

The twins landed next to us. "We can't fly in," Dum announced. "We spotted two hawks circling above.

They're on the lookout for pixies and other small fae trying to worm their way inside. But we have another idea."

"What is it?" I urged, not wanting us to lose the momentum of the distraction. There were still so many guards around, so many eyes.

"We cross the moat and then climb in through the pipes," Dee said.

"And the birds won't get us?"

"If we float in under the drawbridge, they won't see us."

"Yeah . . . But aren't there crocodiles in the water?" I peered into the moat, trying to spot the crocs that a rebel had mentioned when we announced our plan to infiltrate the castle.

"There most certainly are. Monstrous ones," Sansu confirmed, looking uncomfortable with the plan.

"If we float in on leaves or lily pads, they won't notice. Those are always on top of the water's surface," Dee said, although she didn't sound totally confident. "The hardest part would be climbing up the pipes."

I mulled it over. It was better than a mad dash across the drawbridge, where soldiers and guests might spot or trample us, but crawling in through the pipes left a lot to be desired. Particularly when we wanted to mingle once we got inside. We couldn't do that with slime all over our outfits.

I scanned the castle lawn, searching for an alternative, and noticed a carriage encrusted in gold stopping not far away. The carriage door opened, and a pretty, young, teenage fae, maybe a couple years my junior, exited. She was dressed in a light green princess gown that was puffed out with so much tulle that five children could fit beneath it.

"Actually, I have a better idea," I whispered. "See that fae? In the huge green ball gown?"

Everyone nodded because you couldn't miss her.

"We stow away under her skirts." Hatter sputtered, but I ignored him. This would work, if we could get to the girl without being seen.

Once again, I scrutinized the area outside the palace, and my lips lifted. A group of strapping, young fae men walked the moat path, toward the drawbridge. They were dressed well too, likely part of the girl's social class. And every single one of them watched her hungrily.

I took a chance as I brought my fingers to my lips and blew hard.

A whistle pierced the air, catching the girl's attention. She turned and beamed at the guys still staring at her.

"Come on! This is our chance!" I gestured for my friends to approach the walkway that cut through the grass. "She has to walk past us to talk to them. When she does, hop on and hide in her skirts."

Hatter's face flushed. "We can't hide in a lady's skirt!"

But I wasn't about to let his modesty stand in the way of getting inside the castle. The girl was already nearly to us. There wasn't time for hemming and hawing, so I yanked him into position right behind me.

Thankfully, the girl's skirt bloomed so wide that it actually spilled out over the walkway into the grass, which meant there was no chance the guys would see us. Still, we exercised caution. The pixies went first, lifting the back of the skirt enough so that when the rest of us leapt out of the grass, we gripped tulle and not slippery satin.

Once we were inside and accounted for, we spread out, clinging to the fabric for dear life. And then we waited.

And waited.

And *waited*, while the girl laughed at the fae boys' silly jokes, and every single one of them flirted with her.

After what felt like half a lifetime, I was regretting my brilliant idea, not to mention sweating an awful lot under her skirts. I'd just wiped my damp forehead on scratchy tulle for the tenth time, when *finally* one boy suggested that they head inside so they could wish the queen a merry unbirthday before the festivities began.

I exhaled a breath as the girl turned back toward the drawbridge and started walking.

Other voices came closer, and soon, the sound of heels striking a wood bridge informed me that we were almost there. Once inside, we'd need to slip away and find a private place to grow.

"Halt, miss," a gruff voice commanded, and the girl stopped.

I gripped the tulle tight.

"Name?"

"Ginny Grayfoam," the girl chirped.

"Invitation?"

I heard the sounds of the girl pulling something out of her bag and presenting it to the guard.

"Thank you, Miss Grayfoam. We only have one more question."

"What's that?"

"Are you in any way related to the queen, or have knowledge of her blood relations?"

My jaw tightened. Relations? They suspected that I might be glamoured, or influencing someone else. And it seemed they also didn't know that I could lie—otherwise, they wouldn't even ask.

Xavier really had done me a favor, making me drink that potion right before I broke away from him.

"Blood relations?" Miss Grayfoam echoed. "Our dear queen has none."

Because she was young, I figured that the mist that had erased everyone else's memory of my parents hadn't needed to erase hers. Her belief that she told the truth was clear in the smooth cadence of her voice. So unlike the brownie I'd questioned a week ago, who'd had to fight a lie past the enchantment.

Although her infuriating ignorance pissed me off, I'd chosen an excellent guest to hitch a ride in on. There's no way the soldier could suspect her.

"Very good," he replied, confirming that Miss Grayfoam looked as innocent as she sounded. "You may proceed."

CHAPTER 24

Ginny Grayfoam gave us the perfect exit strategy when she excused herself to use the ladies' room to powder her nose. Thank goodness that really was all she planned to do in there. Hatter probably would have flipped out and given us away if Miss Grayfoam had needed to relieve herself. We waited until she exited the restroom for everyone to slide down her skirts. Dee locked the door as soon as Ginny closed it behind her.

"That worked out perfectly," I said, fist-bumping the pixies at their insistence.

"It was a clever entrance," Sansu agreed, looking impressed. "Hopefully, the rest of the mission is that easy."

I wasn't holding my breath, but I also wasn't about to bring anyone else down. Let their hope burn. We'd need the fire.

Knowing every moment was precious, I pulled the second bit of mushroom from my bodice pockets. Like everything else on my person, it had shrunk when I did.

"There's no going back now," I said, and bit into the mushroom. I shot back up to normal size faster and less painfully than I had with the purple drink in the tower.

"Whoa." Alran stared up at me.

I laughed as I pulled off my cloak and hid it in a chest of drawers filled with perfumed sachets and the fae-equivalent of toilet paper. "Bet you're not used to gazing up at others, are you?"

"Not unless they're a giant," the elf replied with a wry grin.

"And here's hoping there are none of those in Heart Castle tonight."

I offered the mushroom to them. The guys each took bites, and promptly shot up like weeds.

"Everyone ready?" I asked once my friends had returned to normal size.

My crew confirmed that they were, and I cracked the door open enough for Dee and Dum to poke their heads out.

"All clear," Dum announced. "I hear music coming from down the hall. I think the pre-dinner socializing has already started."

"Good. Then we can slip in unnoticed." I turned to the pixies. "Remember to remain unseen, high above. Be our eyes and ears. If we need you, you'll know it. Everyone else, if I get the chance, I'm using poison. I'll tap three times on my glass or bodice, whichever is more natural, to tell you when. If I do that, create a distraction."

Wordlessly, everyone slipped out the door. Hatter and I went first, me on his arm, while the other men staggered behind us. As Dum had said, music was playing—a harp, if I wasn't mistaken. We followed the gentle tune to a large, open room bursting with fae.

I took in Heartfire Hall, getting the lay of the land. Streaming in from the entrance, a wide-open space for socializing and dancing split the room in half. The ceiling soared at least fifty feet high. On either side of the divide, tables were laid for ten. Chandeliers hung from the ceiling, illuminating the darkened room, and tapestries decorated every wall—each one depicting the queen or her chosen symbol, a large, red heart.

But most attention-grabbing of all was the head table. It faced the door, so those who sat there could watch guests enter. Candles and red roses flooded the royal table. Two thrones, one larger than the other, but both sprouting a gold heart off their tall backs, were positioned so that three chairs flanked them.

"It looks almost the same as when I last saw it," Hatter whispered. "Except for all the hearts . . . and the name, of course. It used to simply be called 'the Grand Hall'."

I snorted. "She had to erase every remnant of my parents. But seriously, *Heartfire*?" My tone was barely a whisper, it was so low. "What a ridiculous name."

Henri let out a laugh. "I have to agree. You ready?"

I nodded, and we swept into the crowd.

Unsurprisingly, it didn't take long to find my aunt. A group of fae surrounded the Red Queen. All of them were trying to monopolize her attention. I watched her carefully, trying to ignore the way the hair on the nape of my neck lifted at the sight of her. If we were to succeed, I needed to remain as level-headed as possible.

For her part, the Red Queen seemed rather unimpressed, her eyes narrowed as she stared down her long, aquiline nose at her subjects.

Save for the ruby-encrusted gold crown on her head, she looked almost the same as the version of her I'd seen in my vision in the Enchanted Forest. Tall and severe, with inky hair falling in heavy curtains around her face. Her skin was porcelain white, much like my own. Like many faeries and elves, my aunt seemed to have suspended her age—stopping it at thirty.

In the human world, she could have been a supermodel. Her features were just strange enough, and yet still pleasing, in a hardened sort of way.

I leaned close to Hatter as the queen wrinkled her nose at something a subject said. "Does she even like her guests?"

"She doesn't have friends," Henri whispered. "She allows a few duchesses in her inner circle to be her ladies-in-waiting. Other than them, only her soldiers and the king consort escort her."

"Shocker." I tore my eyes away from my aunt and scanned the table again.

All the places were already set, and there was even a goblet of wine sitting in front of the queen's seat, waiting for her. Unfortunately, six guards with hearts emblazoned on their uniforms, to mark them as the most elite of the Red Queen's soldiers, stood behind the table, watching.

"If I can get over there and distract those soldiers, I might be able to deposit poison into her cup."

Hatter gripped my arm closer to his body, as if he was afraid I'd dart off. "Perhaps a better time would be when she calls for the feast to begin. Lots of movement."

As if his words had made it happen, the queen clapped, and everyone in the room fell silent. "I've received word that dinner is ready." She waved her hand toward the tables. "Please take a seat."

Everyone ran to the sides of the room, distracting me from capitalizing on the moment. The guests claimed their spots, and seats filled to the point where there weren't more than two openings at each table.

This posed a problem. Our group wanted to stick together.

"I see that you four are the lucky last ones standing."

My eyes snapped to my aunt, already seated at the head table, and watching us with amusement before shifting her gaze a few feet away to Sansu and Alran, who were looking as confused as I felt.

"Pardon us, My Queen," Henri said, his tone careful and level. "We don't understand."

The Red Queen's lips lifted in a hard smile, and her vibrant, green eyes, which I'd been too far away to notice before, glowed. "This must be your first event at Heart Castle. As you are the last standing, you get the pleasure of dining with me."

Pleasure? Her guests had *sprinted* to their seats. They might have wanted to impress her and earn her favor, but no one was bold enough to sit with her.

She was either blind or delusional. I suspected the latter. And now we were expected to break bread with her —the woman who murdered my parents.

My jaw clenched.

Hatter gripped my arm tight, likely sensing the tension that vibrated from me. "My Queen, we're not worthy of such an honor."

I stiffened. Not worthy? He was obviously trying to cover for what we were here to do, but still, the idea that we weren't worthy of her rankled. Hard.

I wasn't having it.

"Actually, we'd love to join you." I pulled Henri toward my aunt.

"Welcome," the Red Queen said when we stopped before the table. "I must apologize, my ladies-in-waiting sent out the invitations, and clearly they didn't explain the seating protocol to you. That being said, I'm afraid I don't know your names."

"Camilla Thorn." I used the first name I often took when on missions, and then tacked a nature-based surname onto the end, as was common in Faerie.

"And I'm her escort, Ernie Longfog."

Sansu and Alran introduced themselves honestly. Apparently, neither had a troubled family past, or had been involved with the law.

"Now that we're acquainted, please come sit." The Red Queen gestured for us to join her and the king consort.

Henri and I sat next to the queen, while the other two took the king's side of the table. I lowered myself with as much grace as I could muster, hoping that the queen didn't feel the tension rolling off me in waves.

As soon as we settled in, the servants began taking orders, allowing everyone a few much needed minutes to pull themselves together.

And I needed every single one of those minutes.

Xavier had schooled me well in deception, so I managed to keep my face calm, my body loose. But other, more visceral reactions were not so easily dismissed.

Goosebumps pebbled my arms, and I practically had to choke down air because her rose-scented perfume was so cloying.

"So, Camilla," the Red Queen turned to me once the servants had left. "Tell me, what part of Heartstown do you call home?"

Not missing a beat, Henri came to the rescue, leaning forward as if he was an enthusiastic subject. "The north end. We both live in Watercrest."

"What a wonderful area. And do you work? Or are you too young for that?"

"I have no position yet," I replied. "Although my mother is teaching me the ways of the court, so hopefully, I can spend more time here." I gave my aunt a confident, bright smile.

"And I'm apprenticing in my father's trade—personal finance. He's up and coming in the sector."

If I wasn't in character, my jaw would have dropped at that one.

Personal finance? For who? The hundred people in this room?

There didn't seem to be other fae in Heartstown with any sort of financial wealth to speak of.

While I thought Hatter's choice was absurd, the Red Queen didn't balk. In fact, she smiled and leaned closer to us. "Personal finance! In that case, I have many questions."

Henri and the queen engaged in a dialogue about the state of the Wonderland economy. All the while, servants set glasses of wine and plates of food in front of us.

The queen barely seemed to notice the arrival of her food and drink, and I'd just begun to eye her glass and contemplate a poisoning when she snapped the goblet up. Once she drank her fill, she set the goblet down, further away from me, and continued chatting.

I slumped back in my seat.

Henri couldn't help that he chose a topic that interested the queen, and yet if I were to have a chance at poisoning her, I needed her to look the other direction. I wished that Alran or Sansu would step it up and occupy her attention.

"Oh yes!" the king consort exclaimed loudly. My ears perked up. Perhaps the king might provide a better distraction? "The queen and I are very much looking forward to the Wonderland summer games this year. Ezekiel is one of our favored croquet competitors."

A croquet competition? Seeing as I didn't know jack about croquet, the topic was risky, but I could work with it. I only needed a moment of distraction.

"I'm sorry," I leaned back to peer behind the queen, which caught her attention. "Did you say Ezekiel? He's one of my favorite players, too. Who will go up against him?"

The king beamed at me, and as I'd hoped, the queen leaned back into her throne so that one side of the table could see the other.

"Have you never seen a summer game, my girl?" the queen tittered.

Free from royal attention, Sansu nodded vigorously, his eyes locked on me.

"Yes," I replied. "But I can't say I paid the best attention before. It's only recently that I've gained interest."

Henri laid a hand on my arm. "When we started courting, I talked her ear off about croquet." He gave the king and queen a charming smile.

"Then you're doing your civil duty," the Red Queen replied as she reached for her wine glass and took another sip. "Of course, I'll be taking part in the croquet match this year too." She set her glass down, this time closer to me.

My breath hitched. This was my chance.

I grabbed my goblet, and under the guise of casually wrapping my fingers around it, tapped the glass three times before taking a sip, then set it as close to the queen's as I dared.

"And you, My King?" Henri asked, clearly catching my signal as he leaned over the table to lock eyes with the king. "Will you participate this year, too?"

The king boomed out a laugh. "My love has made it clear that my croquet game is a disgrace to the crown. Only she will represent us."

"It's always such a pleasure to watch Her Majesty," Sansu said.

"I'll second that," Alran said, his violet eyes twinkling as he shot the queen a smoldering look.

For the first time since we joined them, my aunt turned a little pink.

"Our kingdom is lucky to have such a lovely monarch who is also very skilled at the realm's game," the elf purred.

Freaking finally, she twisted to face the guys, and began speaking with Alran.

I discreetly plucked the vial out of my bodice, and stuck it in my sleeve. Then I reached for my own wine glass, right next to the queen's, and knocked it over.

I leapt up as if attempting to catch the goblet, and deposited the poison in the queen's glass. I was done by the time my goblet shattered.

The guards a few feet behind us lurched forward, and everyone in the room twisted in their seats to stare.

I threw my hands over my face. "I'm so sorry! I didn't mean to. I—"

The queen's hand landed on my arm, gripping it tight. "My dearest niece, I was wondering when you'd finally show up."

My blood froze as my gaze snapped to her. How did she guess?

"I'm afraid I don't know what you're talking about, Your Majesty," I replied, trying to keep up the charade.

"Don't play dumb with me, Alice!" The queen's composure disintegrated, and she shot out of her seat.

My heart raced as soldiers inched closer. *Her back was turned. There was no way she saw me poison her drink, and she hasn't taken a sip yet. What gave me away?*

"Stupid girl. Returning to Faerie was foolish," the queen hissed so that only those at the head table would hear.

I lifted my chin in defiance. "How did you know?"

The Red Queen laughed. "There have been rumors for days of a blonde girl crossing the island, assaulting my subjects in her wake."

She had to be speaking about the Oyster House. Clearly, the hat hadn't been enough of a cover. I should have just finished those in the room off, when I'd had the chance.

"And then you made such a mess with the bander-snatch debacle, throwing aether everywhere. Only a fae of the White line could produce such a flux—so I took precautions." She thrust a finger to her glass.

My eyes followed and widened.

The wine, which had been red, was now a bright green. She'd put something in it to identify poisons.

I leapt out of my chair, grabbing my dagger from its hiding spot and lifting it high. The weapon glinted in the low lighting of Heartfire Hall, and I was about to bring it down, when a shimmering white force stopped me.

The aether. My aunt was using aether against me, and judging by how I couldn't budge, she was damn strong with it.

"That's better. That's how a *true* White takes what she wants," the Red Queen said, her green eyes narrowing. "Unfortunately, you're not quite up to snuff."

She twisted to face her guards. "Take this girl and her friends to the dungeons. Tomorrow, it's off with their heads."

"*No!*" Hatter leapt up, and a dozen blades thrust out at him from all angles.

He threw up his hands, signaling he was weaponless. "Alice White invokes the right to Trial by Aether!"

Gasps rose throughout the crowd, and the queen's grasp over the aether fell away.

"Impossible!" a fae cried out. "The queen has no family. Only those of the royal line may challenge the crown for the throne."

"Incorrect," Hatter said. "Someone else can challenge the crown to a Trial by Aether—the aether-blessed."

Everyone in the hall fell silent, until finally, after what felt like a year, the king consort spoke up.

"Are you saying that this poisoner is . . . aether-blessed?"

In answer, I called the aether to me, and a ball of white light appeared in my hand.

"I see that it's true," the king said, astounded. "My love, you have no choice but to accept the challenge—a Trial by Aether . . . for the crown."

"I have every right to refuse! I am the rightful queen of Wonderland!" the queen roared. "I'm—"

"No, Your Majesty, I'm afraid you don't," a high-pitched voice broke through the queen's fury.

Everyone in the hall twisted, and murmurs rose from the guests. I craned my neck past the guards to find Herald standing before the royal table, a scroll in hand.

"Oh really, crier?" The queen's voice was oily, full of barely suppressed rage. "And why do you believe that to be the case?"

The paper shook in the pooka's hand, and Herald twitched as though a million flies were landing on him. Still, he mustered his courage and answered.

"This scroll is from your royal library, Your Majesty. The law is clear. It proclaims that should any monarch be challenged to a Trial by Aether by a valid candidate, they *must* compete, or forfeit the crown."

Murmurs ran through the crowd.

The Red Queen's eyes were narrowed, her lips pursed as if she was about to deny the law of the land—the law that she had been stupid enough to leave unchanged for thirteen years.

I couldn't let her do that.

I released my aether. It soared around the hall, exploding into gold and teal fireworks that became confetti before the sparks hit the ground. The queen's jaw tightened. Everyone else in Heartfire Hall gasped at the clear display of power that couldn't be explained by using the other four elements.

"Perhaps you're too scared to take me on? Afraid that you'll no longer be the strongest fae in Wonderland?" I paused, taking great delight in how the queen's face turned as red as her dress. "Or maybe you're scared that, since I'm here, in your home, with aether magic flowing through my veins, you might already have been overtaken?"

The guests cried out in astonishment. Two fae actually fainted, but my eyes remained locked on the queen, and when she turned her green gaze upon me, and I saw how brightly her eyes burned, I knew I had her.

"I'm afraid of no such thing. I accept this girl's invitation," the queen boomed. "Take her and her friends to the North Tower, where they'll remain under guard." The queen clapped twice quickly. "Tomorrow, the Trial by Aether begins."

CHAPTER 25

As soon as the guards shut the door to the North Tower, I whirled on Henri. Rightly sensing danger, Alran and Sansu scattered to the sides of the room.

"What was all that about? Why didn't you ever tell me a trial was an option? You're lucky I can think fast, because what the *hell*, Henri?!" Aether bloomed at the end of my fingertip as I thrust it at him.

He jerked back. "I never thought calling a trial would actually work. I assumed you'd be able to kill her before she *ever* agreed to a Trial by Aether. If we weren't in public, and you hadn't appealed to her enormous ego, I still don't think it would have worked. We'd already be dead."

"You suspected you might need to pull this." I narrowed my eyes. "Otherwise, why would Herald appear with that law scroll just in time?"

"Fine." He gulped guiltily. "I'll admit, it was a backup plan. I had hoped that if things went badly, you'd be able to challenge her. I sent word to Herald to have the law scroll ready."

"That's so messed up."

"No! This way, when you win, it's a fair upheaval."

"What about Herald?! He showed up my crazy-ass aunt." I flung my hand in the direction of Heartfire Hall. "Won't he die for that?"

"This might come as a surprise to you," Henri murmured, "but he was all for it."

I arched an eyebrow. "He's terrified of her."

"True, but he also works for her daily. In my opinion, that makes him one of the bravest in our ranks. He's willing to give it all up to see our cause through."

Damn it all to hell.

The glow of my fingertip lessened.

Hatter's eye went to my hand. "Are your powers up for a tournament yet?"

"Probably not," I huffed, and threw myself upon a red chaise lounge in the center of the room.

After a moment, I took in my surroundings.

Three bedrooms branched off a living area, much like a modern penthouse. Everything in here was plush, luxurious, and not made for prisoners.

When the Red Queen had told her soldiers to put us in a tower, I'd assumed they would shunt us into a moldy, leaking tower with bales of hay to sleep on. However, the tower suite we found ourselves in was nothing like that.

The only objectionable object in the room was the dining-room-table-sized portrait of the queen, hanging on the wall.

I flipped the painting the bird. "Someone take that off the wall and get it out of my sight, will you?"

Alran and Sansu got right on it.

"Why are we here, anyway?" I gestured around the room. "Why didn't she throw us in some terrible cell?"

"She's playing the *gracious host* card," Sansu muttered as he wrestled with the painting. "The queen doesn't want anyone to think she'll cheat or pull anything during the trials. This is one way of doing that."

"He's right," Hatter said, "but don't let her fool you. When the trials begin, watch your back every second."

I rolled my eyes. What did he think I was? An amateur? "So what are these trials?"

At that exact moment, a pounding came on the window. I looked over to find Dee and Dum rubbing their hands up and down their tiny arms and gesturing to be let in. Alran opened the window, and the pixies soared inside and zoomed straight toward me.

"By the old gods! A Trial by Aether!" Dee's pitch was so high, I cringed. "We heard the party guests gossiping about it. Is it true?"

"Yes. In fact, Hatter was about to tell me what the trial entails."

Henri heaved a sigh. "You got the gist that only royalty and the aether-blessed can challenge a monarch for the crown in a Trial by Aether?"

"I have ears," I muttered.

"Well, that's about the only thing that's certain in the trials."

"That's not true," Alran said. "There are always three competitions, and their categories are set in stone."

"And those are?"

"Combat, Creatures, and Conjuring." Alran ticked them off on his fingers one by one.

I inhaled a slow breath. "Okay, combat is obvious. I feel good about my chances there. I assume conjuring means I have to create things with the aether? And creatures . . . help a girl out here."

"Creatures means you have to use the aether to call a magical animal that will fight the queen's creature for you," Dum supplied as she smoothed her blue dress and hair.

"To the death!" Dee added, much more dramatically.

I groaned. The entire herd of bandersnatch had been under the queen's control. "Calling creatures is one of her skills, isn't it?"

"Yes," Henri replied. "Still, there's hope. You'll likely excel at combat."

"But conjuring . . ." I understood how someone might conjure something substantial with the aether. I'd practiced it at least two dozen times, albeit with smaller objects. "I need a lot more practice at creating stuff out of aether. How is the winner of the Trial decided anyway?"

Sansu cringed. "There hasn't been a Trial by Aether

in centuries, but rumor has it the crowd voices their plea-sure or displeasure at the creations."

I threw up my hands. "And we know how that will go! She'll murder anyone who cheers for me—if they even cheer at all!"

"Not necessarily," Henri corrected me. "The trials are performed at random. If the Conjuring Trial is last, and you do well on another one—if you give enough grounds for hope—the rebels will be strong and lend you their voice to oust the queen. It's a gigantic risk, but many would take it for the good of the kingdom."

"It's leaving a lot to chance."

Hatter didn't answer, but he shot a glance at Alran and Sansu, who nodded significantly, like they were a couple of mind readers.

I crossed my arms over my chest. "Care to share with the class?"

"You're right. There is a lot left to chance, and the cards are stacked against you. But if we can get to the witches who created the fog, we could force them to undo their enchantments—"

I sat up straight. "The people who believe the Red Queen is the true queen would come to their senses."

"We've never had the ability to get to the witches before," Sansu said, "but now that we're in the castle, it's a possibility."

I stood. "Well then, it seems like you five have some strategy to discuss. Now, if you'll excuse me, I'm going to prepare for tomorrow."

CHAPTER 26

Early the next day, a knock came at our suite door.

"The first trial will begin in two hours," a guard said perfunctorily when Alran opened the door. He held his arms out, laden with clothing and a letter. "An escort will show you to where it will take place." He dumped his offerings into Alran's arms, and with that, left.

Alran set the clothes on the chaise lounge, and I examined the garments. They were black, with a gold rose over the right breast and another on the back of the shirt. "They look like team uniforms," I said after a moment. "One for each of us."

Henri joined me in examining the clothes. "That's exactly what they are."

"I can't feel any magic on them. What about you?"

After a minute, he shook his head. "Nothing. I'm not

surprised. She's a narcissist, so she likely believes she can beat you without sabotage."

I bit my lip. No one could deny that the Red Queen had been using aether for much longer than me, and knew what she was doing with it.

"Don't look so worried." Dum landed on my shoulder and patted it. "You have us here to help. We will do everything in our power to make sure you win."

I tilted my head. "But it's me versus her in the trials, right?"

"Sure, but we can help you practice every day, and teach you what we know," Dum replied. "Plus, we'll invite the rebels to the events for moral support."

My spine straightened. "They'll be in so much danger!"

After I'd had time to mull it over, I realized that I didn't really want the others to come. I barely wanted any of my friends here. In fact, this morning, Henri and I had gotten into a fight when he'd asked me to remove the glamour I'd made for him. Now that we were no longer going for stealth, he wanted the Red Queen to see his face when he stood against her. Wanted her to know where he'd come from.

Although I hated that it would be putting him in more danger, after a half hour of arguing, I'd agreed, and Henri had become himself once again.

After all, I couldn't deny the value in just wanting to be yourself—particularly if you had a stellar reputation like Henri did.

As for me, I wasn't ready to expose my white-blonde hair just yet. People in Wonderland had been told to be suspicious of the unusual hue for *years*. And I didn't have the same good rep as Hatter. Why would I make gaining their support and trust harder? Just to prove a point?

No thanks, I'd play it safe in the hair department and take my risks where they mattered. In the Trials.

"Alice, you can't control what the others want to do," Henri said, in regards to the rebels attending the Trial challenges. "And they want the Red Queen off the throne. If that means voicing their opinion during the challenges, they'll do it."

"I know that, but maybe we can negotiate with the queen?" I offered. "Make it a condition that no one who supports me gets injured or killed?"

Henri's lips leveled into a flat, sad smile. "The Red Queen might agree to that, for now. But if you lose, I have little faith that she'll keep her word."

I heaved a sigh and glanced at my uniform. "Then I guess that means there's only one thing to do . . . I need to win."

After almost two hours of countless aether drills that consisted of me replicating items and conjuring new ones, and some creature research, my nerves had reached an apex. It was almost a relief when two soldiers collected us for the first trial, and led us into the royal gardens.

Rose bushes as large as Smart cars and bursting with red roses seemed to be the plant of choice, filling in the gaps between other, more varied blooms. Pure gold benches dotted the packed-dirt paths, each with little cushions on their frames for comfort. Fountains featuring the Red Queen, krakens, or a thin but ferocious-looking jabberwocky, cropped up every two hundred yards, reinforcing the message displayed by every tapestry and painting in the castle—that the queen was all-powerful.

"What is this normally used for?" I muttered as we turned onto a garden path, and our destination, an expansive lawn twice the size of a football field and crawling with fae, came into sight. "It seems so out of place in the gardens."

"It used to be an orchard. But now, this is the queen's private croquet lawn," Sansu remarked.

The bitterness in his tone was self-explanatory. I hadn't walked the streets of Heartstown often, but when I did, half-starved fae were a common sight. To rip out fruit-giving trees for a croquet field when your subjects suffered was despicable.

Fae parted as we approached, allowing me passage to where the queen stood in the middle of the green space, her red cloak fluttering in the faint wind. Behind the queen, her Hearts Battalion stood at the ready.

My spine straightened, and I pushed my shoulders back ever so slightly as I went to join the queen. The pixies were off doing their job of playing spy, but with Henri on my right and Alran and Sansu on my left, I was sure I already looked like I'd come to play. Still, a little posturing never hurt.

It wasn't until we got closer that I noticed Herald was

there too, flanked by soldiers. After what he'd pulled the night before, I hadn't expected to ever see him again.

"Good day, Alice," the Red Queen spoke in a low tone so that only those in the center of the field could hear her. "I must say, it's a surprise that you showed up."

"You heard me accept the challenge yesterday, right?" I asked, skipping the niceties.

"Yes, but poison is such a coward's tool. I would have thought after reconsidering, you'd scurry off like a rat in the night."

Her eyes flashed to Henri, seeing him unaltered for the first time. There was recognition and spite in her gaze. "Then again, the company you keep has an idiotic familial history of sticking around at detriment to their own lives. Apparently, the apple doesn't fall far from the tree."

I could practically feel the tension and anger rolling off Hatter.

"Some people call it bravery and loyalty," I said. "But you wouldn't know about that, I expect."

"Darling, you have no idea the many number of things I know about." My aunt chuckled and unclasped her cloak. It fell to the floor, exposing her white uniform with red hearts painted over her breast and on her back.

Her gaudy ass hearts versus the White's roses it is, then.

"What do you say we just get on with this?" I said, ready for action.

"Certainly." The queen gave me a smug look. "Crier?"

The pooka hobbled out of the crowd, a small jar in his hand. Immediately, I took in the bandage on his right foot and the cut on his face, and yet, relief flooded me. I'd been concentrating on learning how to use aether, but Herald had been in the back of my mind all night and day. I was thankful to see that here he was, alive, not killed for insisting that the Trials continue. Insisting that the law be followed. Sure, he looked a bit worse for the wear, but better beaten up than dead.

"The competitors are present and accounted for," Herald announced. "This is the first event of the Trial by Aether. All parts of the trials will be dictated by the godsflame—a physical embodiment of the old gods' aether *and* will, given to the fae." He lifted a small jar he'd been holding.

"The one who opens the jar becomes a conduit for the godly essence. They will inform others of the will of the godsflame. Once the trials are over, the godsflame will claim their life. As the court crier, I volunteer myself to act as the conduit for the flame. Does anyone take issue with this?"

A lump lodged in my throat as understanding dawned on me. The queen hadn't spared Herald at all. She'd given him a terrifying job that ensured his death.

No one spoke up or volunteered otherwise.

"Very well," Herald's voice cracked slightly, but he wore a determined expression on his face. "I will bear the mantle of the godsflame."

As soon as he spoke the words, blue, silver, and green

flames ignited in the jar, and danced and twisted around each other. My lips parted in awe, watching the mesmerizing movements.

"As the conduit, I shall choose at random the first task."

Herald untwisted the lid and plunged his paw inside. The pooka cringed, and a small scream escaped his lips.

Reflexively, I wanted to smack the jar out of his hand, but I knew I couldn't. He'd volunteered for this, knew what to do, and it had to be done.

I wouldn't let his sacrifice be in vain.

His paw flailed inside the jar, until finally, with another scream, he grasped onto the blue flame. The pooka pulled it out, opened his blistered paw, and allowed the fire to dance above the pads.

At first, nothing happened, then suddenly, the blue flame soared into the sky and expanded to form a star with fireworks coming off of it.

"What does that mean?" I asked as everyone else squealed and clapped.

"That is the symbol for conjuring," Henri whispered into my ear. "Your first trial is conjuring."

Fan freaking-tastic

"If you wish to back down, I'll go easy on you," the Red Queen said smoothly. "I'll only punish you—none of the friends you've so blindly led into trouble."

My stomach clenched at the threat. Not for myself, but for my friends. But like the seasoned actor I was, I brushed the discomfort away and smirked. "Not a chance.

To avenge my parents, your *sister* in particular, would be the highest honor."

A ripple of emotion that I couldn't place crossed her face before a mask fell over it once again, and she glowered at me.

I returned her hard glare with one of my own. I'd struck a nerve when I mentioned my mother. I tucked the information away for later.

Herald coughed, breaking off our stare.

I turned to him and jerked back. His eyes, once gold, now glowed the same color as the blue godsflame. The cut on his face had healed too. I glanced up at the sky to see that the symbol was gone, and understanding washed over me.

Herald was the conduit of the trials. For the duration of the competition, he'd absorbed the godsflame. They'd healed him, for now, but later the flame would take his life. A twisted bargain and fate if there ever was one.

"The winner of at least two out of the three challenges takes the crown of Wonderland," Herald said, his voice distorted, more booming and resonant than before. "In the case that a winner cannot be determined in a challenge, leaving the competitors equal, an additional trial will be added. The godsflame will decide *everything*, from challenge locations, times, when the Trial is over, and the winner. Its choice is final." Herald waved his hand, and blue aether—the godsflame—seeped out of him to appear at his side.

My eyes popped open wide. What was this? My team had been wrong?

"That can't be right!" the Red Queen roared. "The crowd is supposed to be the deciding factor on who wins."

Herald shook his head. "Incorrect. To assure that a just and fair monarch is selected, the gods of old have given us the godsflame, imbued with their *essence and will*, to decide the rightful outcome."

The queen's face grew fire engine red. "Well! The Wonderland Court has no need for such arcane rules. We're civilized and can treat others fairly—even if they do wish to overthrow the rightful crown. Isn't that right, my loyal subjects?" She lifted her arms and, as if on cue, the crowd roared.

I stared at those closest to us, and noticed their eyes looked glazed. If I had to bet, I'd guess that the queen's witches were somewhere nearby, working their magic to ensure the queen's support. Or the enchantment that the fog imparted to demand loyalty all those years ago was just that strong.

"We will proceed with the will of the people judging these trials," the queen said imperiously when the cheering died down.

Was this really happening? *Could* it happen?

I glanced at Herald. He caught the motion and shook his head ever so slightly. My breath loosened.

"I'm afraid that's impossible, Your Majesty," he said aloud. "The godsflame assures me that, should any reigning monarch try to alter the rules of a Trial by Aether, the old gods will smite them."

"What?!" The queen rounded on Herald, but the blue fire bloomed and formed a lightning bolt that hovered right over her head.

My hand flew to my mouth. That symbol was ancient, of the old gods, and represented their will from beyond the grave—or wherever they'd gone, no one really knew. It was a threat, a sign that they could still affect us, strike us down unseen.

The Red Queen's eyes grew wide. Perhaps for the first time since she'd taken the crown, she was realizing that she couldn't bully her way out of this. That the old gods' will and raw power, the godsflame, would destroy her if she acted out of turn.

The air stilled as everyone waited for the queen to speak.

"Fine." My aunt's green eyes leveled on me menacingly.

I repressed a shudder. How anyone had *ever* trusted this woman, even if they were blood, was beyond me.

"Very good. The rules of the Conjuring Trial are simple. At the behest of the blue godsflame, each competitor will have two chances to conjure their most magnificent, impressive conjuring. The godsflame will decide the winner at tonight's feast, which will be held in the castle at the expense of the crown as a sign of good will between the competitors. If they wish to attend, no subject of Wonderland will be turned away from the feast."

The queen squawked, which Herald completely ignored.

"Now, if everyone is ready, the first trial shall begin at the godsflame's ready. Please take up your places on the conjuring circle." Herald pointed to a circle already drawn on the ground.

The Red Queen took up position at one pole, and I gravitated toward the other. Our supporters shuffled at our backs, outside the circle.

As soon as we were in position, the blue flame flared and swooped down to hover right at eye-level. I waited, wondering how a bit of fire was going to make clear what it wanted us to do, when all of a sudden, the flame shot a tendril in my direction.

I closed my eyes. *Of course it's my turn.*

I'd been hoping to go second, to see the extent of my aunt's abilities, and try to best her.

"The challenger, Alice White, goes first!" Herald cried, as if everyone hadn't already figured that out.

I pressed my lips together and raised my hands. Ideally, I would like to close my eyes to block out all other stimuli as I conjured, but I wouldn't do that here. In such a public arena, others could take it as a sign of weakness.

"Just do your best," Henri whispered a few feet behind me. "And remind the queen who you are."

Who I am . . .

An onslaught of my newly returned memories came

rushing forth, quelling the adrenaline zinging through me, and pulling the corners of my lips up slightly.

I knew exactly what to do.

I called the aether to me, allowing my magic to spill out and mold it. Shimmering light flooded the air, filling it with electricity, and an astonished gasp flew from the crowd.

I gave them no notice. I remained focused, working, pushing, and sweating as my aether magic transformed the fifth element right before my eyes.

A glass bush appeared first. It grew out of the ground, like a real one would, but its teal coloring veined with gold made it clear that I wasn't using earth magic to create it. Branches followed, and soon enough, buds formed. They were closed, but full and round, poised to shatter and reveal what was inside.

I made the buds wait until the rose bush was twice the size of the others I'd passed in the gardens. When I was sure my creation was as large as I could get it, I gave one final push.

The glass buds cracked. I pushed a little earth magic out to accompany the aether, and to my delight, real white roses bloomed on the glass structure.

The crowd leaned forward, many of them tilting their heads in wonder and confusion.

It was, admittedly, a strange choice, considering none of them remembered my family crest. But I didn't care because my aunt recognized the symbolism. And judging by the clenching of her jaw, she took great offense to me slipping white roses into her sanctuary of red.

Good. Let her simmer.

I grinned and gave a bow. Behind me, Hatter chuckled, and my other team members shouted words of encouragement.

The moment I rose from my bow, the godsflame shot a tendril of blue toward the Red Queen, as if to say *let's get a move on.* And apparently, my aunt agreed, because she launched straight into conjuring.

As much as I didn't want to be impressed, I had to admit that watching her was astounding. She didn't tremble or shake or sweat like I did. The aether came to her effortlessly, and as a mass of glowing air swirled in front of her, I held my breath.

The Red Queen whipped the clouds above into a frenzy, drawing them down and filling them with shimmering aether. Collectively, the onlookers leaned forward, waiting, and when a bolt of lightning burst from the clouds, a few shrieked.

I stood my ground, dreading what would happen next. When the queen pulled the trigger, she didn't disappoint.

The clouds released a deluge of red liquid, possibly blood, and the moment it touched my white roses, the flowers wilted and shriveled. The glasswork followed, melting and seeping into the earth, until nothing was left of my creation.

And then another bush bloomed in its place. A black

metal trunk that expanded and twisted in on itself and grew thorns that resembled deadly spikes. When the skeleton of the bush was even larger than the one I'd created, she stopped, and red roses made of gleaming metal formed from the branches and glinted in the sunlight.

The audience was rioting, jumping up and down in their queen's presumed victory—even if they didn't truly understand the subtext of her attack.

The queen lowered her arms, turned to the crowd, and gave a graceful curtsy, indicating that her conjuring was complete.

Wasting no time, the blue flame shot a tendril of fire in my direction. It was my turn again, my last shot. Clearly, my reminder of her family symbol had gotten to her. I had to do that again, but better. I had to hit her where it hurt most, and I thought I knew exactly what to do.

My second conjuring materialized in disjointed bits and pieces. It hovered in the glittering air, facing me, while I envisioned each piece and painstakingly brought it into being. A solid gold arm appeared first, then a portion of a dress skirt, followed by a torso. I sucked in a breath, pushing myself all the way to my limits as I bid the aether to do as I wished.

The last feature to emerge out of my memory from the Enchanted Forest was my mother's face. It clarified from the aether, so heart-wrenching it made me want to close my eyes. She was all there—how she looked at the exact moment that she begged her sister for her life. Every line, every tear, every feature was perfectly devastating. I turned my conjuring to face my aunt and dropped the statue on the ground.

Her gasp rang through the silent arena as she took in the face of her sister seconds before she killed her. Somehow her face remained hard as stone, but from the way her fingers trembled, I knew my design had to be affecting her.

I smirked, savagely pleased with myself, as the Red Queen dragged her eyes up from the statue to meet mine.

Take that, bitch. Oh shit—

The queen didn't even wait for the flame to dictate that it was her turn. She whipped the aether into a frenzy so hard that the air in the lawn swirled like a cyclone.

Members of the audience ducked, and a few people cried out in surprise. My own heart began beating a mile a minute.

I'd obviously done more than hit a nerve; I'd *enraged* the queen. Was she about to say 'screw it,' and lash out against me? Kill my friends?

I took a half step back, spreading my arms wide to defend them.

However, the queen took no notice of me, or them, as her conjuring appeared and grew toward the sky. The air crackled with energy, and took on a taste—slightly metallic.

Everyone in the crowd tilted their heads, trying to

puzzle out the conjuring. The moment it became clear, I sucked in a breath.

A guillotine crafted of black metal towered fifty feet high, as impressive as it was terrible. A blade glinted at the top, and at the bottom were realistic mannequins of my friends, each kneeling with their heads through the stocks.

And just when I thought she was done, the Red Queen lifted her arms and snapped.

The blade fell, barreling toward the ground until it sliced through the mannequins' necks. Their heads rolled and stopped at my feet.

CHAPTER 27

"Relax." Alran's hand brushed my arm, bringing attention to the fact that I was vibrating with rage as we marched toward Heartfire Hall to the first post-trial feast. "Don't let her see that she got to you."

I inhaled slowly, trying to bring my emotions and reactions under control.

Since the Conjuring Trial, I'd been amped up, unable to concentrate while the others helped me practice with my aether or discuss strategy.

"You're right, but I can't forget the look on her face. There was absolutely no remorse there after either conjuring. I mean, she chopped off your heads . . . how are you all dealing with that so well?"

"We've been her subjects for years," Henri piped up. "We're used to falling back on silence when the queen acts poorly—which is more often than not. Those who don't stay silent often perish."

I shook my head, unable to comprehend such behavior from the queen. She didn't behave as though her subjects, or their opinions, were worth a damn.

"Is there anyone she respects?" I asked.

"Her witches," Sansu, Henri, and Alran replied in unison.

"And maybe the king consort," Sansu added, "a little."

"We need to make getting to the witches a priority," I said.

"Dee and Dum have been on the lookout, learning where the witches' rooms are, watching their movements." Hatter shook the cape he wore. Beneath it, the pixies were hiding until the moment they would split off to spy. "Have you two found anything helpful?"

"Not really," Dum replied. She poked her head out. "We think they have wards up to protect their privacy."

"Keep trying to find a way in," I encouraged the twins.

I knew from years of sneaking into other peoples' lives that no one was totally secure. There had to be a way to get to the witches. And if we could speak with them alone, perhaps we could convince them to lift the enchantment over the subjects of Wonderland.

We rounded a corner, and heard voices coming from Heartfire Hall. My spine straightened. Judging by the noise, there were a lot more people at this feast than at the queen's unbirthday party.

"By now, the entire kingdom has heard about what's happening," Sansu explained. "And Trial by Aether law states that they're allowed to attend feasts revolving around the trial."

"Many will come to get a full meal," Hatter added. "But some . . . want to see what happens."

"Well, then, we'd better give them a show." I stretched my wings. "Chins up. Wings out, if you got 'em. Gait strong."

I marched into Heartfire Hall like I owned the place, all three men a half-step behind me. The pixies, our spies, had already peeled off to continue searching for the witches' rooms.

Our intended table was obvious. It sat four, the number in my entourage plus me if you didn't count the pixies, who had remained hidden from others since we entered the castle. We were to sit next to the queen's head table which was in the dead center of the room. Although I noticed that our table was set back a few inches so that we were subtly behind her. The positioning told me she didn't want me to outshine her, but I also gleaned another, more important tidbit of information from the setup. One that set my nerves on edge.

If the queen thought there was a chance that she would lose this challenge, she wouldn't have put me next to her at all.

She was *positive* that she would win.

Butterflies filled my stomach, right alongside the rage that had been bubbling there for hours.

Needing to calm down, I reminded myself that normal Wonderland politics did not apply here. There was no possible way for her to rig this. The godsflame would choose, and no one could bribe the will of the old gods.

"Alice?" Henri whispered.

I startled to find that I'd stopped walking, and now stood in the dead center of the room. A room full of silent fae, all staring at me.

Hell's balls.

"Are you . . . *ahem* . . . considering a speech?" Hatter arched his eyebrows.

Get your head in the game, Alice.

A delicate laugh came from the head table. I glanced up to find my aunt watching me with a smug-ass smile that was begging to be slapped off.

"Sure."

I hadn't prepared anything, but as I took in the judging smirks of those in the crowd, I knew I had to save face. Reluctantly, I turned toward one side of the crowd.

Right away, a hand shot up and waved.

I let out a tiny gasp. Isadora and a dozen other rebels were present, showing me support at great risk to themselves.

If they can do that, I can deliver a speech. It might even be rousing. Here's hoping . . .

I threw my shoulders back and cleared my throat. "Fae of Heartstown, thank you for being here tonight." I smiled warmly, but predictably received mostly frowns in return. "It's an honor to be in your presence, to witness history in the making—a Trial by Aether unlike our kind has ever seen before."

Someone in the crowd booed. "How dare you attempt to overthrow our dear queen!"

A few others echoed the sentiment, pushing my frustrations to a rolling boil. Drawing in a deep breath, I reminded myself it was the enchantment talking, and pressed on.

"To some of you, the Trial may seem unorthodox, but I assure you, one day, you'll understand. One day, I promise you'll learn the *truth* about your 'dear queen'."

I shot a glance at the royal table. The Red Queen's expression had faltered. Now she gripped her wine glass so tightly that her hands had become napkin white.

"However," I continued, "for tonight, I invite you to enjoy the companionship, the spectacle, especially the *food*. And no matter what the godsflame decides, know that I'm forever pleased to be in your company." I bowed.

Silence rang through the hall, piercing my ears. And then, suddenly, and entirely unexpectedly, someone clapped. Slowly, others joined in.

My lips curled up as I rose and searched the crowd to find who was risking their skin to support me. The rebels were clapping, which made me equally happy and nervous for them. But they weren't the only ones, and when my gaze landed on the other fae who were showing encouragement, my heart clenched.

A table of fae so emaciated that their cheekbones looked like cut glass clapped enthusiastically for me—or perhaps just for my insistence that they indulge in the food. Honestly, they were so small, almost sickly looking that if it was the latter I couldn't blame them.

My fists clenched at my side. How could my aunt look upon these people and believe she was a good ruler? They were starving, and I doubted that she cared at all. It sickened me.

As soon as my team sat, the feast began, and servants offered up platters heaping with all sorts of food. Roasted bird, vegetables, and mountains of creamed potatoes caught my eye, and I filled my plate with them. I'd already dug in when someone stopped in front of our table.

"A word, challenger?"

I glanced up from the delectable potatoes to find one of the queen's witches, both of whom Sansu had pointed out to me as we left the first challenge. She stood on the opposite side of our table, a small, hard smile on her face.

"My name is Alice White, true heir to the throne of Wonderland—although I'm sure you already know that." My eyes scorched through the woman, one of two who created the mist that made everyone forget about my parents.

She was about forty, with black hair that fell to her lower back, and a Marilyn Monroe beauty mark. Undeniably striking, but also creepy, she stood as still as a statue, her dark eyes penetrating me.

"I know who you are," the witch admitted after a long, appraising pause.

"Then why are you here? Why would I want to speak with you, the colluder of a traitor?"

The witch arched an eyebrow. "I'm aware that you likely feel as though you're being watched at every moment. And in fact, you're not far off," the witch said smoothly. "However, you should think twice before sending out any of your *little* helpers. Particularly those who are easily contained."

My heart leapt into my throat, and I gripped my knife, ready to hurl it at her. "Where are they? Did you harm them?"

Her dark eyes fluttered to my knife hand, and she loosed a low laugh. "They're back in your rooms, where they'll remain until I'm sure that you've had a talk with them about snooping. Which you *will* do, or next time I see them sneaking through the halls, I won't be so kind. Do you understand?"

Dammit, there go our spies.

"Yes," I said, not about to try to negotiate.

I hated this woman almost as much as I hated my aunt, but there was no doubt that she was powerful. Negotiating wasn't worth the twins' safety.

"Very good. Now, if you'll excuse me, *my queen* awaits."

The witch left to rejoin her table. When she was out of earshot, I released my breath.

"Do you think she told the queen that the pixies were spying?" I murmured.

"Undoubtedly." Hatter spoke with a wobble in his voice. "But if she's telling the truth, they're safe. That's all that matters."

"True." I leaned back in my chair. "Sucks, though. It would have been nice to have some insider information."

"We'll have to make do with what we have."

"Which is . . .?"

"You."

"No pressure," I muttered.

Hatter chuckled, the first time I'd heard him do so in hours. "I never said that, but judging by that speech, you're quite the weapon. Look at the crowd."

I followed his gaze and saw, to my astonishment, that most of the fae in the room were still watching me. However, this time there were slightly fewer frowns and more interest.

My speech had planted a seed.

"Well, I'll be damned. Do you think—"

The blast of a trumpet cut me off, and my attention snapped toward the door to find that Herald had arrived with the jar of godsflame.

I inhaled. This was it. The moment of truth—one of three chances I had to best my aunt.

"Attention, please!" Herald called, although the crowd had already fallen silent. "The flame has made its choice and is ready to present the winner of the Conjuring Challenge."

Everyone in the room leaned forward. Blood pounded in my ears as I gripped the side of the table.

"Without further ado, I shall reveal the winner."

Herald twisted the lid off the jar. The blue flame flashed out of the container, and then promptly disappeared.

What the hell happened? Where is it? What's going—

My heart stopped as the crowd roared.

Oh no. No. No. No. This can't happen . . .

As I didn't want to confirm my fear, I had to know the truth. I twisted to face my aunt.

She was beaming and waving at the crowd, glowing with a happiness that was enhanced by the illumination of the blue godsflame hovering over her head.

A pit formed in my stomach.

Realistically, I understood that the queen's displays of conjuring had been more impressive. But how could the godsflame be so cruel? Had it not seen the violence my aunt displayed when her conjuring melted my own? Or when she beheaded replicas of the very people who stood behind me?

"Thank you. Thank you, dear subjects," the queen clapped for silence. "I appreciate all your love and support during these troubling times." She brought her hands together, placing them on her heart as if she truly meant the words. "I compete in these challenges for every one of you, so that you might have your rightful queen."

Her eyes slid to meet mine. "And with that, I'd like to say, in all sincerity, let the best aether-blessed fae win."

***

I kicked open the door to our tower suite, grabbed the first thing I saw, an elaborate red and white vase, and hurled it across the room. It shattered, and I pivoted, looking for the next thing I could destroy.

The final hour of the feast had been sheer hell. After the godsflame decided the winner, many subjects of Wonderland felt compelled to tell me how much they wanted me to lose.

Dozens of fae hated me, and wanted me to fail. They called *me* usurper. Of course, they were wrong, enchanted to believe a lie, and I should have felt bad for them.

But it was so difficult, sitting there, sucking it up. The moment that Herald had proclaimed that the godsflame wished for the feast to end and the next trial to commence at midday tomorrow, I'd shot out of my seat and left.

"Alice, you must calm down." Henri walked through the door behind me, as unruffled as ever.

"It's natural to be angry," I shot back. "I lost. Most of the fae here hate me, and I only have until noon tomorrow to prepare for the next trial. What if it's the Creatures Trial? I've never called a creature in my life!"

Henri was about to respond, when the sound of yelling from somewhere in the tower hit my ear.

"What the—"

I remembered that the witch who'd caught Dee and Dum spying mentioned they would be in our suite.

"Oh god! The pixies! Where are they?"

A frenzy of searching ensued, and finally I found the twins trapped in a glass jar with a few holes poked in the lid under my bed. I pulled the jar out and unscrewed the lid, but the pixies didn't fly out.

My brow furrowed. "What's wrong—oh!"

Why they hadn't immediately escaped their prison became clear. Their little wings had been cruelly sealed together to resemble shark fins rather than diaphanous wings.

"Girls! I'm so sorry that this happened to you. How can we get them apart?" I reached into the jar to help them out, and began feeling for a seam along their wings.

Dum pulled away as if my touch had hurt her, and I retracted my fingers.

"You can't," Dee said, her tone full of anguish. "They're spelled together so we can't fly. No one but a witch can undo it."

"Not even an aether-blessed fae?" I asked.

"Well . . . maybe, but you're so new." An uncomfortable expression crossed Dee's face. "Sorry to say this, Alice, but you might mess them up. Then what would we do? Our wings could be ruined forever."

I bit my bottom lip. She wasn't being cruel, she was

simply right. I was still learning my magic, and why would I even want to try it on this, if there was a chance I might injure my friends? It was inconvenient, but they could live without flying.

"We'll get it figured out. Even if we have to make another trip to the human world—eventually," Henri said, his unspoken words louder than the ones he'd voiced.

The girls' ability to fly again depended on me winning the Trial by Aether. If I didn't, it wouldn't matter that their wings were stuck together. Like the rest of us, they'd be executed.

"Looks like you're joining my detail tomorrow," I said.

"We could use their help, anyway," Henri added. "The crowds at tomorrow's challenge will be larger."

"What does that have to do with the pixies?" I asked.

"They can work the masses," he answered. "After all, they're the most charismatic of our group."

Dee brightened at Hatter's compliment. "We want to help Alice! We can encourage people to cheer for you!"

"As long as they aren't in swarms, pixies are almost universally liked," Sansu pointed out.

I exhaled a resigned sigh. "I don't want them to get hurt. What if someone is offended that you're supporting me and steps on you or something?"

"We're fast. They won't be able to catch us," Dum assured me. "Don't worry about us. We should be worrying about you and helping you study!"

"Okay, as long as you're careful."

I tried to appear as assured as everyone else, even though that was impossible. Until I'd won the Trial by Aether, I wouldn't be able to stop worrying.

CHAPTER 28

That night, Hatter drilled the theory and particulars of dozens of magical creatures into my head until my eyelids grew too heavy to lift. And in the morning, the session continued the moment I awoke.

It helped a bit, but I couldn't deny that, after my loss, my confidence remained at an all-time low. I doubted any amount of studying could fix that.

As midday neared, I geared up in my black uniform, and prayed to the old gods. *Please let this be the Combat Trial. I need to give others the hope and strength to speak out against the queen. I need a win . . .*

A knock came at my bedroom door.

"Yeah?"

"The escort is here," Hatter replied.

"I'll be right out," I called back.

When I finished getting ready, I met my team in the living area. "Any last words of advice?"

"Remember who you are," Henri said, repeating the wisdom he'd given me yesterday—a lot of good that had done.

I sighed at the seemingly worthless sentiment, and opened my door to find an entourage of a dozen Diamond battalion soldiers waiting.

My eyebrows arched. Yesterday, our entourage had comprised only two soldiers.

"The pixies heard a few things before they were caught. Things they didn't want to worry you about, and told me once you went to bed," Hatter whispered in my ear as the guards led us through the corridors. "Word has it, the queen tried calling her jabberwocky after the Conjuring Trial. It didn't come, which angered her. Considering the larger escort, I'd say things aren't going her way. I bet she believes throwing you off your game is the best course of action."

"How unnecessary," I muttered.

"Hey." Henri grabbed my hand, and despite the fear and anxiety coursing through my veins, my heart fluttered. "Where's the proud Alice I know? The one who wanted to infiltrate Heart Castle all on her own? The woman who stood up to the caterpillar when he tried to take advantage of her?"

"In case you didn't notice," I murmured. "That girl got her ass handed to her yesterday."

"I didn't see it that way," Hatter's tone was so low, I

could barely hear him. "I saw a woman create something amazing out of nothing. I watched a young faerie fight a more experienced queen, and produce heart-wrenching conjurings. I glimpsed a queen rising—showing her people what she can do, giving them hope."

A lump lodged in my throat. Goddamn, what could I even say to that? The only other person who'd ever believed in me so much had been Xavier, and he'd only built me up for selfish purposes.

"You can do this." Hatter squeezed my hand tight. "No matter what the next trial is, I have total faith in you."

"Thanks." I squeezed back and tried to ignore how tightly my stomach was tied into knots.

We remained silent the rest of the way, until the guards led us back through the elaborate royal gardens and to an enormous amphitheater. The Red Queen stood in the center of the wooden stage. Herald was at her side, but neither of them occupied my attention.

That honor went to the dozens of familiar faces in the crowd that sat on the stone bleachers overlooking the stage. Rebels who I'd met over the last few days beamed at me and waved, even as their neighbors scowled at them.

"Best of luck, Alice!" Isadora screamed at the top of her lungs.

My lips pressed together, unable to believe she was here so soon after Circe's death. She was so supportive— so strong.

"You've got this!" The brownie blew a kiss.

The queen's eyes snapped to Isadora, narrowing with hatred. My heart rate sped up for her. Whatever this trial was, no matter how futile it seemed, I had to give it my all. If only for the people in the crowd who had endangered themselves just by showing up.

"Welcome, subjects of Wonderland," Herald announced as soon as I stepped on to the stage. He no longer wore a bandage on his foot. In fact, he looked vibrant, no doubt from the godsflames' inhabitation of the rabbit. "Now that both competitors are present, we shall see what the godsflame decrees."

He held up the jar housing the blue, green, and silver flames, all separate and yet mixing together like water and oil. With his tiny paws, he unscrewed the top, and without preamble, a silver flame shot out and flared above the amphitheater to form the shape of a sword.

"Combat!" Herald roared, the pleasure obvious in his voice.

The crowd mimicked his joy, going wild—particularly the rebels, who were jumping up and down in their seats.

I blinked. *Combat? For reals?*

I'd been *so* sure it would be the Calling of the Creatures, but now . . . I had a chance—a *real* chance.

My heart began thundering, and my mind went into overdrive, studying the queen like I would a mark—searching for weaknesses.

Physically, she was strong, there was no doubt, and mentally, she was sneaky. I didn't have any idea what her weapons skills were like, or anything about her magic besides what I'd seen yesterday. I'd have to investigate as we fought, which was fine with me.

I was excellent at sizing up combat opponents. Whatever her weaknesses were, I'd find them, and put them to good use. It was just a matter of drawing them out.

Once the crowd quieted, Herald explained that the blue and green godsflame would act as shields for the onlookers so that the queen and her challenger could use magic without injuring the crowd. To win, we needed to either draw first blood, or get the other participant to surrender.

The silver godsflame would mark the start and end of the trial. And should anyone break the rules—such as kill the other person after first blood was drawn or they had surrendered—the godsflame would smite them.

"Are the participants ready?" Herald asked once he'd finished explaining the rules, and had maneuvered us into position.

The queen and I stood across the vast stage from one another, necessitating either an initial long-range magic strike, or a rush to our foe.

"Bring it on." I bent slightly and placed my hands on my knees as I considered my first move.

"Yes," the Red Queen answered, her tone much more dignified than my growl.

Herald released the other two flames from the jar, and they soared over to the crowd and created a sheer, blue-green shield in front of the audience. From behind the shield, Isadora waved, and my confidence ratcheted up a couple more notches.

Then a boom sounded as the silver flame erupted in the sky like a firework, signaling the start of the trial.

"Let the trial by combat begin!" Herald screamed, and in response, the audience began to roar.

Without hesitation, I called the aether to me, and imagined my favorite dagger. It appeared in my hand a heartbeat later, by far the easiest conjuring I'd ever created.

I smirked. "Alice the Dagger is back, baby."

"You'll need more than that to take me down," the Red Queen sniped.

I tore my eyes from the blade to find dozens of small boulders swirling around her. Where she'd gotten them from, I wasn't sure, because there definitely weren't boulders in the gardens. However, their rapid appearance made one thing crystal clear. My aunt was strong with earth magic.

"We'll see about that!" I dashed toward her.

One rock flew past me, then a second, and a third . . . after only a few seconds, I lost count as I dodged through the barrage of boulders. With each one, my aunt loosed a scream—perhaps trying to intimidate me.

If I weren't saving every ounce of my breath for a battle, I would have laughed. Didn't this woman understand that silence was far more threatening?

The frenzied pace of her rock slinging increased as I

got closer, but when I was fifteen feet away, there was a break. A chance. I took it.

I leapt. The Red Queen doubled her efforts, hurling the rest of the rocks in her arsenal, but to no avail. I had become more agile with my wings since our adventure in the Enchanted Forest.

I soared through the boulders without sustaining a scratch, flew right up to her, and swiped with my dagger.

She spun out of the way just in time, darting backward and dropping her rocks in the process.

"You want to do this with steel." A gleaming sword appeared in her hand. "Come and get it."

"With pleasure."

Using aether magic, I pushed the tip of my dagger outward, lengthening it into a sword, and surged to meet her.

Our blades collided, eliciting cheers from the crowd with every attack and parry. It didn't take me long to determine that I was more skilled with a blade, but she was better at incorporating magic when she fought.

She used earth, fire, and water against me—all of which I shielded against. However, one element had been absent from her arsenal: air, my specialty.

I tried to concoct a technique suited to someone who was relatively weak with air. All the while, my blade whistled through the air and clanged against hers.

The queen fended off my attacks, and fluidly responded with her own. It was almost as though we were dancers, the way we played off one another, the twirling, advancing, and receding.

Since the trial began, the crowd hadn't stopped shouting their pleasure or grief, but we paid them no notice. In fact, I'd even begun to enjoy myself a little. My body felt alive in the fight—on fire. We were engrossed in each other, a whirlwind of elements and steel.

And then my aunt caught me off guard.

A vine burst from the floor of the amphitheater and slithered up my ankle, around my calf. I tried to kick it off, and for a brief second, took my eyes off the queen.

She thrust her sword at me and, flailing, I flung my body the opposite way and fell to the ground with an *oomph*. Another vine burst from the wooden stage to wrap around my arms.

I blinked, unable to believe where I was. What had happened? How had I not seen something like this coming? I'd been too caught up in the pleasure of the fight, and now she was towering over me, her sword descending slowly, painfully.

"It's over. You've lost." My aunt hovered her blade inches from my neck. "Surrender."

"Never!" I spat on her.

"Do it!"

I grinned up at her, not about to give her what she wanted.

"Fine, if you insist that I resort to spilling your blood, I will. There's no way you'll get out of this."

"Is that what you told my mother when you murdered her?"

She winced, and her sword drooped a half-inch.

I took advantage of her disarmament, blowing a gust of wind in her eyes as I conjured thorns to rip open the vines and pulled at them. As soon as they tore completely, I rolled away.

She screamed and her metal hit the wooden stage right where I'd been seconds before. I leapt up, twirled in the air, and slashed my blade across the heart drawn on her back. Fabric ripped, exposing a milk-white back and a streak of blood that signaled the trial's end.

The crowd bellowed with anger, except for a few slight cheers from the rebels, letting me know they were there.

"The Combat Trial has ended!" Herald cried.

"*No!*" The Red Queen whirled on me and raised her sword, clearly intending to bring it down.

Defensively, I lifted my weapon, but instead of metal hitting metal, her sword hit a shield of blue-green aether.

I smirked. "It seems that the godsflame won't let you have your way. If I were you, I'd admit defeat now before it sucks the life out of you."

She sneered at me. "I could have slit your throat."

"Close doesn't count."

The Red Queen's cheeks grew a dangerous red.

"Your Majesty, might I suggest that you cease your assault." Herald hopped over. "The silver flame has just informed me that if you continue, the other two gods-flame will smite you."

The Red Queen's jaw worked. "Fine. *I concede*," she spat, and stomped to the far side of the stage.

The shield of blue and green disappeared, and the silver godsflame soared toward me to dance above my head in victory.

The rebels cheered like mad, and I couldn't help myself—I raised my hands and shook my fists, letting the win wash over me.

I did it! I bested the Red Queen in combat. I . . .

All of a sudden, I stilled. Once again, I felt the odd and yet familiar sensation that someone was watching me. Someone whose presence differed from most other peoples. I blinked, trying to figure it out. Before, I'd thought it might be the queen or her little helpers watching me, but now my aunt had turned her back on me. It definitely wasn't her. I scanned the crowd. There were so many people, it could be any one of them. It was probably pointless to try and figure out. I had more important things to be concentrating on. Like the final challenge.

"Yay, Alice! Fist bump me Dee!" Dum's high voice cried out, breaking my concentration and warming my heart.

A body slammed into me from the side, and Hatter, identifiable by his spicy scent, gripped me tight. "You're tied! We have a shot."

"Why the tone of disbelief?" I teased.

"You know I believed in you!" Henri shook his head. "It's just that I've waited to see her overthrown for so long. I can't believe it's almost here."

"It's not over yet," I said. "We still have the calling of creatures. As soon as we leave here, I need to start practicing again—"

All my words fell from my lips as the green godsflame surged above the amphitheater and bloomed into a ball of light the size of a giant trampoline.

Everyone except Herald, who seemed entranced by the godsflame, gasped as the light pulsed and then fell down, straight into Herald's heart center. The white rabbit began to glow green, and his golden eyes took on a neon verdant hue.

Herald had claimed he was speaking to the flame, voicing their will, and everyone had believed him because to go against the aether's will meant death. But now, there was no denying it. The pooka was embodying the message of the gods.

"The Trial by Aether is tied," Herald said, his voice holding more gravitas. "The godsflame has decided that there will be no feast tonight."

The crowd mumbled, displeased that their free meal was being taken from them.

"The last trial, the calling of creatures, will take place at dusk." Herald turned toward me and the Red Queen. "The participants should be prepared to see the end of this trial on this very night."

CHAPTER 29

"Tonight!" I screeched as I threw open the door to the North Tower. My heart was pounding so hard, I felt like it might burst out of my chest. "Is there a precedent for the godsflame just changing things up like this?"

My friends stared back at me, at a loss for words.

I was about to ask again before I remembered that a Trial by Aether hadn't taken place for centuries. They were as shocked over this as I was.

I threw a dismissive wave. "I guess it doesn't matter if it's happened before. Let's be honest, the godsflame can do whatever the hell it wants! The only thing that matters is it's happening now."

"This is certainly problematic," Alran spoke up. He'd situated himself by the pile of books documenting magical creatures, and had already started flipping through them. "Instead of having hours to prepare, you have significantly less time."

No shit, Sherlock.

"Maybe that's why the godsflame is rushing the end," Henri muttered as he laid the pixies down on the red chaise lounge.

Partially from excitement, and partially because their bodies were trying to fight the enchantment binding their wings together, the girls had been exhausted all day. They'd passed out on the walk back to the room. Judging from the sounds of their snores, they wouldn't wake up soon.

"What do you mean by that?" I asked, once Henri had placed a blanket over the girls.

"The amount of time. The Red Queen controls a bandersnatch herd, but she won't call them now, as they're all recovering from injury. She also controls the jabberwocky and the kraken. The sea monster is never very far from the island, but the jabberwocky flies all around Faerie. I wonder if the aether was trying to level the playing field, force her to call a new creature."

"But that still leaves the kraken," I noted. "Can they move on land?"

Everyone exchanged glances. Once again, we were all clueless.

"It has many arms," Sansu offered with a shrug. "But it's hard to say what it's capable of. The only fae who have seen it up close besides the Red Queen have vanished. I suppose it could crawl on land, if it needed to, but I don't see that happening."

"Technically, that's not true," Alran said, pointing to a page in his book detailing the sea monster. "One person has survived a kraken. They claimed it was smaller, about the size of an eight-person carriage. So likely, it wasn't a queen kraken, which are supposedly much larger. Still, the fae killed it by stabbing it through the heart." He pointed to the picture.

I took in the detailed anatomical drawing documenting the kraken. The creature resembled a squid, and its heart was located on the underside, where the two frontmost tentacles met. If the kraken was crawling, the spot would be difficult to get to. The beast would have to tilt on its side to make the area accessible.

"Fine. One person has killed one." Sansu rolled his eyes, breaking my musings. "I still don't think it's likely that the queen will call a sea monster to fight when the island boasts so many other deadly creatures. Unless it's a sea fight, most of them would be more efficient than the kraken."

"I have to agree," Hatter spoke softly, probably trying to ease the rising anxiety in the room. "Wonderland is full of many other dangerous creatures—all wild, but near enough to Heartstown that the queen might call them."

Sansu nodded. "There's a roc's nest nearby, and a manticore lair, too."

Roc? Manticore?

I knew that a manticore had the body of a lion, a

scorpion's tail, and the face of a human. And that a roc was a giant bird. But neither existed in the human world, so I didn't know much else about them.

"Basically," I said, picking up a book, "I need to get to studying."

I buried my face in the pages of books, and the others did the same—occasionally stopping to tell me another interesting tidbit about a creature we'd already covered. Thankful for their help, I stored it all in my mind.

The theory was, the more you knew about a specific animal, the more likely you would be to call it to you. Being knowledgeable of a creature's physical description was the bare minimum I would need.

"Exactly how far away does the manticore live?" I asked after two hours of studying.

"No one has sought her out," Sansu offered, "but she's within a few miles of the city."

"Rumor has it there's a male too," Alran added. "He lives along the coastline, but fae rarely see him. Heartstown lies within the female's territory, and seeing as they're the more vicious sex of the species, he doesn't dare encroach."

"But if she's out flying, she could be much farther away," Sansu said. "Even on the mainland."

I took a big breath and let it all out in one go. Facts and images swam in my head, but I was starting to wonder if that wasn't as useful as others' opinions.

The fae who lived here had been around these creatures their whole lives. Social beliefs held power, and the

Red Queen probably preyed upon them to keep others in line. If I could guess what she'd choose, I could attempt to call a worthy counterpart.

I closed my book. "Which creature would *you* call if you had to choose?"

Alran leaned forward and placed his elbows on his knees. "Probably the jabberwocky or the kraken. I know that they'd be effective. Actually, almost everyone in Heartstown is terrified of them. They've seen firsthand the serious damage that both can do."

I bit my lip. I was going in circles. Those creatures were already firmly under the queen's control. My best hope was that the jabberwocky was elsewhere in Faerie, not close enough to be called in. And that the kraken wouldn't be able to fight out of water.

"So if I call something with wings, I'd have a pretty good chance." A flightless creature wouldn't stand up against a dragon.

"Correct," Sansu said. "That leaves us with the manticore, roc, or gryphons. If you succeed in calling a gryphon, and it's the leader, the whole convocation might follow."

I was drawn to the roc, the giant bird capable of carrying an adult elephant in its talons. It was supposed to be a vicious fighter.

"Would the roc's beak and talons be able to defeat the jabberwocky?"

"That depends on which one you call," Hatter replied.

I was about to fire off a retort that the same might be said for any animal, when a knock came at the door.

My spine stiffened, and I ran to look out the window. We still had hours until dusk.

"Could they have moved up the challenge?" I asked, twirling back around to face my friends.

Everyone looked as stunned as I did, an occurrence that was becoming far too common for my liking.

"I—I don't know," Henri replied. "I'll check."

A hush fell over the room as he opened the door to find two guards.

"Henri Hatter?" One guard asked.

"That's me."

"You've been requested."

The rebel leader took a step back. "By who?"

"Isadora Blackthorn was injured and requires your assistance."

I dashed over to the door. "Isadora? What happened to her?"

"We are not at liberty to say," the other soldier spoke up. "We were told only to retrieve Mr. Hatter, so that he might help her out of this predicament."

I exchanged glances with Hatter. "What do you think?"

"She was at the feast last night, and the amphitheater today . . . and she was vocal."

My throat closed up. He was right. Isadora had been vocal, especially before the Combat Trial. So much so, she'd earned the queen's ire. Certainly, others had noticed her too. What if another subject of Wonderland attacked her afterwards?

"Go." I placed a hand on his shoulder, adding assurance that I meant what I said. "Check on her, and once you're sure she's okay, come back."

"Are you sure?" he asked. "I should be helping you."

I gestured back to Sansu and Alran. "There are enough cooks in this kitchen. Plus, she's as important as family to you. Isadora needs you."

And I wouldn't be able to live with myself if I didn't let him go check on her.

"Okay," Henri said. "I'll check on her, get her whatever she needs, and return as quickly as possible."

I nodded, and then, unable to help myself, lifted up onto my tiptoes and pressed my lips to his cheek for the second time. "We'll be waiting."

CHAPTER 30

Hours passed. I couldn't even count the number of times I caught myself staring at the door to our suite, waiting for Hatter to stroll through with news of Isadora. Waiting to see his brilliant smile, hear his voice assure me that the brownie was fine and that I'd do well tonight. When the evening meal was delivered, he still hadn't shown up. I picked at the food, unable to eat.

Where was he?

And when Henri still didn't return by dusk, I was certain something was very, very wrong.

As a result, my focus was in tatters as my team walked onto the beach in front of the castle for the third challenge.

"Maybe he's in there," Sansu whispered, not wanting to broadcast our worry to the guards escorting us.

A group of at least three hundred fae, many of them

soldiers, stood a couple hundred yards away, waiting. My gaze scanned the crowd. I couldn't find a single person who remotely resembled Henri. And if he saw us, I was positive he'd catch our attention.

My last hope that he'd make it back in time for the Creatures Challenge vanished. I broke out into a sweat.

"There's that horrible witch," Dee growled from her perch on my shoulder. She pointed to one of the two witches.

Both wore striking emerald cloaks that made them stand out in the sea of red and white. To add to their air of superiority, the two women stood on either side of the Red Queen.

"We can sink our fangs into her when she's not paying attention," Dum replied, her voice as venomous as her sister's. "With this large of a crowd, it would be easy to slink away after."

Henri was gone. Both the witches were present, as were *many* more soldiers than before. The hair at the nape of my neck lifted. Something was very wrong.

"Actually, girls," I whispered. "I have a bad feeling about Henri. I know you want to watch the last trial, and get revenge on the witches, but can I persuade you to take on a different mission?"

"For Henri?" Dee stood up. "Of course!"

"Okay." I paused and squatted, earning looks of annoyance from the guards escorting me, which I ignored.

I gently set the pixies on the sand, and brought my

face close to theirs so no one else would hear. "Henri wouldn't miss this. Something is wrong—I just know it. Find him, save him, and, if you can, bring more of our people back to the beach with you."

I glanced at their wings. "This'll be harder now that you can't fly. You'll have to be much sneakier. Are you sure you're up for it?"

"Girl, we might not be able to fly, but don't underestimate us pixies," Dee replied, her chin jutting out. "We're on it."

"*Ahem.* We're on a bit of a schedule here," a guard said.

I didn't reply to him, only held my fist out for the pixies to pound. "I have the ultimate faith in you," I said when their fists hit mine simultaneously, and opened into explosions. "May the aether light your way."

The girls scampered down the beach, their tiny feet leaving small indents in the sand. I watched them go and hoped that I wasn't too late. Or better yet, that my gut was wrong and Henri would show up at any minute.

But when I stood and caught sight of the smug expression on my aunt's face, I couldn't find it in me to believe that.

"Alran. Sansu. Stay close."

The guys flanked me as I strode toward the gathering on the beach, as upright and proud as I could, with my feet slipping in the sand. When I got there, I saw that there were even more soldiers than I thought. Well over one hundred, from both the Diamond and Heart battalions.

My mouth dried up. The Red Queen expected something to happen here, and she had to know that my experience with creatures wouldn't require so many soldiers.

No, if I had to guess, I'd say that my aunt expected to win. And if she expected to win, there was only one reason to have such a large guard.

She thought I'd do what I came here to do, anyway. Assassinate her.

"I see you're one crony short," the Red Queen said, her voice low. "Did he decide he chose the wrong team?"

There was something in her eyes that made me think she knew exactly where Henri was. I was glad I'd sent the pixies to investigate, and frustrated that I hadn't considered it sooner.

"He had to go help someone he loves," I snapped back. "I don't expect you to understand that."

The Red Queen snarled, but Herald cut off her retort when he hopped through the soldiers to stand between us, and called the gathering to order.

"The contestants of the Trial by Aether have arrived." The white rabbit gestured for me to come closer. "And the third competition will take place forthwith."

I watched him, impressed. So far, Herald had performed his tasks unflinchingly. Even now, when he knew this was the last trial and he would die once it was complete, he was all business.

I had to be more like him—to keep my eye on the prize. I had to trust that the pixies would find Henri.

I had to be Alice the Dagger one last time.

"The rules for the Calling of the Creatures are simple," Herald continued. "Each party vying for the crown of Wonderland will use aether magic to call upon their mythical creature of choice. No fae may be called or influenced in this trial, only creatures identifiable as animals. Once the creatures are called, it's a fight to the death. The participant with the victorious creature wins this challenge."

"And if someone's animal doesn't show up?" the Red Queen asked, her lips curled in a smile that I wanted to punch off her face.

"If only one participant succeeds in calling a creature, they are the winner." Herald held up the jar. "The gods-flame chose this spot specifically for its accessibility to animals of the forest, air, and sea. Everyone who is not a contestant, congregate at the edge of the beach. Just as with the Combat Trial, the godsflame will protect onlookers from any animals who might slip from their master's control."

The crowd, including the soldiers and a few rebels I glimpsed in the far back, moved to huddle against rocks that climbed up to the base of Heart Castle.

Once they were a safe distance away, Herald unscrewed the jar's lid. Out floated the green flame—the final godsflame of the trial.

"Are the contestants ready?" he asked.

I glared at my aunt, and she stared back at me, hard and unyielding.

"Yes," I growled.

The Red Queen nodded. "Let's get this over with."

In response, the green godsflame floated up, thirty feet high, and formed the shape of a unicorn.

Herald held his paws to the sky. "Let the final challenge of the Trial by Aether begin!"

The Red Queen leapt into motion, her body turning, her arms extending toward the ocean.

My heart jumped into my throat at the implication. *She must be calling the kraken.*

Mentally bringing up an image of the roc, I called the aether. I bid it to find the closest roc and bring it to me.

I did exactly as the text said. And yet, I felt absolutely *nothing*—no change. No indication that what I was doing was working.

Maybe calling creatures is a more subtle magic.

Keeping my eyes closed, I tried harder and harder. Sweat began to pour down my brow, and my arms trembled as the sounds of churning water and my aunt's laughter filled my ears.

"She's coming!" the Red Queen cackled. "The queen kraken is coming to protect her master!"

She must've looked over at me, because her next jab was directed at my pitiful state.

"You should pull yourself together. Kraken can sense weakness as well as they can smell blood in the water. They might mistake you for a tasty snack, niece."

My teeth gnashed together and, unsure if it was the right thing, I switched targets. Gryphons were more familiar to me. At the very least, I'd seen one in the wild, smelled their musty scent, heard the noises they made.

I pulled up the image of the convocation of gryphon, as vivid in my mind as the day I entered Faerie.

A bird screeched, and distractingly, the hope that the roc had actually arrived leapt in my chest.

I opened my eyes and swore.

It was only an ordinary hawk, cruising the skies.

"It seems you need assistance," a voice, dreamy and familiar, spoke in my ear.

I gasped and twisted, but no one was beside me.

"Who's there?" I asked as a pit formed in my stomach.

Was someone playing a trick on me? Was one of the witches befuddling my senses?

"I've been watching you, Alice. And now I'm here because you have shown which princess you're most like."

Watching me? I gaped. All those times I'd sensed someone nearby studying me came rushing back, just as a pair of glowing amber eyes popped out of nowhere. I inhaled sharply.

"If you want my help," the owner of the eyes continued, "bind me to you."

"The Cheshire cat? The one we met in the woods— the free one?" My words wobbled, but the cat's stare didn't break.

"One and the same," he said as a roar came from the ocean.

I winced at the sound.

"I'm here to be your creature," the Cheshire cat explained. "To help you win this trial. Call to me, share with me your aether magic. Bind us, Alice."

I didn't have a clue how to do any of what he'd just said. But seeing as other creatures weren't beating down my door, I was going to roll with it and do my damnedest to make a binding happen.

I called on my magic and, using instinct, let it pour from my fingers to the space where the cat was hovering. It caught on him, lighting up his fur. Suddenly, purple stripes appeared, and long claws popped out of paws as the cat became visible.

Could it really be that easy?

I bit my lip. "So . . . did it work?"

The cat stretched his paws out in front of him, his butt in the air. "Yes. I'm no longer a free cat. I'm yours to command, as you will."

"You just gave up your freedom? Why?"

Freedom had been my primary driver for so long, I didn't understand why someone would willingly surrender theirs.

"For the sake of the island." His eyes darted toward the ocean. "Now, we're running out of time. Tell me what you need. Be precise."

I gulped. "I don't suppose you could kill that giant kraken?"

The beast roared again and slapped her tentacles against the waves. The Red Queen released an insane laugh, reveling in the monstrosity of her creature as the enormous, indigo cephalopod emerged wholly from the depths of the water. On top of the queen kraken's head, her eyes blinked as she acclimated to air.

Gods, I hate my aunt.

"I will do my best," the cat replied.

I scanned the skies. Still no roc or gryphon had heeded my call, only a cat about the size of a bobcat. I twisted toward the kraken, half the size of a battleship and paddling faster toward us with every second.

The odds didn't look good, but I was out of time and had only one real choice.

"I'd love your assistance," I said. "Let me know how I can help you."

"We're bonded now," the cat said, his voice still dreamy despite the jarring atmosphere. "Feel past your fear, let me in. You will know what I need, when I need it."

I barely had a second to consider what he meant by that, when screams rose behind us.

I glanced up. The kraken had reached land ridiculously fast. She was already crawling toward us, pulling herself across the sand with long tentacles.

The moment had come.

I looked at the cat and nodded. "When you need help, I'm here."

The Cheshire cat bowed and disappeared. A second

later, he reappeared right on top of the kraken's head, and plunged his claws into the creature's eyes.

My hands flew to my mouth.

A guttural, animalistic scream rang out across the beach, so loud I wouldn't be surprised if all of Wonderland Island had heard it.

Blood began pouring down the kraken's face, so dark crimson it almost resembled black ink. The bulbous torso of the beast collapsed onto the sand as its tentacles flew up, trying desperately to bat the cat away.

The Cheshire cat disappeared and reappeared again, only to swipe at one of the tentacles, once again drawing blood. He pulled that move again and again, until the kraken was bled from what had to be many dozen cuts.

While the cat was clever and had made great progress, I still couldn't see how he would win. The kraken was simply too big, too powerful.

Just when I was beginning to wonder what he'd do next, the cat reappeared right in front of me. "Your dagger, please."

I pulled it out. "Isn't this . . . cheating? Don't you have to kill her?"

"Trust me. It's not your fault the Red Queen chose a beast of a creature, and not something with intellect. I need something that will cut deeper, and with a little extra power." He gestured to the dagger. "Imbue it with aether. As long as *you* don't wield the dagger, we're within the rules of the Trial by Aether."

Alrighty then. I would take his word for it.

A ball of aether formed in my palms, and like I'd done with the cat, I forced it into the dagger.

As soon as the blade glowed bright with aether, the cat snapped it up, disappeared, and appeared once again in front of the roaring creature.

Blood pounded in my ears as the monster swiped one of her many arms, narrowly missing the cat.

I shot a glance at my aunt. All of her previous surety was gone as she watched the events of this challenge unfolding.

The cat was a machine, appearing and reappearing seemingly every time I blinked. He stabbed the aether-filled dagger into the kraken over and over and over. He was doing his best, and yet the kraken was inching forward, smearing her blood along the sand, and filling the air with a metallic scent.

I have to help.

I visualized the illustration of the beast in my mind's eye. The area between her front two arms was underdeveloped, soft, so that the creature might swim with little hindrance. So that it could be fast, limber, and effective in strikes. And just on the underbelly of that spot was the creature's heart.

"Cat!" I screamed.

The Cheshire cat stopped its stabbings and glanced my way.

I bent down on the sand and began sketching the diagram. "Over here!"

The cat was at my side a second later, studying the

drawing.

I pointed. "This is where her heart is located. Stab her there with the aether blade, and she'll die."

The cat glanced back at the kraken. "I've damaged so many of her tentacles that she's barely lifting off the ground. Only enough to inch forward. Accessing that area will be an issue."

I followed his gaze and understood what he meant. The beast was leaning forward, using her body weight to move, just as much as she used the least-damaged tentacles.

"We need her to try to turn—sharply. That will lift her front off the sand, and you can gain access. I'll help. I'll distract her, draw her attention away."

The cat hummed, considering my plan. "It *could* work."

"Right now, I'd say it's our best shot."

"I believe you're probably right."

"Then let's not waste another moment."

The cat disappeared, and, pushing back my rising panic, I followed his lead and sprinted for the kraken.

CHAPTER 31

My arms pumped as the toes of my boots dug into the sand. The kraken's arms swung at me, and I darted out of the way just in time for the suckers to miss me and slam into the ground. Water sprinkled my body, and clumps of sand pelted my legs as the ground shook.

Well, shit. This is going to be a real doozy.

Somewhere behind me, the crowd jeered, and a few rebels screamed my name.

I took heart in the few cheers among the heckling, and surged forward. Three more tentacle dodges later, I'd safely rounded the beast, and was waiting to make my move at the water's edge.

The queen kraken was even more spectacular and grotesque up close. Opalescent dots found only on under-water creatures marred what had appeared to be pure indigo skin from farther away. Blood splattered the sand

and water all around us, filling the air with the scent of iron to complement the salt of the sea.

The injuries the cat had inflicted were more vicious-looking and numerous than they had appeared from up the beach. And yet, they still weren't enough to end this.

"Cat! Sever her ligaments!"

Miraculously, the cat heard me over the roar of the monster. Or maybe it was the fact that we were aether-bound.

If I survived this, I would have to ask him to clarify what that meant.

Either way, he materialized down around the creature's arms, and with the aether-infused dagger, slashed horrifically deep lines across her hide.

The sea monster bellowed and attempted to attack my champion. But the cat disappeared and popped back into existence closer to me where he hovered, waiting for the kraken to find him and change direction.

The kraken responded as we'd hoped, trying to turn from her core because she could no longer effectively use the force of her tentacles to twist. Her bulbous torso lifted up and struggled to pivot the bulk of her body around.

Come on . . . Just a little more.

We only needed her to budge enough so the cat could slide beneath the sea monster.

I dashed further into the water and waved my arms frantically, desperate to ensure that the creature didn't change course when the cat resumed his attacks. "Hey! Over here!"

The monster followed the sound, and the front of her body lifted up an inch or so.

"Get ready, cat!" I screamed. "Any second now!"

My focus was intense, solely fixated on the kraken's weak spot.

Because of that, I didn't see the arm crashing down upon me until it was too late.

A sucker slammed into my head, and I fell into the water. A deluge of bubbles left my lips as I screamed and squirmed beneath the weight of the monster. My blood skittered through my veins as her arm pressed down, intent on smothering me between sand and wave. I screamed again, releasing precious air.

Finally, I realized what an idiot I was being for letting my fear take over. If I wanted to survive, I needed to control myself, to conserve oxygen.

I forced myself to keep my stinging eyes open, taking in everything around me, even as the kraken's tentacle tried to press me into a sandy grave. It was about to pummel me again, when I noticed another one of the creature's arms making deep divots in the ground.

Divots that I could wiggle through.

Using earth magic, I hollowed out the seafloor and created a tunnel for escape. However, when I tried to burrow into it and claw away, the sucker of the tentacle bound me and held on tight.

I was glued to the damnable creature.

I switched tack, calling on water next to create a current that ran through the tunnel. It was as strong as a riptide, practically ripped the clothes off my body, and yet, it wasn't strong enough to separate me from the kraken's sucker as she pressed me hard into the sand.

Abrasive grains scratched at my face, and stars formed in my vision. My lungs groaned, and second by second, my fighting spirit lessened.

No . . . this will not be the end.

Even as I thought the words, tried to make myself believe they were true, I couldn't deny the encroaching darkness. Couldn't fight it off. Actually, stillness felt so much better right now . . . easier.

I stopped fighting and closed my eyes, letting my body settle, feeling the strange and terrible bliss that had surrounded me. The sand rubbed harder against my skin as the kraken bore down, and I almost laughed.

How did I ever think I could fight this beast? Something so large and powerful. It was an impossible task—a fool's errand.

I opened my mouth, inviting the water to flow in and take me away from all this, escort me to my ultimate freedom.

But it didn't happen.

The next thing I knew, hands gripped me and yanked. The suction between my body and the sucker broke, and water floated between us. My body grew slack as someone pulled me through the little tunnel I'd made, into the larger sea. I jerked in their powerful grip, nearing death as they pulled my body away from the ocean floor.

Then the surface broke. We soared out of the water

and into the sky. I sputtered and gasped for air, and the scent of spice engulfed me as I coughed the sea from my lungs.

After only seconds, the sensation of drowning lifted. The feeling of being *me*, alive, whole, and ready to fight, returned like a tidal wave—so fast that I didn't understand it.

"Alice! *Alice*! Wake up!"

Hatter . . .

I opened my eyes to find Henri cradling me in his arms as we flew above the sea creature, well out of her reach. As much as I wanted to keep looking at him, staring into his green eyes forever, the screams and cheers and heckling all around us ripped me back to reality.

Down on the ground, the beach was pandemonium. The kraken had nearly retreated into the ocean, trying to gain an element of advantage over the cat as she fought like mad. And my creature, the cat, battled as hard as he could.

This needs to end.

"Fly low." I was surprised to hear that my voice didn't waver. "On the other side of the kraken, toward deeper water. Just out of her tentacles' reach at first, so she sees us."

"Alice, you nearly drowned."

"I'm fine," I said, and even though I wasn't sure how I'd recovered, I meant it. All I'd needed was a few lungfuls of air, and I was ready to continue fighting.

"Are you sure?"

"Absolutely."

He probably thought I was crazy, but Hatter did as I said, soaring toward the bloodied, thrashing arms of the kraken. Closer to the water. Closer to injury or death.

"Hey, kraken! You didn't get me!" I screamed. "We're over here! Come and finish this!"

The monster's head turned toward me and, like all simple-minded creatures do, she followed using the most direct route. She twisted at her center, causing the opposite side of her body to lift off the sand, higher and higher.

This time, since she was half submerged in the sea, her arms could grab at the water and pull her weight more effectively than they could on land. The waves aided her, lifting her higher, until the soft spot above her heart was completely exposed.

"Cat! Now!" A tentacle extended to snap me and Henri out of the air.

Henri diverted, and for a moment, I couldn't see the cat in the mess of seawater, kraken arms, and the mix of black and blonde hair that flew around me. Still, I knew when the cat had landed the dagger in the monster's heart.

The beast made a deep guttural sound that vibrated the air around it.

I pulled the hair from my face, trying to see, and caught the moment that every single one of the beast's arms pulled back into her body. It released another horrible sound, fainter this time, a cry for help. Surprisingly, the kraken's pain cut through me, and my stomach wound up in knots.

It was a little irrational, but feelings rarely were completely rational. And I couldn't help but feel pity for the beast that my aunt had forced me to kill. The beast that probably didn't give a damn about her, and would rather be patrolling the seas for fish to eat or ships to sink.

So much pain, all because my aunt wanted something that wasn't hers.

The thought struck me, made me want to witness the kraken's end, because I was sure my aunt didn't give a damn about the creatures she controlled. Just as she didn't care about her subjects.

"Henri, stop!" I yelled. "Wait. I need to watch her die."

He jerked to a stop, and although his expression was one of pure confusion, he trusted me and twisted in the air.

We stayed there, a safe distance away, watching the kraken queen's final moments.

As soon as her body collapsed into the wake, tears sprang into my eyes. We'd done it. The Trial by Aether was over. Like a movie on fast forward, everything I'd done to get here flashed in my mind. I saw those I'd had to injure or kill, but also those who I was helping by taking on an evil queen.

A lump rose in my throat. The end was bittersweet.

"Alice, look." Henri gestured above us.

I followed his finger to find that the green flame had

appeared. It was hovering over me, officially proclaiming me the victor of the calling of creatures.

Tears pricked my eyes.

"Alice White is the victor of the Trial by Aether!" a familiar, yet deeper and more resonant voice boomed over the beach, stealing my attention.

When I looked down at the crowd, I gasped.

Herald stood alone on an expanse of sand, his white fur glowing with the essence of the blue and silver godsflame.

"The challenger is the new queen of Wonderland!" the pooka continued, as onlookers watched in silent awe. "The Trial by Aether is over!"

Suddenly, the green flame streaked away from me and toward the pooka. My chest tightened as what was about to happen struck me like a slap to the face.

It was over quickly. The moment the green godsflame hit Herald and joined the blue and silver coursing through him, the pooka slumped and fell to the sand, dead. The godsflame flashed and then, as if saying good-bye, twinkled prettily one last time and soared off, over the sea.

My throat constricted. Herald was dead. I'd beaten the Red Queen. And with the godsflame exit, the Trial by Aether truly was finished.

"May the aether light your way, my friend," Henri whispered, his voice thick as he stared at the pooka.

"We should go to him," I said, wiping moisture from my eyes. "We—"

The cat popped into existence at my side, cutting me off. "I apologize for losing your dagger, My Queen. I couldn't pry it out of the beast."

"It's fine—I'll get another," I stammered, as taken aback by the title as I was his sudden appearance.

The cat beamed at me.

It was strange that he was unaffected by everything that had just happened, but then again, everything about the Cheshire cat was off. I supposed I'd just have to get used to that. At least, while I was still here.

"It was an honor to serve you, My Queen. To rid the island of a tyrant."

"Errr, yeah. Well, thank you. Because of you—"

A blood-curdling scream cut through me, only to be followed by four bone-chilling words.

"Off with her head!"

CHAPTER 32

"I'm sorry, but what did she just say? Can she even *do* that?" I leaned out of Hatter's grasp only to have him wrench me back.

"You heard her right. And unfortunately, as the godsflame didn't stick around to enforce its decision, I suspect that she can and *will* do as she wishes," he said. "Thankfully, after the pixies freed me and Isadora, who they'd locked up too, I was able to send out the call."

My gaze latched onto his. "The call?"

He pointed toward the beach. "Look."

Hundreds of wild pixies swarmed toward the gathered crowd. Although it was impossible to tell from this distance, I imagined that I could hear Dee's and Dum's little voices screaming for their friends to attack. Larger fae joined them, tumbling over the boulders and onto the beach below—more rebels, ready to fight.

"How many?" I asked.

"I'm not sure. I had the girls round up the troops. At full strength, we're well over one hundred, not including the many pixies that flooded out of the forest at their summons. But if my plan works, more will join us."

"Do tell." I gestured for him to fly us closer to the beach where we could be part of the action.

"You and I will go for the witches first—get them to break the enchantment on the citizens of Wonderland. Even if that means ending them. Then we take on the queen."

I pointed down toward the mass of people, straight at the witches in their emerald cloaks. They weren't standing by the queen any longer, but on the edge of the swarm of soldiers, who, after sighting the incoming rebels, had rushed to protect the queen they were enchanted to follow. "That's them in the green cloaks, one blonde, one black-haired."

Hatter nodded, and we streamed toward them, me in his arms. The witches watched us carefully, perhaps sensing the incoming danger. When we were only six feet away, still in the air, I pushed myself out of his grasp and let my wings catch me.

"Your leader isn't playing by the rules, I see?" I sneered at the witch.

Magic bloomed in the witches' hands, and their stances fell into a position suited for battle.

"The godsflame is gone. Why should she?" the younger one asked.

"She's the rightful ruler of this court." The older, raven-haired witch spat at my feet.

Fury bubbled in my stomach, partially from what she'd said and partially because I was pissed at the godsflame for ending the Trial by Aether suddenly and leaving. And yet, there was nothing I could do about it. In the tales the old gods truly only cared about themselves. The godsflame had probably figured that after it made its decree everyone would simply fall in line—just like they had in the days when the old gods ruled magicals and humans alike.

But those days were long gone. In the present, we had to fight for ourselves, and what we wanted, every step of the way.

"You know that's a lie," I said to the witch. "She's never been the rightful ruler. You know who she killed."

I released the aether's hold over my hair, and my glamoured red locks turned white-blonde, the color of my mother's hair. The hue that I hadn't wanted to claim in front of so many who had been taught to be suspicious of it.

But now? Screw 'em.

The young witch sneered.

"What do we care who whelped you?" the older one said, her voice gravelly. "Your mother hated us, but our queen took us in. For that, we're loyal to her, and her *only*. You shouldn't have returned."

I forced myself not to attack, if only because I'd learned in my aether studies that having an enchantment lifted on purpose was less painful than when its caster died. And thousands of fae were under these witches' spells.

"You shouldn't have helped her. But seeing as I'm reasonable, I'll give you a chance to repent. Undo the enchantment on the fae of Wonderland," I ordered. "*Now*. Or I'll end you."

"We'd never betray our queen's wishes," the raven-haired witch growled.

The hard way it is.

I darted toward the older witch, cutting a hard right to dodge her magic. Then I twirled and spun back toward her. Using the aether, I conjured a new dagger as I sent a blast of air her way.

The air picked up sand, and the witch dropped her hands to cover her eyes. A cry of pain had just left her mouth when I slit her throat.

A chorus of screams rang out on the far side of the beach. I glanced over, wondering if it was because of the fighting or the fact that hundreds of fae had gotten their memories back.

"It's this one!" Hatter screamed as he thrust a sword at the blonde witch. "She's the primary mist caster!"

I didn't know how he knew that, but after a single glance, I believed it.

I'd seen a lot of witches fight. I'd battled with, and against, many myself. But I'd never witnessed someone move like this witch. She might have been younger than her counterpart, but she fought as if she'd been battling for a thousand lifetimes. Every motion was efficient and powerful, reminding me of a snake striking to kill.

Still, I wasn't cowed. She might be a strong witch, and skilled at fighting, but she was no match for me. I was Alice the Dagger. I hated it, but killing was what I did—and I did it better than anyone I knew.

Henri and I tag-teamed her, swooping low and attacking with our magic or a blade every chance we got. In the distance, I heard my aunt screaming in fury, and other battles being fought.

I chanced a glance up, and all my air left me. The rebels were fighting bravely, but we were still sorely outnumbered. I needed to end this and go to them, help them, and finish the queen.

The blonde witch's blue magic soared by me, yanking me back to the battle at hand. My eyes narrowed. If only she would fall, we might have the clear advantage.

And then, as if my desire had conjured it into being, I saw it—our shot.

Behind her, Hatter was swooping down again, ready to attack. I only needed to keep her busy.

Calling earth magic, a vine whip appeared in my hand. I snapped it at the witch, whose eyes grew wide as she darted out of the way. My lips curled up, and I snapped the whip at her again.

She leapt to the left, directly into Hatter's path.

I raised the whip again, preparing to time my next snap so she'd run right into Hatter's blade, when the witch sneered, twisted, and shot a barrage of magic at him.

Her power hit the unsuspecting Henri like a boulder. He fell to the ground, his body seizing. I saw red and, using the aether, muffled her face like I had with the bandersnatch. Then, mercilessly, I went for her, another conjured blade extended in front of me.

Before she could fight off the aether and turn to face me again, I'd slit her neck.

Hot blood splattered my cheeks and forehead, but for once in my life, I didn't recoil at the sensation. I barely noticed it. My only concern was for Henri.

"Hatter! Are you okay?" I asked, fluttering over and kneeling at his side.

A groan assured me he was alive. I rolled him over so that his face was up. I gasped. That bitch had hit him right in the face with her magic. Whatever spell she'd used had caused an enormous amount of swelling, particularly around his eyes, which appeared sealed shut.

"Alice?" Henri wheezed. "What are you doing?"

"What? I'm checking on you, I . . ." I trailed off as what he meant to say hit home.

What *was* I doing? I needed to be going after my aunt. Others had sacrificed everything for this moment, this chance. I needed to end it as soon as possible.

"Stay here, I'll be right back." I set his head softly on the sand, and burst out of my crouched position, into a sprint.

The queen was easy enough to find. She was in the

thick of things, fighting any fae who dared to come her way. It seemed that half of her guards had regained their memories and had turned on her. But for some unknown reason, perhaps because they were just used to taking orders, the other half continued to fight on her behalf.

Not for long.

My wings snapped open, and I launched into the air.

"Cat!" I yelled.

The Cheshire cat appeared at once, flying alongside me as if he had wings. "You called?"

"We need to finish the queen. We—"

The cat held up his paws. "I'm afraid that's all on you, Alice."

If I'd been walking, I would have stopped dead in my tracks. I was sure he had reasons for not wanting to help, but what could they be? Of course, now was not the time to ask, so I moved on.

"Fine, I'll do that myself, but I need your help with the soldiers." I gestured to the melee that we were rapidly approaching. There had to be two dozen soldiers between me and my aunt.

The cat glanced down. "Fine."

"Let's go." I zoomed toward her, my dagger raised, poised to strike.

A part of me hoped that she'd never see me coming. That I could end this bloodshed quickly. But another part wanted her to know it was me who was ending her reign —the daughter of the woman she'd killed.

All around, fae screamed and fought with everything

they had. I heard the sounds of a swarm of pixies, bolstered by the twins' commands, attacking soldiers with their tiny fangs. Cat battled in my periphery, appearing and disappearing as he ripped open throats and moved on.

But I set my sights on the Red Queen, who at that very moment was turning toward me. Her green eyes fell on me, and the hatred I saw there blazed through my soul.

I raised my dagger and extended my other hand, prepared to battle her with magic and steel.

"Alice! *No!*"

Before I had time to pinpoint the person calling for me, Isadora hurled herself out of the crowd. She flung her body straight at my aunt, fist-first, and with a punch upside the jaw, knocked the Red Queen out cold.

I stopped flying as if someone had slapped me.

As the queen fell, others stilled too—disbelieving what had happened. A small, unassuming brownie had taken on the powerful Red Queen.

Only Isadora moved, leaping up from where she'd landed atop my aunt, and spreading her arms wide as if protecting her. "You can't, Alice!"

My brows furrowed, and slowly, the familiar sensation of anger began to bubble inside me.

This was what I'd come here for. This was what everyone wanted of me. It was expected—my part to play. And now Isadora was telling me I couldn't kill my parents' murderer? I couldn't do the one thing I truly excelled at, and avenge my parents and this kingdom? But why?

She must have a reason.

Keeping that in mind, I fluttered over to the brownie, who was now giving orders for others to tie up the queen in iron-laced rope.

"What's this about?" I asked. "You brought me here to end this, and now . . . nothing?" I was unable to keep the anger out of my tone. I felt used and useless. "This might sound selfish, but I had a stake in this too. I want to avenge my parents."

"As do we," Isadora said. "But not now. Not like this."

She stepped away from the fallen queen. Only then did I notice the bruises all over her arms and the one spreading across her cheekbone. My grip around my dagger tightened. Someone had hurt her.

"Alice, we want a trial," Isadora's voice was softer now. "*All* the fae of Wonderland deserve to see the Red Queen fall for her crimes. Not just the ones here."

"A trial?" I was pretty positive that, as a monarchy, a real trial had never happened in Wonderland. "You want to see her thrown in jail?" It made even less sense why they would need me, if that was what they wanted.

Isadora blew out a half-amused breath. "No, dear. No doubt she'll lose her head for her crimes—a suitable end. But we don't want that on *you.*"

The brownie approached me and took my hand, hers slick with blood. "You gave us the strength to rise up. You opened thousands of eyes to the truth. You've done enough. No one needs you to draw the blade again—you deserve better. To make your own choices, to live your life how you want. If that includes killing, so be it, but we shouldn't *expect* it of you."

I blinked, unable to believe what I was hearing. My anger dissipated slowly as a lump rose in my throat.

"You can start a new life now," Isadora pressed. "One that's not drenched in blood, if you wish." Her dark eyes drank me in. "You can help us—everyone here—but it doesn't have to be by the edge of a blade."

Dammit, my eyes were leaking. I sniffed and hurriedly wiped away the evidence of almost-tears, only to have more appear.

How had Isadora guessed what I really wanted? How was it that so many people here saw me more clearly than anyone I'd known in my old life?

The conjured dagger trembled in my hand, cold and ready to do my bidding. Behind Isadora, fae were lifting the queen, talking about preparing a dungeon cell.

The cat popped into my view, baring his strange and slightly horrific human smile. The words he spoke to me before he disappeared the night we met came rushing back.

"It remains to be seen which princess you'll turn out to be most like."

My fingers loosened, and the hilt of my blade slipped from my grasp as the dagger fell to the sand.

CHAPTER 33

The cold and damp chilled my skin as I descended the steps deep into the bowels of the dungeon. My footsteps rang through the cavernous space each time they touched down on stone, and the satchel I wore bounced against my hip.

I wouldn't be sneaking up on anyone down here. Not that there were many people imprisoned right now. Only the Red Queen—Sela as I tried to think of her now to strip her of her power—and a few soldiers who remained faithful to her. Out of a whole army, there had been no more than two dozen such soldiers. They were nasty individuals who I suspected liked her violent, cruel style. They probably wouldn't ever have needed the enchantment to follow her in the first place. These men were being kept far away from the Red Queen. And so I wouldn't be tempted to poke them with my dagger, I wouldn't be going anywhere near them.

When I reached the bottom of the staircase, I turned right and cruised past a stretch of newly emptied cells. The fae who had been contained here before, on death row or simply imprisoned, had been released two days prior—after witnessing my aunt's walk of shame to her maximum-security cell.

She was being kept in the far reaches of the dungeon, behind trusty bars of iron and new walls of aether that I had personally put in place. As if that wasn't enough, a dozen soldiers, most who felt wronged by the queen, volunteered to watch over her until her trial.

The guards parted as I approached, wordlessly allowing me through. I nodded to each of them, and they bowed.

I breathed out a soft sigh. Now that the fae of Wonderland remembered my bloodline, people knew me. And they expected me to rise and claim the crown of the White line. They wanted it.

And yet, I still did not.

Although, I couldn't deny that certain people made it difficult to leave Faerie. So, I'd decided that I'd stay, at least until I found Elise.

I passed through my protective wall of aether before turning to the guards. "I'll take some privacy. Please wait down the hall."

A low chuckle came from the cell at the end of the corridor. "With an imperious tone like that, it's a miracle anyone believes you when you say you don't wish to take the throne."

I rolled my eyes. "It's a miracle that anyone believed you should have ever sat upon it."

The traitor to the Wonderland Court laughed again. "No miracle, dear niece. Only leverage, magic, and knowing what people wanted."

I was close enough now to see her face, shining in the light of the single lantern she'd been given. Her black hair still hung in thick curtains and shone like polished glass, not yet dirtied or oily. Her porcelain white skin, however, was marred. Patches of dirt dotted her cheekbones and the underside of her chin. She'd been tossed down here in the clothes she'd worn during the Calling of the Creatures Trial. Judging by the way she was shivering, they weren't nearly warm enough for the cold of the dungeon.

"The people have spoken. Your trial starts tomorrow." I pulled a bag of food out of the satchel I wore against my hip. It was common food: crackers, dried meat, hard cheeses, and a jug of water. I passed it through the bars, and my aunt snatched it up.

"You should know many of them are already sharpening their knives. We won't be using your executioner— he died in the battle. There are so many people vying for the privilege of chopping off your head, I expect it will take some time to decide the best person for the job."

"Then there isn't much difference between them and me after all," the former queen snorted. "Will I have a final meal?"

I shrugged.

Sela popped a cracker into her mouth and chewed it loudly, as if she were trying to make a lot of noise.

I shuddered. "I have questions for you. If you answer, maybe I'll see to it you get a final meal—exactly how you like it."

Sela raised her eyebrows, and popped another cracker into her mouth.

"Where's my sister?" I wanted to continue talking, to drown out the noise of her loud chewing, but I knew better than to jabber on. It made people look weak, and my aunt would never respect or respond to someone who appeared weak. Even if they had her locked up in a cell.

"Elise . . . what a darling girl. Much more malleable than you." She stood and came closer to the bars separating us. "She's kept in this realm, under lock and key of my allies."

The Dark Court. It has to be the Dark Court.

In the two days that my aunt had been imprisoned, I'd been learning much about the various Faerie courts. As far as I could tell, the Dark Court was the only kingdom to ally with Wonderland after my parents' deaths.

"All right."

I took a long slow breath. My next question was harder. And yet, I needed to ask it, needed to know.

"Why did you kill your sister? Why did you hate her so much?"

The vision I'd seen in the Enchanted Forest ran through my mind, unstoppable as a freight train. Sela had seemed justified when she ended her sister, and furious as she struck down my father. I knew from experience that powerful emotions always had powerful stories behind them.

I had to hear this tale.

Sela made a clicking noise. "I'm surprised it took you so long to ask. Clearly, you learned that I killed her, even how."

Her poisonous green eyes bore through me. She was obviously wondering how I'd figured it out and been able to conjure the image of her sister pleading for her life before being struck down. But keeping her pride intact, Sela didn't ask.

"Everyone loved your mother. They couldn't help it, something about her drew them in like flies." She shook her head, still peeved that her sister was so charismatic. Then her gaze flicked back to me, and she paused. "You obviously did not inherit that from her. In fact, I see many similarities between *us*, which is . . . curious."

If I weren't trying to be strong, I would've shuddered.

Perhaps my aunt had been a good person once, but that had been long ago. And while I'd committed atrocious acts since I was a child, I had hope that someday soon the pattern would change. When I returned to the human realm, I fully intended to turn over a new leaf.

"Anyway," she continued, "most of the gossipers at court swore that I'd hated your mother since she'd stolen your father from me. We had been betrothed all our lives, but the moment he laid eyes on Isabel, he lost interest in me."

Her lips tightened, and she looked away, focusing on the stone floor. If it was possible for someone as cold-hearted as her to cry, I think she would've at that moment.

"It hurt, I'll admit." She glared at me again, as if I'd been the one to slight her. "And yes, at the time, I was livid about the situation. Particularly when our father forbade me to leave the court and hide from my shame. But all that pain was *nothing* to what happened later. The moment that tore my world apart and ensured I would end Isabel's life."

"And that was?"

Her lips curled up. "Your birth."

CHAPTER 34

I ran my finger along the rim of my goblet. Around me, fae danced, celebrating both their freedom from a tyrant, and the upcoming trial of the Red Queen. Occasionally, someone would come up and thank me or talk. I tried to be polite, but I wasn't completely there.

"Hey." Henri laid a hand on my shoulder, and sat down next to me.

Our table was located among a sea of other tables. Although many wanted to honor me and what I'd done, and place me at a head table, I'd refused. Just like I'd refused an official coronation ceremony and requested that people call me Alice. Or if they *absolutely* must, Princess Alice. Although the godsflame had proclaimed me the winner of the Trial by Aether, that didn't mean I had to *accept* the title of queen.

I had already felt this way, but the information my

aunt gave me the day before had made me even less inclined to be in the spotlight.

"Are you okay?" Hatter asked, his dark eyebrows furrowed in concern.

He looked as handsome as ever, dressed in a regal, dark navy tunic and black pants that made his green eyes even more vibrant.

"Fine," I said. "What makes you think otherwise?"

"Oh, I don't know. Maybe that you've been walking around in a daze since you visited your aunt. And you haven't celebrated at all since the party started. What did she say to you?"

I shook my head. "Nothing."

For the millionth time since I arrived in Faerie, I was thankful that the potion Xavier had given me hadn't worn off. I wasn't ready to discuss what my aunt had told me. I was barely able to think about it without breaking down.

"You realize that I know you're lying, right?" Henri placed his hand over mine, and shivers ran down my spine. "But if you won't tell me, the least I can do is try to cheer you up. How about a dance?"

I rose and took his hand.

I didn't feel festive, but even a sulky Alice couldn't pass up this chance. If there was one thing I was certain of, it was that I had feelings for Hatter. That I was even possibly falling for him.

And our time was short.

As soon as I saw to it that my aunt got what was coming

to her, and found Elise, I would propose a new sort of leadership. One in which a single person didn't hold all the power. A style of government not exactly like where I was from, since that wouldn't be compatible with fae customs. But one that was a little more equal—and I'd suggest that Henri be at the head of it. His talent for leading people was too strong to ignore, and everyone already loved him. It should be easy.

But for now, while he still had his hand pressed against my lower back, I would dance.

We stopped in the center of the dance floor, and Henri took my hands. I fell into step with him as naturally as I breathed, not at all fighting his lead. We floated among the other dancers, though it didn't take long for me to notice that we were out of time with them. It took only a half-second more to realize why.

Henri was leading me through the dance he'd learned at the age of eight. The one he'd wanted to impress a five-year-old princess with.

"Everyone watching must think that you're terribly behind the times."

"Who cares what they think? I've wanted to show you my improvement for years. I'm not about to pass up my chance in such a perfect setting."

Years . . .

My heart began to thud in my chest. For the first time since my aunt had spelled out my potential future, the secret prophecy, I forgot about the lingering threat.

And yet, as good as it felt to be dancing in Henri's

arms, to have his biceps wrapped around me, and smell his spicy scent, it troubled me too.

"Henri, you know I still don't plan on staying, right?"

Hatter gulped. "I know," he said, his voice thick. "But can you blame a guy for wanting to make the most of the time he has? Or hoping that maybe you'll change your mind?" He offered up a slight smile. "After all, you still have some time here."

There was no denying that. Even after the trial and the execution of Sela White, I still had to find Elise.

My aunt had claimed that she was in Faerie, with her 'allies,' of which there was only one: the Dark Court, the fae court who treated their subjects even worse than the Red Queen had treated those of Wonderland.

If she wasn't there, I would scour this realm to find my sister. And if I didn't find her here, I'd do the same in the human world. I wouldn't stop until we were together.

"I didn't mean to upset you again," Hatter whispered, his lips close to my ear.

I shivered, realizing that I'd fallen into an almost trance-like state, thinking about my sister. "I'm sorry. There's just so much on my mind."

"Can you forget about it? Just for tonight—for right now?"

"I think so." I gave him a smile. "I'll try my hardest."

He stopped dancing. "Good. Because a lot of people want to see you, to know you." He gestured to the surrounding dance floor.

My lips parted. All around us, the dancing had

stopped, and fae were watching us, waiting. Smiles laced their faces, and a few of the females were clutching their hearts, in clear danger of swooning over Henri.

Isadora stood closest to us, a box in her hand.

"What's all this?" I asked as sweat began to slick my palms.

"We want to thank you," the brownie said. "For standing up for us, for freeing our memories and our will. And most of all, for bringing happiness back to Wonderland."

She waved a hand around, indicating the entire room of smiling, celebrating fae. "None of this could've happened without you, Princess Alice."

Suddenly, a pit formed in my stomach.

Was this an ambush? A ploy to get me to try to take the crown for reals? What was in the box?

"You really don't have to—"

Isadora shook her head and placed a hand over mine. "We don't *have* to do anything. That we know. But this is what we desire. The subjects of Wonderland would like to present you with this."

I took the box, trying to hide the shaking of my hands as I did so. Carefully, I opened the lid, and instead of the crown that I feared would be inside, a cuff-like bracelet glinted up at me within a bed of teal velvet.

The cuff was about three inches wide, large but also thin and delicate. The gold had been hammered, and etched on its surface was the design of a rose amidst a field of thorns.

"I didn't go into the details of how I knew your family when we met, but I actually worked for your mother, long ago. She was my queen, and dare I say it, a friend. This bracelet was hers. One of the only items she wore religiously," Isadora whispered. "Before she left to take on the Red Queen, she bid me to give it to you. So you would always know where you came from."

A lump rose in my throat. I'd never had a family, let alone a family heirloom. In the span of two seconds, this bracelet had become the most precious object I'd ever seen.

With trembling fingers, I reached into the box and picked it up, placing it on my left wrist. It was a perfect fit, not too tight or too loose. After taking a second to admire it, I dragged my gaze back up to Isadora's.

"Thank you. You have no idea what this means to me."

"I hope that when you wear it, you'll think of the Wonderland Court. Think of us. And your family, of course."

"Of course . . ." My voice cracked. I was seconds from losing it completely.

Thankfully, Saint Henri cleared his throat. "Thank you to everyone for attending the celebration this evening. The princess, and all who stood with her before and during the Trial by Aether, appreciate it very much."

Politely, people began to clap, and Henri waited until they finished before he continued.

"Enjoy yourself. Eat your fill, drink, and be merry. If

you wish to attend the trial of Sela White, join us tomorrow at noon."

Murmuring flew from the attendees. I could tell that even if people had already made plans, they were going to drop them. No one wanted to miss the trial of the Red Queen, and I honestly couldn't say that I blamed them.

"But until then, let us continue to revel in a new era of the Wonderland Court," Henri said.

Someone offered him a goblet, and he took it and held it to the sky. "To Princess Alice."

"To Princess Alice," the crowd echoed, and my stomach wound into tighter knots.

CHAPTER 35

The courtroom was simply Heartfire Hall, already renamed 'the Grand Hall,' repurposed. Sort of.

The thrones had been removed, but other chairs, almost as grand, sat on one side of a table long enough for ten. Because in this trial an ex-monarch would be judged, which very rarely happened in Faerie, we had to dig deep into the record books to learn the correct protocol.

As it turned out, in the case of a monarch, or ex-monarch, breaking the law, and actually being called out on it, the fae reverted to a governing style similar to that of the old gods.

A jury of six sat alongside the head judge; in this case, me. My vote carried the weight of three other jurors, and I would be the one to cast final judgment on the former queen.

When the guards brought her in, thinly padded iron shackles still ringed Sela White's wrists and ankles. The scent of burnt skin from where the metal had touched her filled the room. As fae were allergic to iron, and if cut or dosed with the metal it could be lethal, the shackles had to have been painful. But the Red Queen didn't let it show. Even when the crowd began to boo and jeer, her face was a mask, haughty and proud as ever, as if a crown still perched on her head.

The guards led her to a chair positioned off to the side of the jurors' table. She lowered herself into the creaking wood with the utmost dignity and grace.

On cue, Sansu rose from his seat at the far end of the jurors' table and approached the accused.

As he did so, I thought of Herald. Had the godsflame not killed him and later devoured his body, this would've been his job. He would have seen this proceeding. The pooka would have known that every sacrifice and danger he'd put himself through had been worth it.

I made a mental note to have a statue dedicated to the pooka, displaying him in his favorite form—a white rabbit in a waistcoat.

"We're here today to witness the fair judgment of Sela White, previously known as the Queen of Hearts, or the Red Queen of the Wonderland Court." Sansu gestured to my aunt, who scowled. "Does anyone here object to the trial of this faerie?"

No one spoke, no one even blinked.

The Red Queen didn't seem an ounce surprised.

"As no one wishes to stand up for this woman, I shall continue to read the counts of atrocities committed by Sela White against the fae of Wonderland."

Sansu pulled out a scroll at least three feet long, and began reading the list of crimes, one after the other.

For each horrible act named, a fae in the crowd snarled, sneered, growled, or made a rude hand gesture. My aunt had made enemies everywhere, and I had absolutely no doubt that today, she would see a reckoning for her actions.

Once Sansu had finished, he rolled up the scroll. "This concludes the reading of the charges. The trial shall now commence, Judge Alice."

I gulped. At my side, Henri snaked his hand onto the armrest of my seat and patted my arm.

"You've got this," he whispered. "It'll be over soon."

I nodded, not exactly sure sure why I was nervous.

My aunt deserved everything she was getting. She deserved death. She deserved an eternity in the dungeon. She deserved to feel everything she had made the fae of Wonderland feel, times a thousand.

And yet, the smallest iota of me, the part that Isadora had breathed life into when she gave me permission not to be the one to kill my aunt, was screaming for me to stop.

It was frustrating as hell. It made me want to throw things. It didn't make any sense.

But no matter why I felt this way, I knew I should be thankful. It showed I was more than just a killing machine, that there was hope for me to change my life after all this was over.

"Sela White," I began, and was surprised to hear my tone so strong. "Do you deny any of the charges made against you?"

"I deny all of them," the former queen said smoothly. "Save one, of course."

Although it wasn't professional, I rolled my eyes. "And what would that be?"

"That I stole the crown. Shall I go into the reasons why I did so?" Her lips lifted in a sly smile as her gaze locked with mine, challenging me.

My throat closed up, and I broke out in a sweat. The crowd murmured, clearly curious as to what the Red Queen would say. But as long as I was in power in this room, they would never know what my aunt believed. They could never know of the prophecy.

I slammed my fist onto the table in front of me. "Quiet!"

At my single word, the onlookers fell silent.

I turned to the accused. "An explanation will not be necessary. Your admission of guilt of a single crime, which you've just given, is sufficient."

The proceedings continued smoothly. Even if my aunt denied all the other charges, there was more than enough evidence to prove that she had in fact committed every single atrocity she was convicted of. So when, hours later, the jurors and I retreated into a separate room to deliberate, I knew there would be only one outcome.

"This should be quick," Alran said, echoing my belief.

"Who doesn't believe that the Red Queen deserves to be executed?" Sansu asked. "Raise your hand."

No one did.

"Then it's just a matter of how she'll meet her end," Henri said.

"And I think we all know what that will be." Alran drew a line across his throat, and all the fae in the room, save for me, nodded.

I didn't disagree, but I felt my verbal agreement would be inauthentic. And if I was to do what I must after the execution, I needed to stay as true to myself—the new me I was discovering—as possible.

"Ready to give the verdict?" I asked.

After what must have been the shortest deliberation known to fae, we marched back into the throne room. All seven of us faced the crowd, and I asked the guards standing around the accused to step back so that we might see her face when we delivered the sentence.

"I, Alice White, head judge, alongside the six jurors, have come to a unanimous conclusion. Each juror will state their conviction at this time." I nodded to one end of the line.

"I, Alran Rivers, sentence Sela White to death by beheading."

"Death by beheading," another fae said.

"Death by beheading," Sansu echoed.

Two more went the exact same way until we got to Henri, whose eyes hadn't left Sela's since we entered the room.

"I, Henri Hatter, son of Ernie Hatter, who you mercilessly killed, sentence you, Sela White, to death by beheading."

Everyone turned to me. It felt as if the entire room was holding their breath, waiting for my word.

"I, Alice White of the royal line White, daughter of Isabel White and Frederic Torna, and rightful heir to the Wonderland throne, sentence you, Sela White, to death."

The crowd leaned forward, waiting for the final ball to drop.

I sucked in a breath. "Off with her head."

Everyone in attendance burst into applause. Some fae hugged their neighbors; others wept, clearly so relieved they would see justice for the wrongs that had been done to them.

I just stood there, silent, soaking it all in. Finally able to breathe.

The execution would take place within a few days. Until then, I would keep busy by helping rebuild the Wonderland Court. Soon, I'd set off to find Elise.

Hatter's hand found mine, and squeezed it tight. "Thank you for giving us our lives back."

"Thank you for bringing me here," I said, meaning every word, and for now, allowing myself to believe that the hand that held mine would always be there.

"You know that, when you're ready, I'm coming with you to find Elise, right?" Hatter's green eyes gazed deep into mine.

"I know," I said with a smile. "I would expect nothing less."

ALSO BY ASHLEY MCLEO

<u>Coven of Shadows and Secrets</u>

Seeker of Secrets

Hunted by Darkness

History of Witches

<u>Spellcasters Spy Academy Series (Magic of Arcana Universe)</u>

A Legacy Witch: Year One

A Marked Witch: Internship

A Rebel Witch: Year Two

A Crucible Witch: Year Three

An Academy Witch: Prequel

The Complete Spellcasters Spy Academy Boxset

<u>The Wonderland Court Series (Magic of Arcana Universe)</u>

Alice the Dagger

Alice the Torch

<u>Standalone Novels</u>

Stealing Maid Marian's Heart (Magic of Arcana Universe)

The Alchemist of Silver Hollow (Magic of Arcana Universe)

<u>Fanged Fae Series - A Bonegates sister series</u>

Blood Moon Magic

Faerie Blood

The Bonegate Series - A Fanged Fae sister series

Hawk Witch

Assassin Witch

Traitor Witch

Illuminator Witch

The Royal Quest Series

Dragon Prince

Dragon Magic

Dragon Mate

Dragon Betrayal

Dragon Crown

Dragon War

The Starseed Universe

Prophecy of Three

Souls of Three

Rising of Three

The Starseed Universe (five-book boxset with two bonus novellas)

Acknowledgments

Thank you to my husband for being so very patient during the writing of this book (and every other book), and assisting me in every way that you could. You're a freaking saint.

Special thanks to my editor, Jen McDonnell for helping me whip this baby into shape. I love working with you.

To my dog, Flicka, thanks for all the hard work you put in by my side, day in and day out.

And finally, thank you to all my readers. Without you, I couldn't do what I love.

All the magic,

Ashley

About the Author

Ashley lives in Portland with her husband, Kurt, their dog, Flicka, and the house ghost that sometimes makes appearances in her charming, old home.

When she's not writing urban fantasy and portal fantasy novels she enjoys traveling the world, reading, kicking butt at board games (she recommends Splendor and Dominion), and frequenting taquerias.

For all the latest releases and updates, subscribe to Ashley's newsletter, The Coven, today. You can also find her Facebook group, Ashley's Reader Coven.